Praise for *Ten Men:*

"A wicked whisper through the West End world of dating—billionaires, film directors, toffs and more." —*Tatler* (UK)

"A *Sex and the City*–type look at the ups and downs of dating—a quirky and humorous read." —*Belfast Sunday Life* (UK)

"A first novel that reads like an autobiography . . . You'll soon warm to a heroine who gets hurt but never bitter in her quest for The One. . . . While you're looking for Mr. Right, you can still have fun with Mr. Wrong." —*In Style* (UK)

"We all know true happiness lies within, but as *Ten Men*'s heroine discovers, flings with actors, lawyers and even a billionaire make the search way more interesting. Add the complication of a mum who doesn't believe in sex before marriage and you have a brilliant read." —*Cosmopolitan* (UK)

"If I were speaking to any of the men I've loved in the past, I would tell them to rush out immediately and buy *Ten Men*. . . . It's shockingly good." —Suzanne Finnamore, author of *The Zygote Chronicles* and *Otherwise Engaged*

"Reminiscent of Lucinda Rosenfeld's *What She Saw,* Gray's debut brings warm, bracing insight to the classic chic-lit story of a young woman in transition." —Misha Stone, *Booklist*

"A witty, sophisticated novel about the ups and all too many downs of modern dating . . . Gray's portrayal of modern dating is wryly accurate. Her debut novel is endearing and humorous but her point is a serious one: don't go looking for love until you know yourself."
—*Waterstone's Books Quarterly* (UK)

"Alexandra Gray's wickedly entertaining novel introduces a heroine for the noughties."
—*Western Mail Series* (UK)

"Does not disappoint . . . This is an intelligent book. . . . What lies behind that cover is a well-written and acutely observed novel; an intellectual woman's read—and a diamond in the rough of mass-market tosh."
—*City Sheffield* (UK)

Ten Men

ALEXANDRA GRAY

Grove Press
New York

First published in Great Britain in 2005 by Atlantic Books, an imprint of Grove Atlantic Ltd.

Printed in the United States of America

FIRST GROVE PRESS EDITION

Library of Congress Cataloging-in-Publication Data

Gray, Alexandra.
Ten men / Alexandra Gray.
p. cm.
ISBN-10: 0-8021-4252-4
ISBN-13: 978-0-8021-4252-8
1. Man-woman relationships—Fiction. 2. Young women—Fiction. 3. Happiness—Fiction. I. Title.

PR6107.R4T46 2005
823'.92—dc22 2004062781

Grove Press
an imprint of Grove/Atlantic, Inc.
841 Broadway
New York, NY 10003

Distributed by Publishers Group West

www.groveatlantic.com

06 07 08 09 10 10 9 8 7 6 5 4 3 2 1

Of all thy suitors, here I charge thee, tell

Whom thou lov'st best. See thou dissemble not.

❖

Shakespeare – The Taming of the Shrew

One

The Virgin

It is one of the wonders of the twenty-first century that a beautiful, brilliant and broad-shouldered man could reach almost forty without someone, somewhere convincing him it was time to drop his guard – or his underpants. God knows having sex is not difficult. It's not meant to be. Celibacy leads to extinction. But if nature and nurture conspire to inhibit the sexual impulse, we would all be virgins, every one of us. Or so the Virgin said. And I believed him, not just to be gracious, but because I understood how it could happen.

My mother's doctrine, inculcated in me as completely as her DNA, was that I should remain a virgin until the day I married. As an obedient daughter, I did my best to follow this command, hence an early engagement, subsequent marriage and a hasty divorce. My husband was mine for only a year. Divorce, however, did not liberate me from my mother's doctrinaire view. In the face of contrary evidence, I took longer than a lab rat to grasp that whenever a man wanted sex with me, marriage wasn't also on his mind. Today I understand what every woman eventually understands: there is sex without marriage, just as there is marriage without sex.

And so to the Virgin – my first – who completed the circle. I was back where I started, in bed with a beginner, except this time it wasn't me. Here was a man who embodied the qualities my mother so cherished, a man with the character to wait, and go on waiting, for Miss Right to show up. By the time we met, Mr Right Now was my philosophy, so when he looked at me I didn't step back and wonder why, but stepped forward thinking optimistically *why not*?

I certainly had questions about what made the Virgin's patience possible. I just didn't ask them before responding to his plea to 'Please, please, please be my teacher'. I should have noted at the time that he did not say, 'Please, please, please be my wife', which is why I assumed he'd waited.

We met on the night of a General Election. Phoebe and her husband, Charles, had invited me to a charity fundraising party in a decrepit but still elegant building in Belgravia. Downstairs, below the bland party in the grander rooms, drunken men and women filled the bar, oblivious to the television coverage of the British General Election. In the midst of this smoky noise, an Aryan-looking man, head tilted up at the wall-mounted television, was watching the Conservative Party lose constituencies throughout the land. Charles, I would later discover, had in mind the downfall of one more conservative stronghold.

'Would you do me the honour of allowing me to introduce you to one of my oldest friends? We were at university together,' Charles said, armed with champagne as we walked towards the Virgin who shook my hand, smiled a little too widely and pulled up a chair for me. He had all the manners. Nobody could have guessed at his lack of experience.

The Virgin was glamorous in the way few objects or people are any more, and his distinctive style was a reminder of a more gallant age. His Savile Row suit was a classic, he wore a striped shirt open at the neck and his brown hair fell in a Brideshead flop – a seductive touch.

Midnight, and the results were in: Tony Blair for another four years. The drunks cheered, but none of us cared. We dismissed politics, Charles ordered another round of champagne and, as we drank to a brighter future, out of the corner of my eye, I saw the Virgin stare at my bare feet through the silver threads of my shoes.

Later I watched him nod vigorously at Phoebe as they said goodbye, before hailing a cab to his part of London, which from the look of him had to be Chelsea. Meanwhile, I drove Charles and Phoebe to Notting Hill, our part of town.

'Well? Do you like him?' Phoebe asked from the back seat, eager as a stockbroker pushing equities, watching my response in the rear-view mirror.

'He's nice. Yes … I think he's nice.'

'He'd like to see you again,' she said.

'Really?'

'Yes. You're the reason he came tonight.'

'But he didn't know me.'

'I told him about you. Don't be put off. His body's fantastic, he's really clever and he's from a good family.'

'Can I give him your number?' asked Charles, getting straight to the point.

Charles didn't give a damn about his friend's physique or family, but he wanted the Virgin to be happy and enjoyed playing his wife's game. Phoebe's mission was to bring her single friends to the state of marital bliss and for that I saluted her, irrespective of the results. Most married women don't socialize with single women, unless it's alone during the day when their husbands are safely out of the way. But Phoebe was different. She promoted her single friends, matching men with women at every opportunity, and I was her latest project. She took too long to tell me that the

Virgin had been a work in progress for sixteen years.

The Virgin called the very next day to invite me to the theatre (he'd get the tickets) and dinner (he'd make the reservation). Here was a man who knew what he wanted, and I liked that. Bearing in mind Ralph Waldo Emerson's caution to 'beware of all enterprises that require new clothes', I picked out my favourite black dress, pair of black Chanel sling-backs and a classic handbag I'd found that summer in Portobello market. The look was Ralph Lauren without the price tag, and sexy enough. Best of all, I hadn't dashed out to buy any of it. There was no reason to beware on a first date with a man I'd only met for an hour, sustained by champagne and a midsummer's midnight. No new clothes, no nerves, no tension. He seemed to be a courteous, trouble-free zone and I was convinced he would cause me less pleasure and pain than his magnetic predecessor – a man across the Atlantic it had taken me too long to forget.

That evening I slung on my familiar clothes and looked in the mirror. Needs a belt, I thought. I've got a waist, I may as well show it. It was six o'clock. I had a credit card, and just enough time to dash to one of the boutiques on Ledbury Road. Fifteen minutes later I jumped into a cab for the West End, a big buckled belt around my waist. But this wasn't any old belt. This was a £200 handmade belt. Consequently I was no longer going on any old date. I had stupidly raised the stakes.

I arrived at the theatre ten minutes late to find the Virgin waiting in the empty foyer, clad in a bespoke suit that certainly wasn't new. I followed him up to the dress circle. His loafers were plain black and he wasn't wearing socks. I noticed how the hairs on his ankles curled provocatively, and I wondered about blisters. I should have guessed he wasn't a summer-sock kind of man.

After forty minutes it was apparent that our front-row dress circle seats were better than the play. Getting fidgety, I crossed my legs and knocked his. 'Sorry,' I whispered, placing a hand on his knee, which I couldn't help noticing was strong and perfectly formed. Later, at the restaurant, he took off his jacket to reveal more of the physique Phoebe had recommended. Buttons were missing from his shirt, and his smooth tanned chest was exposed as if by accident. To counteract this impression of laissez-faire vanity, the Virgin carried his possessions in a transparent plastic carrier bag. Gym kit, newspapers, notebooks, house keys, even his wallet was stuffed in there. But no car keys. The Virgin was averse to modern cars and had never learned to drive.

Halfway through dinner, and all the way through a bottle of wine, I was beginning to like this rather irregular man. I just couldn't believe that he didn't have another woman lurking around and eventually felt confident enough to ask: 'When was your last girlfriend?'

'Ah ... girlfriend ...' He stumbled into silence.

'You've got one?'

There was a longer silence.

'A girlfriend is something, I mean a girlfriend is someone I've wanted in my life for as long as I can remember.'

'Do you mean you've never had a girlfriend?'

My question sounded like an accusation and the Virgin blushed, then laughed. Actually it was more of a bleat, for I had taken the lamb to slaughter. He wasn't the only one to be embarrassed: in the light of the Virgin's willingness to wait, I regretted my own impulsive past. I didn't want him to feel inadequate, but I especially didn't want him to think I'd had one boyfriend too many. But whichever way I looked at it, our different attempts to find a mate had yielded the same result: we were both still single. There could be no judgement on either side.

'We've approached the same dilemma from opposite directions,' I said, trying to find common ground. 'But how did you, you know, get this far — '

'Quality control. I'm famous for it. I'm a pretty austere judge.'

I chose to ignore this blaring warning signal, and responded to the Virgin as a challenge, a man to convince of my worth.

Over dinner I encouraged him to talk and was being open myself. 'My sister and I have clocked up three marriages and two divorces. But she's happily married now,' I added.

This failed to reassure the Virgin, who smiled maniacally as he gulped more wine. Regaining his composure and, with eyes fixed on his medium-rare steak, he asked, 'Do you have children?'

'No,' I said. I don't think I sounded rueful.

'And your parents ... are they divorced?'

'They were together and in love until the day my father died. What about your parents?'

'Alive and kicking, happy to say.'

❖

We met several times after that first evening and, because I'm not good at small talk, I rushed the Virgin into conversations he had spent his life avoiding. He was a restrained English man, who spent weekends in the country with his parents, or with friends from The University, engaged in activities that were familiar and safe. The prospect of widening his horizons was part of the appeal, but I should have read the label. He didn't do wider horizons. Away from polite society, his antiques business and occasional work for the posh people's travel guide, this man had amassed little experience. In retrospect, I should have abandoned the whole affair and let him down gently with the suggestion that we should have met twenty years ago when our personal histories were in the same ballpark. Instead I found his innocence endearing and, in the mistaken belief that it was his secret wish, I decided to help him open up – a phrase he wouldn't have understood unless I meant with a cleaver. I reassured the Virgin that it was admirable to wait for the perfect girl and, oh vanity, began to believe that perhaps he had been waiting for me.

'So how did you manage to stay single for so long?' I asked the Virgin over supper one evening.

'I'm a terrible example of what can happen to love unrequited. Sadly the girls I fell for didn't fall for me. And now one sees one's friends married with children, leading full lives …' He trailed off. 'You see the thing is, I'm shy,' he said quietly.

Profoundly shy, I thought, or gay. Looking across the candlelit table, I couldn't believe that love unrequited accounted for this good-looking man's celibacy. Sexual persuasion aside, the Virgin was ambivalent at best, because there comes a time when either you want it or you don't.

'Surely there were women who fell for you?'

'I'm told some did, but I'm an absolutist. I could only see the girls I fell in love with, and none of them noticed me.'

I should have guessed that the Virgin had never listened to popular music. His favourite singer was Noël Coward, who, to be fair, was popular once. But while listening to those witty tunes, Mick Jagger's wise counsel had passed the Virgin by. He had failed to understand that sometimes in the absence of what you want, it's perfectly reasonable to get what you need.

Twenty years on and tired of waiting, getting what he needed was on the Virgin's mind most of the time. A few weeks after our first date, and yet another polite dinner, we were sitting in my car outside the Virgin's white terraced house, when he told me about the Vegas girls. More than a year before he had taken a flight on an appropriately named airline for a stag week in Las Vegas. In the company of entertaining friends and strangers, the Virgin had found himself in a strip joint where pretty girls cavorted on his lap, their long hair draped over him as their nipples grazed the tip of his nose. One dancer had broken all the rules and placed her ripe, sweet nipple between the Virgin's open lips and he could not forget it. That girl was the closest the Virgin had got to sex, and her memory gave him hope, plus some, for each of the three hundred and ninety-five days since he'd slipped a fifty-dollar bill into her red sequinned panties.

Before we'd met, the Virgin was contemplating a return to the infamous oasis. Finally he was prepared to renounce the dream of happily ever after with the perfect girl in favour of one happy night with a perfectly willing Vegas girl. By the time the Virgin had finished his saucy tale, my car windows were quite steamed up, but the Vegas girls did not intimidate me. I knew the Virgin wanted to invite me in – if only he could find the words.

'Would you, er … Would you do me the … Are you … ,' he began, before giving up. He leaned back, closed his eyes and sighed. After a second he looked at me with uncertain eyes and smiling sheepishly said, 'Would you like a cup of tea?' Hardly seductive, it was effective. A few seconds later we were at the front door. Perhaps the Virgin wouldn't be returning to Vegas after all.

The Virgin was surprised and a little embarrassed to discover his house looked like a laundry. Unironed shirts hung from the corners of doors and the back of every chair.

'Sorry about this. Maria can't have come today.'

Maria was the woman in his life, 'a Spanish angel' who was his confidante so far as a stiff upper lip allowed. She cleaned and ironed for him once a week, although for some reason not today.

He pushed on the cassette player, and Nina Simone sang the eerie melody, 'Strange Fruit'.

The Virgin hummed along as he gathered up his shirts and put the kettle on. I sat on the edge of the sofa. The drawing room had a bare wooden floor, a few sombre prints featuring dead animals, or fighting soldiers, and an antique desk.

'Earl Grey?' The Virgin called from the kitchen, his head in a battered pine cupboard, as he rummaged through stacked-up packets of dry goods. 'Or Darjeeling?'

'Any herb tea?'

'God no. Do you take milk?' He was in the light of the fridge now, sniffing an open carton. 'Ah – milk's off.'

He poured congealed milk into the sink. To his credit, the Virgin sensed that this was no seduction scene. 'Do you want a tour?' he said, as though we were in a stately home, rather than a narrow house in Fulham.

Without waiting for the kettle to boil, we mounted the stairs. More pastel-coloured shirts hung on the banister. He swept them up as we passed, pressing the fine cotton shirts to his face.

'They don't make cotton like this any more. These belonged to my grandfather.'

His bedroom was white with a low bed, a chest of drawers and a hard, wooden chair. Apart from an orange bed cover, which provided the only note of colour, the theme was Monastic Bachelor.

'This is from Thailand,' he said, folding the bright cloth, 'my second favourite place, after England in June.'

We perched on the edge of the bed, fully dressed, and kissed. Actually, it would be more accurate to say we pressed our mouths together. I tried closing my eyes, but it didn't feel right and opening them, I found the Virgin staring at me, eyes popped, comic-strip style. We pulled our lips apart to draw breath.

'I don't know whether you can tell, but I'm a bit nervous. I've lived here for twelve years and you're the first girl to sit on my bed.'

I tried to be positive. 'I find you very attractive,' I said, thinking something was badly wrong if I was coming up with that line at such a moment.

I sympathized with this man with his impressive intellect and body to match, who was stuck in a rut that should have lasted a few months when he was seventeen and not dragged on longer than anybody could have imagined. A fatal mix of vanity, hope and pity compelled me to persist. I felt it was up to me to help him, convinced that, given the right encouragement, the Virgin could be moulded into a lover with a smooth hand. I needed to instil confidence, but I wasn't sure how to proceed – and the Virgin certainly wasn't. The prospect of getting laid for the first time had paralyzed him. A grin was fixed in the centre of his face and his hand stuck to my breast like Velcro.

I peeled off his heavy hand, and took a deep breath. He took this as a cue to stand and remove his jacket and shoes (no socks to worry about). It was no good. I couldn't go through with it and I was about to tell him so, when the Virgin removed his shirt. His commitment to the gym, pounding the treadmill and pushing weights, had not been time wasted. The Virgin's torso was sculpted to perfection. He glistened with a freshly showered cleanliness that was cut with his own smell.

We attempted another kiss, which was marginally more successful than the first, and he stood again, this time to remove his trousers. When the blue polka-dot boxers came off I appreciated every finely muscled movement: the Virgin's body was London's best-kept secret.

He fumbled with my bra for a full minute until finally I was unhooked. My breast fell into his hand. He looked – and kept looking as if overwhelmed. I touched him and he lay back, wide-eyed amazement replacing the rictus grin. He was so hard, it was a delight. Perhaps, I thought, just perhaps it pays to be a virgin, regardless of age or gender. And then, without warning, he exploded. Semen flew everywhere; his neck, my face, even the wall five feet behind us got splattered. And that was that, the Virgin's first time with a woman brought to a premature end.

Our first night together wasn't a complete disappointment though. There are many varieties of come, from super spunk, the 'grand cru' with highly creative potential, all the way down to the dirty dishwater variety, which is less plentiful and altogether less appealing. It was some kind of compensation to discover the Virgin's semen was so pure it looked like double cream. It even smelled sweet. Here was a man, if ever there was one, to get a woman pregnant, and while that thought had yet to cross my conscious mind, my ovaries thought of nothing else.

❖

In the summer months that followed the Virgin and I saw a lot of each other. Nothing could beat breakfast in his garden, going through the papers, discussing the news. The Virgin was well informed and witty and at first I was amused by his particularly English superiority complex, characteristic of someone sent to public school before they could tie shoelaces. But as time went by, the Virgin, who never questioned his own views or intelligence, began to question mine.

'Of course I don't think you're stupid,' he'd say. 'It's just a pity you didn't have a teacher like my English master at Eton. If only you'd gone to public school. And it's a tragedy you didn't go to The University.'

'Why? I'm glad I went to the States to get my degree. And as for private school, I don't think it's — '

'Public school, darling. Private school is so American.'

'So?'

'We're English.'

The Virgin went to great lengths to point out my political naivety and my intellectual inferiority, while I tried just as hard not to remind him of his sexual inexperience. When it came to the bedroom, we scored highly for effort, but not for execution. Having fantasized about the female form in abstract ways, when the Virgin was confronted with the reality of a woman's body, something got lost in translation. It wasn't so much that the treasure that had taken so long to attain, once possessed, lost its lustre; it was more a question of proximity. Stripped of numinous qualities, the female form in all its glory was a little gory for the Virgin.

His idea of sex was more convoluted than was my custom. He wanted a shimmering sex goddess who tantalized and teased. In short, he wanted a lap dancer. I bought the heels and lacy underwear, but putting on that outfit to make love felt like hard work and I began to wonder why being naked together wasn't sexy enough.

While we battled on in the bedroom, the word was out: the Virgin had a girlfriend. We received invitations to spend weekends in glamorous places, which distracted us from our difficulties, but also caused some. At the end of a long summer of socializing in the Mediterranean, and stalking in Scotland, the Virgin was commissioned to write about the old inns of Cornwall. It was the perfect opportunity to spend time together alone.

'My assignments are frequently indecently exotic,' he quipped, 'but be a darling and join me.'

The Virgin went on ahead so that he could get some work done, and I arrived a few days later. The inn where we met was ancient from the front, the original rooms dark, low-beamed and unchanged for three hundred years, but at the back of the building newly-built bedrooms transformed olde England into Americana. I walked down a long glass corridor to find my once Virgin male sitting in a conservatory, talking with the proprietor – a self-made multi-millionaire from Australia. Introductions were made and we listened to our host's rags-to-riches tale before he turned to me and said, 'Where are you from?'

'England.'

'But I can tell you haven't always lived in this country.'

'I've lived in New York, and Paris.' Paris was an exaggeration, but it was what the Australian wanted to hear.

'Exactly. International,' he said, and I smiled because he was trying to flatter me.

A few minutes later, our host summoned a porter to take us to our room. The Virgin whipped out pen and notepad. 'What's wrong with this room?' he asked.

I spun around. 'Bed's too big?' I said, falling back onto it.

'Wastepaper basket, that's what's wrong,' he said. 'There should be one in here,' and he noted that fact down. 'Hotels must provide their guests with all their needs. And I don't mean shaver sockets, which should be turned into glue, or something useful.'

The Virgin was a wet-shave devotee, and divided men into those loyal to the blade, and those common enough to shave electrically. While he scribbled down details of the prints – copies of nineteenth-century hunting scenes – displayed strategically on pale cream walls, I crept up behind him and covered his eyes with my hands.

'Darling, I'm working,' he said.

I kissed his neck and he squirmed, dropping his pad to the floor, and we fell together on to the wide bed.

'You mustn't distract me. I've got to meet our host in the bar for a tour in twenty minutes.'

'So there's time to play.' I kissed his neck again.

'The original rooms date from the fifteen hundreds. God knows why our host stuck us in this monstrous room tacked on at the back of the building.'

'He said I looked international,' I said, undoing the Virgin's shirt and kissing his chest.

'International hooker more like.'

'What?'

'Joke, darling.'

'It wasn't funny.'

'Oh God. Sense of humour failure.'

The Virgin tried to conceal his sense of inferiority with suggestions that I had too much experience, but I refused to be amused.

'I'm joking,' he insisted. 'We have to be able to laugh together. It's crucial.'

The Virgin was right, but we didn't have many laughs that weekend, not simply because I was furious at his comment, but also because wherever we went his notepad was pressed to his nose. He jotted down descriptions and locations of fixtures and fittings; soaps, lack thereof; the textures of cushion covers; the source of marmalade, bread, candles, sheets and even headed notepaper; the time it took staff to respond to room service; whether the restaurant waitresses were as efficient as they were pretty. The list was long, for the Virgin had a meticulous and critical eye, and as the weekend wore on, the more inclined he was to focus it on me. Resentments were stacking up on both sides and we jumped on them like bickering siblings. But I was entrenched and on the way back from the Cornish trip, I found myself meeting the Parents. Another mistake.

❖

I drove us back to London and as we passed through Wiltshire the Virgin pulled his mobile out of his pocket. 'I'd better call them.'

'Who?'

'Mother and Father. They live around here,' he said, punching in the numbers. 'Hello, Ma. No, I'm pretty close actually. I was thinking of dropping in. Don't worry about supper. Sausages? Fantastic. And Ma – I'm with somebody I'd like you to meet. The sausages will go round. I don't think she eats them. Vegetarian apparently. There's a long list of what's off the menu, including butter.' He laughed. 'See ya.'

'That wasn't so difficult. Sausages for supper, I'm afraid. But homemade, and the purest thing on the planet.'

I was more worried about my skirt.

'What's wrong with it?' the Virgin asked.

'It's very short.'

'Exactly.'

'Shouldn't I change into something more suitable?'

'I can't think of anything more suitable than your legs in that skirt.'

We drove on in silence through more quaint villages and more ploughed fields, until the Virgin directed me to take a narrow lane off the main road.

'We're quite close, but don't be nervous. It's crucial you're not nervous.'

This ritual wasn't new to me and I had no nerves, while the Virgin, I noticed, was actually sweating. He had brought other girls home, girls from The University, women who were friends, but nobody Significant.

'I think you're the one who's nervous,' I said.

'I'm fine.' He pushed in a cassette of John Betjeman reciting his poetry. The Virgin's lips moved silently in time with Betjeman's meticulous pronunciation.

From the geyser ventilators,
Autumn winds are blowing down
On a thousand business women
Having baths in Camden Town.

Those rounded vowels, so correctly pronounced, echoed the Virgin's own precise diction, and as we drove past ploughed fields flat as wallpaper, I longed for variety. I was not about to get it. The five-bar gate was open and we swooped onto a gravel drive around the side of the house to park opposite a rosebed. It was late September, there had been no rain for a week and the air was rich with the scent of heavy-headed flowers. The fine Georgian house was smaller and less opulent than I had been led to believe. Its classic simplicity was balanced by an English country garden and elegant trees.

The Parents, in anticipation of an event for which they had waited many years, were there to greet us before we got out of the car. Their youngest child was bringing a girl home, and expectations were almost as high as the hem of my denim mini, which I could tell already was not a good idea. I extracted myself carefully from the driver's seat, edging my skirt hopefully in the direction of my knees.

The mother extended her hand: thin lips, full skirt, red cardigan, a slash of neon pink lipstick. Her mouth moved into a rigid smile. I think she decided not to like me even before she shook my hand. Her husband hesitated, a glint in his eye, and a pleasant smile. Father, like son, wore the summer uniform: white cotton trousers and beige, light-weight jackets – classics straight out of a Noël Coward play. And just as Coward would have had it, we were all terribly polite.

Handshaking and first impressions done with, we stood for a second not quite sure what to do next. The Mother took the initiative. Turning to her husband she said, 'Why don't you two go into the garden?' And to the Virgin: 'You, darling, can help me with tea.'

The Father and I walked in silence across long lawns towards an imposing avenue of trees. The old man didn't try to be polite, or force a conversation, and for that I was grateful.

'I planted these from seed over forty years ago,' he said, as we walked down an avenue of poplars which resonated with the spirit of a cathedral. We made our way in the shade of the tall trees towards open sky and open fields, and I knew that no architect could have created anything more impressive.

We returned to the house, which was crammed with quiet good taste, to discover that mother and son had decided that we would stay the night. I was shown to the guest bedroom, and the Virgin told me he would sleep in the bedroom above, a civilized distance apart and next to his parents' room.

Over a sausage supper (I had four), mother and son enthused about books, shared disappointments about Radio Four's left-wing news coverage and swore they couldn't listen to *The Archers,* which was a travesty with its regional accents, weak plot lines and middle-class gossip.

During their enthusiastic conversations, the Virgin's Mother turned to ask me for the salt. 'There you go,' I said, passing it to her.

The Virgin flinched. 'There you go', he later explained, was a common phrase that debased the language and was consequently on the family's black list.

'So I understand that you lived in America?' the Mother said, no doubt prompted by my slang.

'Yes. New York.'

'And liked it?'

'It's a great city.'

'It's somewhere we've thought of going, isn't it, darling?' she said to her husband. 'But it seems so American somehow.'

'I still want to visit one day,' he said.

'When this country has become so Americanized, one hardly needs to travel to see what we have more than enough of at home.'

'Smart casual,' said the Father, chuckling.

'Oh darling, don't start,' said the Mother.

'Smart casual?' I said.

'American phrases; anathema to Pa. But we've heard them all before, Pa, so don't start,' warned the Virgin.

'Smart casual – terrible phrase, terrible idea. And chinos. What in heaven's name are chinos?' asked the old man, encouraged by my support to override the opposition.

'You're wearing a pair,' I smiled.

'Am I really?' He seemed amused. 'America. The best and worst country in the world. I'll get there before I die.'

'Oh, darling. Let's not exaggerate,' said his wife, pouring herself more red wine, winking at her son over the rim of her glass.

After supper, the Virgin announced we were going for a walk. For a second I thought his mother was coming too, but after we had helped clear the table, as good children should, we escaped from the confines of the house. It was liberating to be outside on that late summer's evening, the air cool and clear. In the middle of the lawn, where the light of the house couldn't reach us, the Virgin laughed with delight, swinging me around and around. The moonlit garden was the pastoral paradise of True Love, where young lovers hide from parents and the rest of the world to steal chaste kisses. The Virgin was transported. 'I've longed for this moment. And they think you're wonderful.' His face was flushed, excited as a teenager in love.

'Are you sure your parents like me?' All I had detected was disapproval.

'Darling, they love you, I can tell.'

We kissed again. It was all so new for him, not just the kissing, but kissing at home under a full moon, his parents so near but out of sight.

'Could you imagine living here with me?' he asked, stopping to hold both my hands, our arms extended towards each other.

'We could live here one day … once your parents have died.' I had tried to be tactful, and failed.

'Darling, how could you?' The Virgin's face fell. 'Ma and Pa have years in them, thank God. They're fantastic people.'

'Maybe, but not to live with.'

'I want to live here with them *and* you,' he said.

'We'd all go nuts.' I let go of his hands. For a second he looked crushed, as though I had robbed him, but my reality could not destroy his quixotic ideal.

'Just wait, you'll see. The more we come here, the more you'll learn to love Ma and Pa,' he said, stepping up beside me as we walked down the avenue into the darkness of the deep trees.

❖

The following morning I went down for an early breakfast and, approaching the kitchen, overheard hushed voices. I strained to listen.

'She's marvellous, isn't she?' said the Virgin, sounding proud.

'She's not exactly what we were expecting, darling,' the Mother said.

'I know she's got a different idiom from living in America. And she goes to therapy,' he added.

'Goodness, darling, *therapy*. Thank God none of my children have needed that mumbo jumbo.'

'But what do you really think of her?'

'I'm ambivalent because you are.'

'Am I?'

'You're not sure about her, darling, I can tell. And another thing — '

'What?' He was eager for her words. 'Go on.'

'If you stay together you'll never have children. She'll soon be too old.'

'We've talked about our great antiquity.'

'It's her great antiquity, not yours. A man of thirty-eight is so much younger than a woman of the same age.'

Mother and son sat in silence, and I was about to sneak back to my bedroom and sob into my starched, white linen pillowcase, when I heard the Mother say, 'Whatever happened to that lovely girl Lady Annabel Pitt-Ponsonby?'

'What, Lady A?'

'The photograph of you both on her parents' estate is still by my bed. You were deliriously happy, darling, and she was so in love with you. I remember getting down on my knees, praying you would marry her.'

'Ma, she was just a friend.'

'Friends make us happy, darling. Don't think you'll find happiness with a girl just because she's different and has long legs.'

❖

A month before I'd met the Parents, in spite of the obvious hurdles, the Virgin had talked about commitment and having a family of four children – never mind that I was in my late thirties, and one child would have been a miracle. The Virgin had given no indication that he wasn't ready to walk his talk. He'd even asked me where I would like to get married.

'Depends who to,' I'd said.

'To whom,' he'd corrected, and once we'd got the grammar straight, 'To me, for example.' Indeed.

However, the Virgin hadn't mentioned marriage, children or moving to the country since I'd met the Parents. Meanwhile his tendency to correct my speech had become a compulsion. The more he insisted that I conform to perfect English usage, the more I refused to fall in line, particularly when to do so would have made me sound like a character from an Edwardian play. The Virgin's adherence to convention was driving me mad. I no longer saw it as charming eccentricity, but a blinkered adherence to his mother's worldview. My fear that we were incompatible was brought into focus whenever we tried to have sex. The Virgin was ambivalence in action, keen to initiate, but unable to finish what he'd started. Increasingly we settled for a brief hug and quick peck on the lips, rather than face the horrible truth that the Virgin couldn't rise to the occasion. And as we fell asleep, back to back, I would remember his mother's comment: 'I'm ambivalent about her because you are.'

One minute I was convinced I should ask the Virgin whether his mother's opinion was affecting his erection, the next I feared this conversation would take him over the edge and our relationship with it. And so I kept quiet.

Then one evening, driving over Westminster Bridge after the theatre, I was about to express my love for the city at night, when I realized there was no point. The Virgin was sitting beside me but in every way that mattered, he wasn't there at all.

'Are you okay?' I asked a second time.

'I'm fine, darling.'

'It's as though you're not here,' I said.

'Really, darling, I'm fine.'

He was dismal, staring ahead, unaware of the dark, broad expanse of water that reflected the riverside lights and buildings.

'It was the play. A twenty-four-carat downer. Blacker than a power cut.' His usual façade of carefully chosen words was in place.

'You don't think it's got something to do with your mother's comment?'

'What comment?' He was impervious to me. 'I think it's my ind —'

'Indigestion?' I interrupted, because dinner had been as indigestible as the play.

'No, my dyspepsia hasn't bothered me for a while,' he said.

'What then?'

'My indecision,' he said flatly.

Perhaps the mother had identified her son's ambivalence towards me before he'd been aware of it, or perhaps she had sowed its seed. Either way, I had an indecisive man on my hands. We drove back to my flat in silence and as soon as we were through the front door he held me tight, arms heavy around my shoulders, his face pressed into the curve of my neck. The dead weight of him was terrible.

'Are you depressed?' I asked, trying to dislodge his buried face. I needed to see his eyes, but he wouldn't look at me.

'I'm not right in myself,' he said, extracting his body from mine. He sat, eyes downcast, on the edge of the sofa, and I realized that whenever he was with me, the Virgin perched like this. I was looking at a man who couldn't even commit to sitting comfortably.

'Would you like a cup of tea?'

'Yes please, darling.' He grimaced at me, presumably from gratitude because I'd changed the subject. But not for long.

'How long have you been feeling like this?'

'I don't know. I don't think about feelings.'

'Not ever?'

'Not especially. Feelings aren't that important. I think you've made the mistake of believing how you feel inside matters. Feelings are a luxury for people who haven't got something else to worry about.' He looked me sharp in the eye.

'If you mean they're a feature of civilization, then being aware of feelings could be seen as an advance for mankind,' I said.

We were both quiet. He stared at the floor. Honestly, it was as though somebody had died.

'You're not happy, are you?' I said, stating the obvious.

His response took a while. 'I remember the last time I was happy. I was walking out of my house to the tube,' he said in a soft, small voice.

'When was that?'

'Four weeks ago last Tuesday.'

'Would you be happy now, if you were at home, the prospect of a morning walk to the tube waiting for you?'

'I don't know.'

I handed him a cup of steaming tea, no milk, thick slice of lemon.

'Thank you, darling,' and then he said, 'Perhaps I'd be happier if we could just date.'

'What does that mean?'

'You know, see each other once a week.'

'Once a week?'

'Once – or twice. I don't know, I've never dated before so I'm not quite sure how one does it.'

I was confused. There seemed nothing left to say and we went to bed without another word.

❖

The following morning, in white cotton knickers, I lay on my back between white cotton sheets, both hands resting on my abdomen. It was twenty to six and my ovaries had woken me up. It hadn't happened before. I looked at the Virgin sleeping beside me in the cool morning light, our late-night conversation in my mind. The suitable boy was backing out. Dating was all he could cope with. My ovaries, meanwhile, were in rebellion, tantalized by the hope of healthy sperm that was only an ejaculation away.

'We don't care about dating,' they screamed at me, shrinking from their suspensory ligaments. Ovaries are ruthless, dismissive of convention, marriage and even Love. They didn't care about the Virgin. All they wanted was his sperm.

'We're emptying out down here. Make use of our eggs,' they pleaded.

However much my reproductive organs wanted me to fulfil my biological destiny, and as much as I liked the Virgin's talk about having children, I was yet to be convinced. In the restaurant the previous evening during our pre-theatre supper, while the Virgin was building to his black moment, I had watched a perfect baby eating a paper tablecloth, sticky yellow food running down its chin. My instinct – to which I did not respond – was to pick up the baby, wipe its chin, kiss its cheek, hold it and then hand it back to the mother.

'Have one for yourself,' whispered the primordial part of my brain that was crying out for such moments, not in a restaurant for five minutes, but for as long as it takes for a child to learn to eat without losing its food down its face.

The Virgin turned in his sleep. I wanted to talk, but feared what we would say.

'I couldn't sleep last night,' he said from behind closed eyes. 'And you slept like a baby, which made it worse.'

'I can't sleep now,' I said, tears filling my eyes and running down my cheeks.

'Oh, bubba don't cry,' he said, and reached out to hold me. Although deep sobs went through my whole body, a part of my mind was wondering about 'bubba'. I hadn't heard the Virgin use this term before – it seemed most uncharacteristic.

'I've been thinking: we can't go on like this. You're right. Let's date. We can see each other once a week,' I said.

'Oh, darling.' He moved closer, the soft warmth of his body pressed against mine. We kissed, our mouths full and open, his hands smooth on my body and we made love for the first time in a month, perfect timing beginning to end. Afterwards, resting together, heads touching as we drifted close to sleep, it was as though there was a connection between us, stronger than ever before.

'Perhaps you should build a wing at your parents'. It wouldn't be so bad, we could spend weekends there …' I said dreamily. I wanted him to know that I could conform to his wishes, and anticipating his happy response, I turned towards him. He was staring, wide-eyed at the ceiling, and once again had checked out.

'Are you okay?' I asked. And then I heard myself say, 'Are you thinking of another girl?'

'Yes,' he said, just like that. I rolled onto my tummy and, propped up on my elbows, began to ask him the kind of questions that are necessary when a person is confused and that confusion involves you. My voice was slow and steady, without emotion.

'What kind of girl are you thinking about?'

'A laidback American girl.'

'Have you ever met one?' (I hadn't.)

'Once, for ten minutes. In a pub. She was laughing, and she made me laugh.'

'How did you meet?'

'We had friends in common.'

'When?'

'A year and a half ago.'

Ten minutes ago we'd made love and it was intimate and strong, and here he was reminiscing about a girl he'd met briefly in a pub over a year ago. What's more, she was American. What about her grammar? They'd never get beyond his corrections. It didn't add up.

'I used to be certain of everything, now I'm not sure of anything,' he said, eyes still fixated on the ceiling.

'Are you sure you want to run your antique business and write for the travel journal?' My voice was neutral, and suddenly I was numb, asking questions as though his response had nothing to do with me.

'Yes.'

'And that one day you'll want children?'

'Yes.'

'And you believe in children within marriage?'

'Yes.'

'So you want to be married?'

'Yes.'

'So the only thing you're not sure about is me.'

'Yes.' At least he had the decency to hesitate.

I climbed out of bed. He was no longer 'The Virgin.' Now, if he chose to be, he was a Lover with a Smooth Hand. I ran the bath, made a pot of tea, burnt the toast, spread it with English butter and marmalade that was not homemade. And once he'd bathed and breakfasted, I showed him the door.

'Oh, darling,' he said, standing on the doorstep clutching his trademark carrier bag. He was about to rest his head in a sorrowful heap on my shoulder, but I stepped aside.

'Goodbye,' I said firmly and shut the door, determined never to talk to him again.

Five weeks later I found out I was pregnant.

Two

The Schoolmaster

We were all virgins once, intact and incomplete, and few forget when the veil was lifted on that state of purity. I had anticipated the moment with delight, but losing my virginity was a more solemn and solitary experience than I had imagined. On my knees, eyes screwed tight, elbows digging into the soft mattress of a single bed, teetering on the precipice of original sin, I prayed: 'Our Father who art in Heaven.'

The man about to transform me from fantasizing girl into a woman was looking for a condom in the bathroom.

'Hallowed be thy name.'

I wished he'd put one under the pillow. When we were kissing, I'd felt ready.

'Thy kingdom come, thy will be done.'

But now I'm not so sure. God? Is this meant to be?

'On earth as it is in Heaven.'

Even though my mother says men only marry virgins.

'Give us this day our daily bread.'

But he loves me.

'And forgive us our sins as we forgive those who sin against us.'

And this won't be a sin if we get married.

'Lead us not into temptation.'

Oh dear Lord, please forgive me.

Before I got to the power and the glory, I heard him coming down the hall and leaped back into bed. Through eyelash tips I watched him walk into the room.

'Behind the shampoo,' he laughed, holding a single condom like a prize.

I took a lung-expanding breath, as if to extend time. He pulled his blue bed shirt over his head and stood naked at the foot of the bed. Even if he had approached in slow motion it would have seemed too fast.

He bit the silver condom packet, tearing the corner with his teeth, stroking himself with his other hand. His testicles drew up into him. I wondered how that happened and why.

Suddenly he was so erect I forgot my nerves and sat up, curious as a cat. He unrolled the transparent disc down the shaft of his penis, which glinted like a blade in the sunlight passing through a crack in the closed curtains. Dust particles floated in morning air and, caught in their suspension, I watched him move towards me. He pressed close, warm breath on my shoulder. 'I want to be careful,' he said gently.

The bed was so narrow there was nowhere to put his hard penis, apart from into me, which is where it went without much ado. I thought about joining in with the moving around, but pinned to the mattress I couldn't work out the rhythm. A sandpaper sensation deep within made me catch my breath and suddenly it was though I wasn't there at all.

This isn't really happening, I said to myself. Our Father who art in Heaven, please may this not last long. Hallowed name, hallowed ground. Forgive me, Father, for this sin, which feels punishment enough. I escaped to a memory of the day before, walking through a field, when my boyfriend had knelt and lifted my skirt to kiss between my legs. The force of my orgasmic cry

unrebellious student, but all those 'Hail Marys' couldn't stop me longing for a man about the house. By the time I was fourteen I had stuck first a poster of Donny Osmond, then one of tennis star Arthur Ashe on the back of my bedroom door. The posters, tacked at a height that placed the men's mouths above mine, were hidden from my mother by my dressing gown and beneath the eyes of God (whom I'd decided was more benevolent than the nuns would have me believe), I engaged in unresponsive kisses on unconventionally large lips. One-sided kisses with poster men did not lessen my frustration at being trapped within the female matrix and I could not understand why my mother and sister didn't seem to need a flesh and blood man in the family. Every day I encouraged my sister to help me look for a man for our mother, but the candidates in our village were either married, or eighty. 'You're wasting your time,' my sister advised. 'Even if you found Paul Newman, our dear mother wouldn't succumb.' Fuelled by my own curiosity to know men (one would do), I refused to be deterred.

The man I was searching for was nearer than I had imagined, so close in fact he was calling at our door twice a week. Regular visitors included the milkman, postman, a man who sold cleaning fluids and another who sharpened knives, but it was the greengrocer, Mr T, his van loaded with homegrowns, who caught my eye. But I think he caught my mother's first. Certain afternoons she would paint her lips, casually and without the slightest vanity. It took me a while to make the connection between this embellishment and Mr T's visits. If his Romany good looks had inspired my mother to lipstick, I felt it was my duty to encourage a more intimate relationship. Mr T was dark-haired and lean, and I found him as dramatic as the Catholic Church. He always wore a black shirt, open to the centre of his chest, black trousers and a silver chain that glistened on his skin. In my attempt to draw Mr T into our world, I went with my mother to talk to him at the back of his van and a few weeks later three tickets for the latest local amateur dramatic society's production were tucked in with our vegetables.

My mother scrutinized the tickets. 'So, Mr T's a thespian,' she said in such a way I couldn't tell whether that was a good or bad thing. '*My Fair Lady*. I wonder what part he'll play?'

'Let's go, then we'll find out,' I said.

'We should go, it's only polite,' said my sister, snatching the tickets from my mother and sticking them on top of the fridge under the Bible, as if conferring God's blessing on their use.

The day came for us to see *My Fair Lady*, in which Mr T played Eliza's father, even though he wasn't much older than Eliza herself, but we all agreed he could act and sing. Shakespeare's *Othello* followed, in which Mr T played the lead and we got to see him naked from the waist up and discover it wasn't just his face that was dark. After his persuasive performance as the Moor, I was convinced my mother wouldn't need any more encouragement to appreciate the charms of our travelling greengrocer. But I couldn't even persuade her to invite him in for a cup of tea – and I tried for three whole years.

By the time I was seventeen a summer heatwave stimulated a desire for more intimate male company. The long hot days had prompted my mother to cut down our attendance at Mass (she was from the Mediterranean and adored the sun almost as much as she adored the good Lord), and we spent afternoons roasting naked on the flat roof at the back of our terraced house. I was studying for A Levels, my sister for nursing exams and, lying between us, my mother took it in turn to test us both. My sister's first choice had been art college, but such a precarious way to make a living made my mother anxious. Nursing was the permissible alternative because my sister had shown compassion beyond her years at the bedside of our dying father. I admired my sister's stoic acceptance of a path so far from her heart's desire and feared that I would never be allowed to go to university to study drama.

'The world needs secretaries,' my mother said to me whenever I brought up the possibility of being an actress. 'A girl who can type will never be without a job.' I applied to secretarial college, but was haunted by a red-haired girl at the convent studying for Oxbridge. She sat alone, pale and dour, in an empty classroom every lunchtime, working her way through the study guide and endless packets of salt and vinegar crisps. I knew I should be in that room with her.

I couldn't argue with my mother when she insisted I train to do something that would guarantee an income. She wanted her daughters to have a level of financial security, and nursing and secretarial work provided enough income to avoid the ignominy of second-hand shoes, but not enough for us to lead lives of Decadence and Trouble. That perfect summer seemed to be a consolation for the lives my sister and I were preparing to lead. It was bliss to lie side by side, talking and taking the sun on our naked bodies. Apart from the sun, nothing much had changed – Mass on a Sunday, Mr T twice a week.

He would knock on the back door, and knock again, before a theatrical call: 'Ladies, girls.' We would wrap towels around our breasts and shuffle to the edge of the roof, and there was a delicious moment when he didn't know we were watching him. My mother would call down in her café noir French accent, 'Mr T, we are up 'ere. I'll have whatever you've got that's fresh.' Mr T's dark eyes would glint and he'd whip his tongue around his chipped front tooth that was capped with gold. I was mesmerized.

The summer came to a stormy end, but not before Mr T produced three front row tickets for *As You Like It*. He had always given us good seats, but the *As You Like It* seats were the best. Beside me was a tall, clear-faced man, sitting so close I could smell his skin, fresh as earth after rain. I also spotted two hairs sprouting on his neck, which both beguiled and repelled me. On his other side sat an old woman, presumably his mother, who handed him a small tub of chocolate ice cream, which he scoffed even before the lights went down. The man may have looked adorable, but he was a fidget. Shuffling in his seat, he brushed the back of my hand with his. This unexpected touch sent a thrill through my body and a vision of my own future into my head. I was cured for ever of the notion that my mother should marry Mr T.

During the interval the good-looking man caught my eye above the crowd and offered to buy my sister and me an orange juice 'with two straws'. This turned out to be his idea of a joke because he brought us a glass each and a cup of tea for my mother. His mother stood by, resisting conversation and civility, rattling ice in her drained glass of gin and tonic. Her son was oblivious, talking to me about flaws in the production my naïve eye had no wish to see.

'The cast's a bit too enthusiastic,' he said.

'But I love it,' I cried, wounded for Mr T's heartfelt performance.

'Have my programme as a souvenir,' he said, and before my mother and his, wrote his telephone number on the top. 'Let's keep in touch,' he said.

My sister gave me a discreet but knowing wink, which made me suspect that she knew more about men than she'd let on. Later that night, when we were lying in our twin beds in the dark, I whispered, 'Have you got a boyfriend?'

'I have,' she replied coolly.

'Who is he?'

'Nobody you know.'

'Obviously, but since when?'

'None of your business.'

'Does Mummy know?'

'No, and don't you tell her.'

'Are you still a virgin?'

'Of course not.'

Of course not? I was scandalized and sprang from my bed, desperate to find out more.

'When did you lose it?'

'Over a year ago.'

'When are you getting married?'

'Who said anything about marriage?'

'Mummy and the Bible for a start.'

I couldn't believe that my dutiful sister, studying to be a nurse and to all appearances my mother's 'shining example', was hiding a lover whom she may, or *may not*, marry. I could only suppose that her nurse's training had inspired a liberal attitude to making love (we never called it 'sex'). Her casual revelation challenged the foundation of my life. She had defied the authority of our mother and the Catholic Church and, worse still, done so without telling me. Once I'd recovered from the shock, I was grown up enough to realize that if my sister had a boyfriend, I could reasonably expect to have one of my own quite soon. I lay in bed reconstructing the man I had met at the play and the way he had said, 'Let's keep in touch.' I so longed to be touched I committed to memory his telephone number and, just in case, hid the programme he had given me beneath the bed.

It took me a while to call him. It wasn't just courage that I lacked, but conversation. What did I have to talk about, apart from secretarial college and Church? When finally I called I was surprised to hear a young boy answer the phone, telling me that he would 'go and get sir'. It turned out my new friend was a schoolmaster in a boys' boarding school, and lived on an island off the coast of France. Fantasies about his island life filled my head, and by the time we said goodbye and he had promised once again to 'keep in touch', I think I was in love.

Order was restored to my world when my sister announced her engagement to the man in charge of snakes at the local zoo. He was so passionate about reptiles he kept them in his bedroom and it had been a venomous bite from one of these that had led him to Accident and Emergency, where he'd met my sister. They married in our local church, a white wedding that thrilled the village. I was more interested in the photographs of their Spanish honeymoon in a coastal town with views of Morocco. My sister had not only seen Africa, she now lived with her very own man – albeit only five miles from home – and her adventures conspired to make me even more anxious to discover the world.

After A Levels I dragged myself through secretarial training and regular attendance at Mass. However, shorthand typing and communion with our Lord could not sustain me. My only joy was the long distant communication with the Schoolmaster, which dramatically progressed after I sent him a photograph. 'I'm beginning to forget what you look like,' he had complained. A few weeks later he invited me to the island for a long weekend.

Once my mother had granted permission (with surprisingly little resistance), I withdrew all my savings from my Saturday job and bought my first aeroplane ticket for my first date with a man.

After ten months of long-distance courtship the Schoolmaster and I stood at the altar of my village church and said, 'I do,' at least until death do us part. I chose not to say obey because I wanted to be modern, but I was so happy to be married that whatever my husband wished was my command. Even before we walked out of the church into a rainy October morning, I accepted that my life would be his. Marriage, the blessed union that confirmed my womanhood, signified the beginning of our life.

After the ceremony we flew to the island where he lived and checked into a luxurious hotel. That night we made love in semi-darkness in a four-poster bed, enclosed in brocade. The following morning room service arrived and I pressed into my Bible the pink rosebud that had decorated our breakfast table.

'Our life together will be fun, won't it?' I asked, doubt surfacing a little late.

My husband, a good-looking, gentle giant who played rugby and the violin, didn't understand my question. He was committed to life being fun.

'So much better to have fun in the present, than to wonder about it happening in the future,' he said, leading me back to the bed where he wriggled down my body to settle his mouth between my legs.

❖

Darling Mummy

I will never be able to thank you for all you did to make our wedding day so memorable. It was more than I could have dreamed. I hope I will be as dedicated and loving in my marriage as you were in yours, for therein lies true happiness – regardless of the rest.

I think I have found paradise. The island is beautiful, and I am at one with myself.

I hope you like the headed paper. This hotel is very grand. I've never seen such a place. I think I could get used to it! Unfortunately we could only afford one night, but it was a lovely surprise. The term starts soon, so a longer honeymoon would have been impossible. Tonight we are going to a restaurant, overlooking a bay on the other side of the island. It sounds most romantic with views of the sun setting slowly in the west, as long as it stops raining.

Will write again soon.

So very much love.

❖

My husband was assistant housemaster at Soane House where he helped the housemaster look after the boarding schoolboys who lived there. Our first home would be a flat in a neo-classical building on top of a hill overlooking the sea. When the taxi dropped us at the front of the House, I was impressed. I gazed at the monumental building and then out to the misty sea view, all my dreams coming true at once.

'Come this way,' my husband said, picking up our bags and walking around to the back of the House where waste bins and old bicycles occupied dark recesses beneath windows without a view. Once inside we passed the boys' kitchen, climbed spiral stone steps to a first-floor landing, then went through a fire escape and down a narrow corridor. I couldn't think what we were doing in such a grim place when suddenly my husband picked me up and carried me through to a tiny flat. 'This is it,' he said, setting me down. *This* was a sixties' extension built above the boys' kitchen. The hall was covered with brown carpet that looked like underlay (and probably was) and had a solitary lavatory at one end. The black plastic lavatory seat was forever raised to expose a cracked white enamel pan, and around the stand was a fluffy pink mat.

'The flat's more about convenience,' said my husband as he showed me around the cramped rooms with views onto the flat roof below the windows.

'You're right,' I said, trying to conceal my disappointment.

'The housemaster doesn't want me tucked up in here. He wants me in the main house keeping an eye on the boys. It works.'

The kitchen, painted a solid sixties' blue, was lit by a bare bulb and its sash window had no blind to block an unobstructed view of the bins. A deep crack in the wall above the sink was partially concealed by a poster of Olivia Newton John's beatific face, hovering like the patron saint of washing-up.

Our bedroom at the end of the corridor was no more inspiring. Another poster, this one of Bruce Lee, was stuck above the single bed and, once again, there were no curtains.

'Anyone can see in at any time,' I said to my husband, standing at the window, staring at the flat roof and the bicycle shed.

'You'll soon get used to it.'

'I'm not sure that's the point.'

We found a spare bed in the boys' sick room, which, pushed next to the existing single, made an unsteady double, and curtains from a Soane House store cupboard were shaken of cobwebs and stretched to fit the bedroom window. Every dusty surface in the bedroom was decorated with official photographs of boys holding sports trophies. More mini-trophies, some engraved with boys' names, some still waiting to be assigned, lined the window sill in the hall, along with more dust. The airing cupboard was stacked with sports kit and every kind of ball – rugby, cricket, football, hockey, tennis, water polo, squash and volleyball. There didn't seem to be much room for me.

'Don't ask me to move that lot,' said my husband, watching me pull the contents of the cupboard on to the corridor floor.

'What shall we do with all these balls?'

'Leave the balls to me. What about a cup of tea?'

We took our mugs of tea on a tour of Soane House. It was a relief to be out of the cramped flat. There was a huge games room with a full-size snooker table, a television room with staggered seating and a bright dining room with long sash windows that looked onto a cricket pitch. Iconic posters of sporting heroes and wet T-shirt women personalized identical dormitories, and in their midst on the top floor, was my husband's study.

'This is where I spend my time,' he said opening the door.

It was easy to see why. A panoramic view of the town and the sea beyond filled every window, there was a glass-topped desk, deep sofa and an open fire. The bachelor flat seemed all the more depressing.

We had four days to settle into married life before seventy boys returned from half-term. But this prospect was less daunting than an invitation to have dinner with the housemaster and his wife.

'What shall I wear?' I asked my husband.

'Something grown-up but let's not be late.'

With ten minutes to spare I was still rummaging through my clothes, which were scattered across the bed.

'It looks like a jumble sale in here,' my husband said, as I picked out a tweed mini-skirt and black roll-neck.

'I'll need a cupboard for my things,' I said, brushing my still wet hair. 'And where's your hair-dryer?'

'Men don't use hair-dryers. Come on. Let's go. I hate to be late.'

I whipped my hair into a knot and we ran down to the housemaster's apartment, which occupied a whole wing of Soane House. The wood-panelled entrance hall was grand with a fine wooden staircase that led to four bedrooms on the first floor, the same level as our flat on the other side of a fire escape, a whole world away.

The housemaster, Eric, appeared from the kitchen to greet us. Petite, bearded and bald, he was dressed top to toe in navy-blue and silver zippers dangled from the pockets of his crimplene trousers. He didn't walk so much as mince us through to an elegant sitting room: a wood fire was blazing, there were Persian rugs, comfortable sofas and fine Chinese lamps. In the corner stood Eric's wife, Helga, with her back to us, pouring nuts into a silver dish, munching as she went. She hadn't heard us walk in and to let her know that we were there, Eric rested his hand on her upturned bottom. She turned with a flushed face.

'Velcome,' she said, her accent unmistakably Austrian.

She was the stout wife to Eric's Jack Sprat, her features unfortunately porcine. She shook my hand with salty, damp fingers from picking at the nuts, and she stuck her tongue beneath her top lip to clean away the cashews. Her smile was restrained.

Eric served dry sherry and sat beside me on one sofa while Helga sat beside my husband on another. My husband winked at me as if to acknowledge this wasn't going to be easy, and painfully a conversation was chiselled out.

Helga poured herself another sherry and, returning to my husband, placed her hand on his thigh and announced in a stage whisper, 'Nobody on ze staff has a vife like zis. Congratulations.'

'To you both, and your future,' said Eric quickly, raising his glass.

'How old did you say you vere?' Helga asked.

'Twenty-two,' I lied.

At nineteen I was too close in age to the precocious boys in the upper sixth and a little too far from my 32-year-old husband. Twenty-two was the diplomatic and credible alternative the Schoolmaster and I had agreed upon.

'When I married for ze first time I was twenty-two,' said Helga. 'But zat ended in disaster. Shall we go through?'

Dinner was served in the kitchen. There was an Aga and a refectory table with five places set. I was wondering who would dare to be so late, when the kitchen door opened. 'Got delayed sorting out the beds. I think we're missing one,' said a pale woman with dyed black hair, tottering in spiked heels. Her skirt was candy pink, her legs were bare and her white stilettos clacked on the stone floor. She must have been freezing. And, I guessed, about fifty-five. Helga stopped slicing the roast pork with an electric knife and announced, 'Matron, meet our new housemistress.'

They all chuckled, even my husband. An embarrassed silence followed, which was broken only when Helga switched on her electric blade to resume hacking through the meat. Eric served red wine, subservient in his wife's company, like an overqualified waiter.

Matron sat opposite me and extended a bony hand, her long fingernails covered with vermilion varnish chipped at the tips.

'Welcome. It's quite something to uproot your life to come to this island,' she said.

'Surely she's zo young,' said Helga, 'zere wasn't much life to uproot?'

'What did you read at university?' Eric asked, covering his wife's tracks again.

'I didn't go — '

'What, she didn't do A Levels?' Eric turned from me to my husband, as though he were a more reliable source of information. I was about to reel off my list of exams when a movement at the window made me jump.

'Are you all right?' asked the housemaster.

'Yes, but I think there's a policeman outside the window.'

'Zat's my boy,' said Helga.

She unlocked the door to her six foot four uniformed son, who kept his helmet on as he walked in.

'He always forgets his key – don't you, darlink?' said Helga, kissing him on the cheek, as he eyed the joint of meat resting by the Aga.

'You're all served up, right?' he said and, without waiting for a reply, plonked the joint of pork on a plate, grabbed a knife and fork and walked out.

As if the presence of his wife's son was too awful to bear, Eric closed his eyes and drank more wine. The policeman towered over Eric and when they were in the room together there was no doubt about the dominant male in this ménage.

❖

That night, lying in bed, my husband and I agreed that if Eric and Helga ever invited us to dinner again, we would find an excuse. We needn't have worried. They never did.

On the third day of our marriage a letter arrived from Eric in which he took pains to point out that I should not consider myself a member of the Soane House staff.

'So much for my idea of being the perfect housemistress,' I said.

'The school doesn't have the money to pay you and we can't afford for you to do something for nothing. You're better off not getting involved. But look at this, Office Angels needs temps.' He tore an advertisement out of the paper and handed it to me. 'I think you should look for a job today,' he said, turning to the sports pages and tucking into his sixth slice of toast.

Later that morning I walked down the hill into town. The October sun was so surprisingly warm that even Eric's dismissive letter and my appointment with Office Angels couldn't affect my spirits. There was a café by the flower market with tables set outside and I had a cup of coffee and a croissant, which reminded me of breakfast at home with my Mother. And then I realized this was my first time in a café alone, which made me feel more grown up than being married. The prospect of hedonistic hours with Baudelaire, Balzac and Flaubert unfolded in my mind. Inspired and ignited by caffeine, I continued down the high street to Office Angels, who promptly ruined my heavenly day by sending me to Crapper & Jarndice, Solicitors, Advocates and Notaries Public. I was to be the temporary secretary in the Conveyancing Department.

'Let's hope you stick it longer than the last girl, and that your copy-typing is good and your French is better,' said Terry as he sucked on what was left of his cigarette. 'I need this contract in an hour.' He dropped a lengthy legal document in old French into my tray.

I spent the day behind a cranky golf ball typewriter in the darkest corner of a drab office, but soon got to like Terry. His manner was sharp, which suited his appearance – even his head came to a point. I thought he ran the department until a small round man they called the Gladiator emerged from his opaque glass lair followed by a lanky woman submerged beneath a stack of files. She was the Gladiator's secretary and sat outside his office door, which was always shut. Her focus was his work, unless Terry was really pushed.

'We carn't get a temp to stick it 'ere for love nor money,' said Sandra, arching an over-plucked eyebrow and filling my in-tray with contracts. 'You'd better get them lot done this afternoon or Terry'll be in the shit,' she said.

My unsteady typing announced that I was new but the clerks appreciated that I had a thankless task, and included me in their jokes and made me cups of tea.

'All right?' Terry was standing over my desk at the end of the afternoon, enjoying a fresh cigarette. My fingers were passing over the keys with more confidence and even though I was nowhere near fast, by the end of the day I had re-typed all the contracts. He signed my time sheet and grinned. 'See you Monday, if you've got nothing better to do.'

I had typed non-stop for five hours, my eyes stung, I was tired and hungry and my hair stank of cigarettes, but when Terry said that, I knew I'd be back. The office was familiar. As I walked up the hill in the dark, all I wanted was home and a bowl of the onion soup my Mother made most Thursday evenings. I missed her and I hoped my husband would be in the flat to greet me from my first day at work. Without him my island life didn't make much sense.

I opened the door and knew instantly that the boys were back. The House was filled with noise and in the kitchen six women in white hats and overalls were preparing vatloads of food, shouting over the clatter of industrial-sized stainless steel trays. Not ready to meet more new faces, I ran past and up the spiral stairs. All I wanted was the seclusion of the flat, but when I stepped inside it was unrecognizable. The kitchen had been raided, the fridge door hung open and when I walked into the sitting room, thirteen junior boys were sprawled across the floor, feeding on chocolate biscuits and orange juice, glued to a cartoon on the television.

When the six o'clock school bell rang, the boys rose as one, passing me as though I were invisible, to join more boys running down the stairs to stand in a distant room for roll call. I turned off the television and stood in the silence. The smell of the boys' supper intensified. Sausages and baked beans.

I cleared away the biscuits, washed up the mugs, hated Olivia Newton John for smiling and was scrambling eggs for supper when my husband came in studying a timetable.

'I can't believe he's put me on duty five nights a week,' he moaned, pouring himself a glass of milk. 'Sorry, sweetheart. That looks tasty,' he said, grabbing a slice of toast.

'Do you want some eggs?'

'Had supper with the boys.' He disappeared into the sitting room to watch the news.

Later that evening as I went to find my husband in his study, the boys I passed on the stairs glanced and looked away.

'The boys don't seem to know who I am,' I said to my husband, who was marking books at his desk.

'I didn't have time before the holidays to tell them that I was getting married. We'd better introduce you before you cause a riot.' He glanced up and winked at me.

I looked around the study, which seemed to encapsulate my husband's life. Photographs of beaming boys in winning teams were pinned on a corkboard around a timetable mapping out my husband's responsibilities, which were all perfectly achievable, provided he was willing to work twenty-four hours a day.

'You love your job, don't you?' I said, standing behind him, scrutinizing the coaching sessions, duty nights, weekend sporting fixtures and academic classes.

'This is my vocation,' he said, 'not to be confused with vacation. I couldn't imagine working for a living.' He laughed.

'I worked for a living today,' I said.

'Well done you,' he said, moving to a nearby armchair and

another stack of textbooks. 'Gordon Bennett, the third year are going to have to pull their socks up.' He scribbled in a margin.

I leaned my forehead against the cold glass of the window and stared for a long time into an indifferent night. The sea was blacker than the sky, and I watched the play of colours, the varying shades of darkness. I felt alone and was fearing that I had made a terrible mistake, when suddenly my husband was beside me, easing my shirt out from my skirt, resting his warm hand on the small of my back.

'Was it that bad?'

My steamy breath clouded the window and I covered my eyes with my hand to hide my tears.

'The first day's always the worst. Stick with it until you feel settled here, which you will once you know everyone.' He drew me towards him. When he held me like this I felt calm. I knew everything would be all right. A knock at the door jumped us apart.

'Sir, can we watch *Star Trek*?' A junior boy stuck his head into the room.

'Only if it ends before lights out.'

'Thanks, sir.' The boy ran off with the good news and my husband led me to the sofa, but within seconds there was another knock at the door.

'Sir?'

'Come in.'

In the doorway stood an exceptionally tall, lean boy who was so beautiful I wiped my eyes and pulled myself together. I recognized him from my husband's sporting photographs, except he was no longer an innocent child but a golden-skinned teenager, so sure of himself he seemed no less a man than my husband. They greeted each other like old friends.

'Is signing-out with you tonight?'

'The sign-out sheet is in the kitchen on the window sill.'

'Can I have an extension, sir?'

'Not tonight. I'm too tired.'

'Okay. Congratulations to you both by the way.' He flashed me a brilliant smile and sloped off with a graceful swagger.

'That's the Head Boy,' said my husband, his head back in the textbooks. I wished he'd introduced me, and wondered why he hadn't.

❖

Darling Mummy

I have been here three unbelievable weeks and C- has been on duty almost every night, but even when he's not, junior boys are in the flat. One of them told me I'd been adopted, which sounds endearing, but there are disadvantages to being the only girl in the house – such as no privacy. Boys come in any time, day or NIGHT. One junior boy knocked on the door at three o'clock this morning. He'd wet his bed. Apparently he couldn't find Matron, but I don't think he looked. I changed his bed using sheets that were a wedding present – they were still in the wrapping paper.

The junior boys follow C- around as though he's their champion. In a way he is: he stopped fagging in the boarding school and the tradition of naked swimming. Can you believe it was a school rule for the youngest boys to swim without trunks? What kind of mind thought that one up?

The boys are a mixed lot. More than three-quarters have divorced parents, and last year one boy's mother was shot by her ex-husband – not the boy's father, thank goodness. Relations get complicated. A middle school boy – who I thought was a bore – actually cried when he told me he hadn't talked to his mother all week. He's kind of arrogant, and a precocious fourteen year old, but he still needs his mother… I will try to be nice to him from now on. A lot of the boarders seem like the lost boys. Sometimes I feel like a lost girl.

The senior boys, however, are nothing like lost boys. Most of them steer clear of me. C- says that's a good thing because they're a 'different ball game'. I laughed, but he was serious. I don't think he likes the older boys very much. He is fond of a boy called David. (I think I'm about third in line – not in affection but viewing time). C- says he's normal, which is rare. He's fourteen, his parents amazingly aren't divorced, and they live in England in the country, not far from us. Most of the boys seem to live in exotic places I can hardly pronounce. David loves chess and he and C- play often, sometimes to 10p.m. which seems pretty late to me.

The Head Boy is half-German, half-American, and he's a fantastic sportsman and very bright. Of all the boys I like him the best, and I'm grateful every time he clears the flat after a couple of hours' occupation by the juniors. At least they listen to him. It's hard for me to shout at them loud enough to get them moving. Last night the Head Boy came to the flat looking for C- who was at a football match with a few teachers and their wives. Can you believe he forgot to buy me a ticket? He said he hadn't got used to the fact he was married. Wonder how long it's going to take?

I ended up talking to the Head Boy for an hour. What a pity we don't have another sister to marry off, as he is quite the best-looking boy in the school and his father is very rich! He wears jeans and silk shirts, and C- told me he's a count in Germany. I don't know about that, but I do know I mustn't serve him teabag tea. He can spot a cheap bag a mile off.

Yesterday played five-a-side football and this evening basketball with the juniors. They said I was their honorary boy – apparently the biggest compliment. C- says the juniors don't have convoluted minds, and their hormones are less imposing than those of the older boys, which makes them nicer to be around which is why he prefers them.

Love to my darling sister, and to you.

P.S. I've got a job. There are plenty of agencies here, like Top Personnel, but I don't think I'm top enough for them yet. The boys are fascinated by shorthand, which they think is a secret language. I'm not using it at the lawyer's office as it's only a typing job – hell, but bearable. I'll stick with it for a bit.

Love,

❖

Gradually I became part of Soane House. I knew the names of all the boys, and all the staff. I understood the significance of the bells, which rang periodically from seven in the morning to ten-thirty at night, and I shared some of my husband's duties, signing boys out, doing the junior dormitory round. I learned the etiquette of House dining, such as the Latin grace and who sat on which table. And I watched forever hungry boys devour pale slices of grey meat in thick brown gravy and vegetables served from stainless steel containers – a reminder more than any other that we lived in an institution.

If the juniors came to our flat to escape feeling institutionalized, the seniors went to Matron's studio, where behind constantly-drawn curtains, they watched videos and drank orange juice, which I suspected was laced with vodka. Apart from opening the First Aid room every afternoon after school, Matron stayed in her studio flat with her favourite seniors for company. A couple of nights a week, a young woman with bone-thin arms and long red hair also dropped by. Matron didn't seek friendship with the other adults in the house and we never had a conversation that went beyond the weather.

'Why don't the older boys talk to me?' I asked my husband after the Head Boy, in the company of his senior friends, had ignored me on the stairs on his way to Matron's den.

'Don't take it personally. It comes down to testosterone. Spending time with you isn't worth the bother,' my husband replied.

I told my husband that I wanted the seniors to visit our flat but it was the Head Boy's company I craved. We had met in the library a few days before, and he had invited me to his study for a cup of tea. I sat on his sofa while he sliced the cherry cake his mother had sent from Germany. We talked about his plans to go to Oxford, then Harvard, and Argentina in between to play polo. We talked until the outside light faded and conversation turned to my future – which seemed too predictable to me. I had expected a friendship to develop, but the Head Boy, like the other seniors, only came by for permission to sign out, I envied their sophisticated social lives while my husband and I stayed in clock-watching, making sure they returned on time. If I was a confusing presence for the upper sixth, they were no less so for me. They did all the things I had never known about, but now that I did, wanted to do too. They had places at university and plans for such bright futures that my own depressed me.

It wasn't long before I wanted to leave the island. I dreamt of going with my husband to live in Paris, or England, where I would go to university while he worked as a schoolmaster. But my husband resisted my visions of our future. We had married to share one life and the longer we were together the more I resented that that life was his. The only future he could imagine was his bachelor life, proceeding unfettered by me and babies tagging along behind.

'If we start now we'd have a five-a-side football team by the time you're thirty,' he'd say with an amused grin.

Children surrounded us and I couldn't imagine having my own. I had seen the reality of the laundry room, which was a full-time job for a kindly, white-haired lady, who sorted endless socks and spent hours ironing and shaking static from acrylic sports shirts.

'In between giving birth, I'll have just enough time for cooking, cleaning and ironing,' I'd sigh.

'Darling, don't worry. You won't be stuck at home, you'll be back at work because we'll need the money.'

'I don't want to be a secretary in between having children.'

'But it's what you trained to be.'

My husband genuinely couldn't understand, and I couldn't explain, why I had trained for a job I didn't want to do. The Schoolmaster had always known his own mind, which made my lack of clarity incomprehensible.

'One day you'll get promoted to personal assistant for one of the partners. Then you'll love it,' he'd say enthusiastically, as though I'd be spending my days at the right hand of God.

❖

Darling Mummy

Today was boy-filled. Apparently the spring term is always a happy one and this afternoon the boarders got together for football. It was like being part of one big family of brothers. Thankfully everybody forgot that fifteen minutes earlier the son of a top psychiatrist had a fit and kicked the toaster around, dived at another boy's throat and threw an egg across the dining room, which hit an unsuspecting boarder on the back of the head.

Last night I persuaded C- to take me dancing. A new nightclub sent invitations to the office so everything was on the house. C- loves going out when it's free. The women from the office thought he was so good-looking.

He is very fit at the moment. Constantly worrying about money though, and understanding about my lack of it. I use his car sometimes and must remember to refill the petrol. He is funny. I don't think I understand him. He worries that he doesn't have enough time for me because of his work, but never does anything to cut down his commitment to the boys and their sport.

Last weekend the seniors and matron organized a three-legged volleyball match and I played for the ladies' team, mostly the cooks, a cleaner, Matron and her niece. This girl, by the way, is twenty-eight years old, attractive in an ethereal way and likes to ask out seventeen-year-old boys – which is what she did after the match. The game was a shambles, and after twenty minutes the cooks disappeared inside to open a bottle of martini. C- wanted nothing to do with it.

I've been allowed to open a tuck shop – after much deliberation by Eric who really didn't want to approve the idea, but had no choice, as the boys wanted it so much. One of the seniors, Peter – nursing a broken heart because his girlfriend just dumped him – helped me clean out an old storeroom and paint it red. We had a great time transforming the place and cut a stencil saying, 'The Red Room, a Gentleman's Club', for the door. So far Eric hasn't mentioned it.

It's time-consuming but it involves me in the House and in one week we've made quite a lot of money. The plan is to buy a canoe with the profits and start a canoe club next summer.

I live for Fridays and 5.30 p.m. Such a relief to have a weekend to break the weeks, although sometimes it all feels like work.

So much love,

Life with the Schoolmaster was one long sports match, and the surfaces on which our relationship played out were the dining table and the mattress. Our marriage came down to sharing food and sex.

Spending time alone together otherwise was almost impossible. There were so many demands on my husband's time, our marriage had to wait until the boys weren't there. Trouble was, by the time it came to lights out, my husband was the first to fall asleep. The only thing I could do to guarantee his wide-awake presence was to cook. I would put on a pretty dress and prepare extravagant dinners for two and, once my husband was inside, we'd lock the door, light candles and play music. The boarders still came by every five minutes calling, 'Sir', but if we kept quiet, they soon went away.

But boys weren't our only obstacles to intimacy. To meet stringent safety regulations, Soane House was rigged with a heat sensitive fire alarm and even when I hadn't burnt anything, my cooking would set it off, sending the whole House into fire drill.

I'd call the station every time. 'It's me. I've done it again. Please don't send the firemen.'

'Regulations, love. Can't ignore an alarm.'

'But there isn't a fire.' The fire engine would be screaming up the hill even before I'd put the phone down.

'All right love, let's have you,' one of the firemen would say, standing in the entrance to the flat.

I tried hiding to avoid the humiliation, and once even crouched on the other side of the bed. I thought I'd got away with it, but they found me even there. I felt such shame, not for inconveniencing the Emergency Services, who always seemed rather entertained by my antics, but for my private efforts to please my husband, which were now so public. The firemen would grin under heavy helmets, each one dressed in fireproof coats and carrying pick axes, with nothing to extinguish except my spirits.

'Can I stay here?' I'd beg. I didn't want the boys and staff to see me all dressed up for my not-so-secret dinner party.

'You've got to do the drill.'

'I know the drill. I did it two weeks ago.' I never convinced them, and every time was sent out to the front lawn where the whole of Soane House was waiting. Sometimes the boys would cheer, sometimes they would whistle, but when it was raining, nobody was amused.

❖

Darling Mummy

Sorry for not writing but life is busy. I am in the local netball team and I've been asked to play tennis for the island, less a reflection on my tennis than the lack of girls on the island between 18 and 25. Where are they and what do they know that I don't?

Meanwhile, most of the boys play tennis and I had a good game last weekend with the Head Boy who finally deigned to speak to me again. After his easy victory he invited me for a drink in town as C- is away for a weekend sports fixture. I said no because Eric and Helga would disapprove and we settled on a cup of tea in his study, which surely couldn't offend anyone. We talked for hours.

While Eric and Helga keep an eye on me, Matron gets to do whatever she wants with the boys. She bathed one of the seniors last night in her own bath. Apparently he needs some special ointment applied to his back … She is also suspected of serving the middle school boys alcohol and letting them have the occasional peep at 'rude' magazines. Also, it turns out, her 'niece' has little relative value. One of the boys saw them kissing in Matron's car. She's certainly got her finger in a lot of pies. No wonder we hardly ever see her.

Helga has just invited me over for a glass of wine. Wonder what that's about? Hasn't happened before.

I was right to be suspicious. She wanted to know how much profit the tuck shop was making. While we were talking, Eric walked in and out sighing, 'Isn't life awful,' then he'd disappear, and come back saying, 'I've got an awful headache,' or 'I've got to take two additional periods tomorrow with an awful class.' Finally he said, 'I'm awfully tired, I'm going to bed.' I think they're both bloody awful.

C- has acquired weights from the gains of his sponsored bike rally. He has been using them in the gym to improve his physique, and this week eleven boys arrived to shape up with him, including the Head Boy, who is as tall as C- and almost as strong. I watched, and got the giggles because they were all so serious. I might join in next week.

Must go, getting late and C- has just come down from his study.

Love,

P.S. C- has asked for your cherry cake and flapjack recipes, not that he'll be the one making them …

❖

Baking did not set off the fire alarm. It took a while to master my mother's flapjack recipe but once I had, my husband was powerless to resist them. After working in his study, or checking the House for lights out, he would often bring one to bed with a cup of hot chocolate, which hadn't been the point at all. If he was going to eat something sweet in bed, I wanted it to be me.

'I don't know which I like best. Sex with you, or your flapjacks,' he said, standing by the bed, mouth melting around the gooey, syrup-soaked oats. He placed his late-night snack on the bedside table, removed his dressing gown and picked up the latest Wisden.

'If the Head Boy scores a century tomorrow, which on his current form is quite likely, then he'll have a better average than any boy in the country last year,' he said, consulting the cricketers' bible.

'That's good. I like him,' I said.

Watching the Head Boy in cricket whites was the reason I sat on the boundary line every weekend, but recently he floated through my mind even when I wasn't.

While my husband read on, I stroked his chest, slowly unbuttoned his pyjama top and put thoughts of the Head Boy out of my mind. I moved my hand across my husband's tummy, and as he turned another page, I edged lower. Then he took the last bite of his flapjack, closed his book and switched off the bedside light. 'Night-night, darling.'

Too frustrated to lie beside him, I crept out of the bedroom. Wrapped in a shawl, I sat in the dark on the stone stairs staring out of the window. Then I heard a scuffling sound and muffled voices from the roof below.

'They've been in bed ten minutes.'

'They must be doing it by now. Let's go.'

Peering out of the window I saw five middle school boys, duffle coats over pyjamas, creeping in crocodile formation along the roof. One of the boys sighed orgasmically which made them giggle, and a spectacled boy who I had helped with homework the day before, tiptoed to the crack in the bedroom curtains.

'What's going on?' whispered another fourteen-year-old.

The bedroom light came on.

'*Jeessus*!'

'What? They're doing it with the light on?'

'He's reading.'

'What about her?'

'She's not there.' At that, the boys fled back to the dormitory window. Watching the housemaster read in bed wasn't worth the punishment coming their way if they got found out. The next day I invested in a pair of heavy brocade curtains that reminded me of the four-poster bed on our honeymoon night and more loving times. The curtains stayed closed for the rest of the term.

The boys weren't the only ones curious about my marriage. I had seen shadows on the other side of the fire escape and was convinced that Eric and Helga were trying to gather information to justify my husband's dismissal. His easy popularity amongst the boarders made them nervous and I suspected they feared he was planning a coup d'état. Once they realised such militant thoughts did not enter my husband's head they turned to me. I was an easier target.

One morning while we were eating breakfast, Eric interrupted us to convene an emergency meeting with my husband. He had overheard a dormitory of middle school boys masturbating in unison as one of them described their fantasy, which just happened to be me.

My Schoolmaster pointed out that I could hardly be held responsible. 'Boys will be boys,' he'd said.

But Eric was on a witch hunt. 'Matron tells me there's too much semen on the sheets. We must stamp out this behaviour before it gets out of hand.'

Out of hand was the only solution, but unless he was going to handcuff the boys, Eric was powerless to implement such a policy. I knew then that if anything was going to be stamped out, it was going to be me.

That Saturday night my husband was on duty, and, as usual, we were in his study playing cards with a group of boys having a high-spirited good time. It was no different from any other Saturday night, until Eric and Helga burst through the door in matching dressing gowns.

'Get to bed now!' Eric screamed.

The boys vanished.

'Ve need to talk,' Helga said, dragging me off to the boys' sick room. 'The boys are masturbating themselves to bits over you. And I've seen the way you touch Peter's hair,' she said, referring to my easy friendship with one of the seniors. 'He's in love with you, you stupid girl, don't you know that? They all are. You make me sick just to look at you.'

While I sat through Helga's bitter attack, Eric was informing my husband of the latest Soane House rules. He and Helga believed that for the sake of decorum and the boys' sanity, my access to certain parts of the House should be restricted. I was not allowed to use the swimming pool, or the sports room. I was not allowed to wear my bikini in the school grounds during term time, or to sunbathe on the roof. I was not allowed to use the senior boys' corridor or go into any of the dormitories at any time for any reason 'whatsoever'. I was not allowed to walk barefoot around the House and the tuck shop had to close immediately. I was permitted to eat in the dining room, but only on a Sunday, presumably because I'd be appropriately dressed for Church and the boys' minds cleansed by their attendance.

'The whole house is an excluded zone. What's left for me?' I asked my husband as we lay in bed that night.

'My study. Our flat.'

'Is that it?'

'Seems so. But we won't be here for ever. In the meantime, watch your step,' he said, kissing me on the forehead.

I longed for the Schoolmaster's support, but being told to watch my step made me feel guilty. My husband's calm acceptance of Eric's new rules felt more excluding than the rules themselves.

❖

Darling Mummy
Please forgive the lack of letters. Usually as soon as I settle to write, a boy comes in to the flat looking for C- , but for the first time in five weeks that hasn't happened because it's half-term. The boys went home today, and of course now they're gone, I miss them.

Last night, in defiance of Eric's veto on my right to roam, I went with C- on the lights-out dormitory round. All the boys were in bed, quiet and sleepy except for one of the Indian boys who was saying his prayers, chanting in front of a picture of the Indian god Ganesh. And to think he was one of the boys spying on the roof that night. In the junior dorm one boy said, 'Trubshaw wants a kiss, miss.' They all bully Trubshaw so much I'm sure that's why he wets his bed. I went to the boy who'd shouted out and gave him a kiss instead. He soon shut up after that.

C- is exhausted but will coach tennis every day of half-term so that he can save money. He says he wants to leave the boarding house sooner rather than later.

Work tomorrow, which is much the same. Tedious and tiresome.

I do miss you and my darling sister. How is she? I haven't heard for ages.

Love as ever,

❖

The following week I received a letter from my sister to tell me she had separated from her snake-charmer and was filing for divorce.

So marriage didn't have to be for ever.

Three

The Lawyer

If Eric and Helga saw me as the evil siren who had infiltrated the Testosterone Fortress, my husband hardly noticed me. He treated me more like an honorary boy than his young wife. I dreamt of escape and distant places, but on my secretarial salary, and with only two weeks holiday, I couldn't hope to go far.

One summer evening, while my husband marked books, I stood behind his desk scanning the calendar which was full of sporting fixtures and academic deadlines. I'd known them all: the cricket teas, the swimming galas, the inter-house matches, the farewells at the end of term. My husband's life was predicted, his position and purpose confirmed, but as the disenfranchised housemistress his status did not ratify mine.

'You're coaching every school holiday. We'll never get away,' I sighed.

'We need the money,' he said, turning to a stack of sporting photographs for the school magazine.

'Sport and school are your life,' I said.

'I'm a sports master dammit. What did you expect? You can't wait for me to make you happy.'

'I don't expect you to.'

'That's what it feels like. Now here's what I call happy,' my husband said, holding up a photograph of five beaming juniors, thrusting their hockey sticks into the sky. 'They were certainly the happiest days of my life.'

'What? When you were twelve?'

'Absolutely.'

No wonder my husband loved the juniors; they reminded him of his glory days. 'What if I can't be happy where you're happy?' I asked.

'You'll be happy once you set your mind to it.'

'That's like icing a fake cake,' I replied, petulantly.

'Darling, you'd be a lot happier if you weren't so impatient. You wait, once we start trying for babies everything will be fine.'

The only emotion my husband could acknowledge was happiness, which left me nowhere to go with the confusion and disappointment that beset me. His philosophy shielded him from anything that might threaten his worldview and left our conversations wanting. My sense of isolation intensified daily and I began to behave in ways stranger than I could have imagined.

I would wake in the middle of the night and wander in my nightshirt through the downstairs rooms and corridors from which I had been banned. In that dark silence the big house felt like home. I'd raid the House fridge and eat strawberry ice cream in the blue neon light of the kitchen's flytrap as electrocuted flies hit the floor. In the library I curled up in a cushion behind the bookcase to read prospectuses for universities by torchlight, dreaming a future that had nothing to do with the island and till death do us part. When the summer nights were warm, I'd swim in the outdoor pool, the water cool on my naked body, and when the moon was full I'd walk the lanes around Soane House. Sitting by the gate, staring across the empty playing field towards the cricket pavilion, I'd imagine the Head Boy playing cricket on the moonlit pitch, bowling and batting only for me. Now that the senior boys' corridor was out of bounds, I no longer visited his study for cups of tea, but nobody could censor my mind, and during those summer days he was with me all the time. I recalled the winter afternoons when it had seemed natural to spend time together talking in his study. I couldn't believe how unselfconscious I had been in his company. I imagined what it would have been like to kiss him, to have felt his soft mouth on mine in the half-light, when eyes are bright. These velvet dreams put heat between my legs, even sitting on a cold stone step in the middle of the night.

❖

Darling Mummy
Sorry for not writing before now. Things have been a little strange recently. I beg C- every day to apply for teaching posts on the mainland and all I think about is escape. Last night when I asked C- if he had to choose between working on the island or me, without hesitation he said the island. Mind you, it was a stupid question. I must find something to absorb me to balance things out. Helga closed the tuck shop last week, and bought a big barbecue with the profits. She intends to barbecue the boys' lunch every Sunday and doesn't care they'd rather have canoes.

There's nothing for me to do at Soane House now, except keep out of trouble and help David with his French. He was the bottom of the class, but yesterday got 100% in a test. C- said the hour we'd spent revising was too long for a 15-year-old, although as I pointed out, he and David play chess for an hour or more. Getting told off by my husband for helping a boy with homework confirms that I can't do any thing right.

Work is mind-numbing – mostly copy-typing and, heaven help me, filing. It is time to look for another job. C- says I'm moping around and should snap out of it, and I know you'd say that too, but I don't know how. Will write when I feel better.

Haven't been to Church for a while. Perhaps Confession's the answer, although God knows, life's so dull it would be a pleasure to have something to confess.

Forgive me …

Your loving daughter

❖

If living among boys was problematic, then working for men at the office was no less complicated. It didn't help that I was under scrutiny in both places. The office gang, a core group of women who lived for gossip, colonized the kitchen every lunchtime, gathering around the table with cigarettes, microwaved meals, their knives out for whoever they were carving up that day. The unfriendliest to me, and the most vicious gossip, was also the fattest. She was so fat that one day she came into work with her jaw wired, but not even that could stop her talking or eating. Through clamped teeth she forced out vitriol and sucked up melted ice cream through a straw.

In my part of the office, lunch came in a box, but the higher up the hierarchy, the longer the lunch and the finer the restaurant. Apart from the clerks and the lawyers, the other men in the office were company administrators who set up off-shore companies for wealthy clients to avoid tax. They were the most self-satisfied bunch, for while they weren't as qualified as the lawyers, some were better paid. Much of the tax business came from France, but apart from the lawyer who owned the firm, only Terry spoke the language and he was bombarded with translation requests.

'Where's Terry?' asked Sebastian, a punctilious administrator, who arrogantly assumed superiority over the conveyancy department.

'Right behind you,' I said.

He turned as Terry walked in holding a tray of steaming mugs. 'Terry, I need your help.'

'Not now, I'm busy.'

'What, making the secretaries coffee?' Sebastian was desperate, 'My biggest clients are sitting in the boardroom right now. They're French. And they don't speak English.'

Terry opened a file, lit a cigarette, said, 'Sorry, I'm busy,' and switched on his Dictaphone as if to prove it. Sebastian, red with frustration, stormed out muttering about priorities, nicotine and caffeine.

'Can I translate for him?' I asked.

'Be my guest,' said Terry.

I was a girl and a typist, and men in the office didn't do lateral thinking. Sebastian was incredulous that I spoke French. The French clients were delightful, and Sebastian was suitably grateful. When we walked out of the boardroom an hour later, ten secretaries behind a line of computerized workstations pinned me with their eyes. The French men kissed me courteously on both cheeks, and there was such a jolly stir the head of the firm came out of his office to join in the farewell.

I returned to sit behind my battered typewriter and something had changed: for the first time, I had enjoyed my work.

I was soon the office's unofficial translator, staying long after half past five to finish copy-typing for the Conveyancing Department, and translating for everyone else.

'They're exploiting you,' Terry said one evening, when we were both working late.

'At least I'm learning — '

'To work twice as hard for the same money. Ask for a promotion. This firm can afford to pay you for the job you're doing.'

The next day I met with the personnel director, a pompous man with a handlebar moustache whose office was spacious and new.

'I'm surprised you've stuck it out back there,' he chuckled.

'That's what I'd like to talk about.'

'What have you got in mind?' he said, pulling at his moustache with mock solemnity.

I longed to be taken seriously but I was young, blonde, had breasts and copy-typed – and so far as most men are concerned, that package doesn't come in 'Serious'. The canny women in the office didn't let the patriarchy get them down; they knew that if they flattered the directors, it would be reflected in their pay. I wasn't that savvy.

'I was wondering — ' I began.

'Let me guess. You want to get out of Conveyancing?' he said, leaning back in his chair, chest to the ceiling as he burped beneath his breath.

'That's why I'm here.'

'Sorry, my love, we've got no other secretarial jobs at the moment.'

'I don't want to be a secretary.'

'What do you want to be?' he asked, and I half expected him to add, 'When you grow up.' Suddenly it took courage to suggest that I should be paid for a job I was already doing.

'I'd like to be the firm's official translator,' I stammered.

'This firm doesn't have such a job specification.'

'I've been translating for over a month,' I said, my insecurity overcome by indignation.

'We can't create a job without a specification. I'm sorry, my love.'

If I had been willing to beg, he might have granted my request, but I was so angry I was already at the door. I turned to say goodbye but decided not to bother – the personnel director was transfixed by my departing bottom.

Back in the antiquated Conveyancing Department, Terry asked how the interview went.

'There isn't a job for me.' I choked back tears.

'Go to the top. Ask the boss. Friday after lunch is a good time to catch him.'

That Friday I wore a business suit that suggested potential beyond copy-typing and waited for the Lawyer to return from lunch. As Terry had predicted, the Lawyer's lunch was suitably long. At half past four he staggered into the office and went straight to the men's cloakroom. This was my cue to stand by the filing cabinet and turn into his path.

'Oh, I'm sorry,' I said, meeting him face to face.

'Not at all.' The Lawyer was reluctant to walk on.

'Could I talk to you for a minute?'

The Lawyer smiled. He liked private conversations. 'Come to my office in ten minutes.'

I knocked, the Lawyer indicated for me to enter and I shut the door. He sat in a designer chair at a vast desk, fine white curtains behind him letting in the sun, a smouldering cigar balanced on a crystal ashtray. The Lawyer looked at me beneath arching eyebrows and said, 'What can I do for you?'

Within ten minutes I had convinced him that I was worth promoting, but the only place he could offer me was assistant to the bumptious Sebastian.

'He's not so bad,' the Lawyer said, seeing my expression. 'And if all goes well, I'll give you your own office – and a secretary. I'm counting on you not to let me down.' His lips trembled on the damp end of his cigar.

Within months I had a sufficient number of French corporate clients to be granted my own secretary and a glass-sided office opposite the personnel director, which must have made him sick. But the last laugh was his: he decided my salary and never paid me more than the firm's head receptionist.

The Lawyer had promoted a junior filing clerk to become my secretary and the resistance we faced from our office colleagues united us. We were new and very young, and got things done in a chaotic way. I gave her a chance, and she gave me several as I learnt what it meant to have somebody work for me. While I welcomed my new responsibilities, my secret ambition was to move to Paris. Whenever I spoke to my French clients I told them how much I adored their city (even though I had never visited it) and would happily save them the bother of coming to the island, should they have any business to discuss. Each day I learned more about the relatively simple procedure of setting up off-shore companies, and it wasn't long before the Lawyer asked me the question that would change my life: 'Do you think you could manage a trip to Paris to meet a couple of clients who want to set up a company?'

I didn't even hesitate.

Soon my work demanded regular trips to Paris and I was happy to make work my priority. I spent less time at Soane House, and when I was there, shut myself away in the flat, waiting for my husband to come off duty. I saw Helga and Eric so rarely it was a surprise when the housemaster came to the flat late one afternoon. 'Just got the message your husband won't be back tonight. The fog's too thick, his flight is grounded,' he said, trying to look sympathetic.

Several Saturdays a year my husband took a group of boys to France for sporting fixtures, and he had promised to get back that evening so that Eric and Helga could go to the headmaster's party – the most prestigious invitation in the school year. With my husband unexpectedly away and Matron nowhere to be found, Eric and Helga wouldn't be going anywhere unless they found somebody to cover their duty.

'Are you in tonight?' Eric began, as though testing a tightrope.

'I am.'

'It would help us awfully,' both feet on now, edging towards oblivion, 'if you would do duty tonight.'

'Okay,' I said, overlooking his hypocrisy to accept responsibility for seventy boys.

'No need, of course, to let them know you're the only one here.

You could probably skip the dormitory round, too,' Eric called, as he disappeared up the corridor.

The juniors wanted to watch a television show that ended after lights out, and the seniors signed out to a party with a promise to return by midnight. I thought I'd dealt with everybody when at nine o'clock there was a knock at the door and the Head Boy walked in. I had assumed that he had gone out with the other seniors and his unexpected appearance made my stomach leap.

'Can I sign out?' he asked.

I tried to sound indifferent when I asked, 'Where are you going?'

'The Trattoria for a friend's birthday.'

'I've always wanted to go to that restaurant,' I said.

'I'll take you one day.' And then, as though it were nothing special, 'Can I have an extension until one?'

I handed him the sign-out sheet, taking in his freshly ironed shirt and faded jeans that hung on his hips. He was a long-limbed man, with a lean waist buckled with a belt from Argentina where he went to play polo.

No master would sit up until one o'clock in the morning for a boy but, curled up in a beanbag watching the late night movie, I did. At five past one the sliding door opened and the Head Boy called, 'I'm back.'

'Okay, thanks. Good night.' I didn't want to see him or to hear about his good time, but there were footsteps down the hall. He stood stock still in the sitting-room doorway as if deciding what to do next.

'I love this movie. Can I watch?'

He sat on the floor leaning into the beanbag, so close it made my heart race. Thankfully I had been watching the film in the dark and he couldn't see that I was nervous. He was so relaxed, his arms wrapped around his knees, his left hand clasping his right wrist.

'A girl like you shouldn't be alone on a Saturday night,' he said.

I glanced at him and caught his eye on mine. 'I've got used to being a sports widow.'

'You're too young to say that.'

'Some days I feel too old to be twenty.' I revealed my age because I wanted to share a secret with him.

'I've dated women older than you.' The implications of his remark hung between us like ripe fruit.

'I'm married,' I said, keeping my voice flat with resignation.

'It's strange he chose a girl like you. I've known him ten years and he was great when I was a kid. But he's not at all curious, and I think you are.'

It was unbearable that he understood me in ways my husband didn't. I couldn't let him know me more, or see the trouble I was in. There was nothing we could safely do apart from go to bed alone, so I got up and without saying goodnight, left him in the dull grey light of the television. And, just in case, turned the key in the bedroom door.

❖

Life in Soane House was so tedious, the Head Boy's presence so torturous and my husband so oblivious, in those days I was only happy in Paris. As my French clients grew in number, I was there at least twice a month and planned my meetings to leave me time to explore the city. I visited museums, bookshops and Café de Flore – my favourite because in my fantasy Samuel Beckett still lived around the corner and might walk in any minute. I always took the last flight back to the island and got to Soane House around midnight. Dressed in heels and swinging my briefcase, I'd enter the House using the senior boys' entrance. This was my one rebellious action which was harmless enough as the house was silent and everyone in bed. It was easy to be cavalier, until one night I turned the corner and walked straight into the Head Boy.

'What are you doing?' I screamed in a whisper.

'I heard your car — '

A torch beam bounced off the corridor walls.

'Who iz zere?' It was Helga.

The Head Boy pulled me into the doorway of his study.

'Who iz zere?' The torch beam brightened.

If using the seniors' corridor was bad, getting caught in the shadows with one of them was infinitely worse. The Head Boy signalled towards his study door, turned the handle and silently we slipped inside. Helga was right behind us, and my heart almost stopped when she shone yellow torchlight beneath the door and said in a weighty whisper, 'Are you zere?'

I screwed my eyes shut as the Head Boy pulled off his shirt, jumped into bed and, in a sleepy soft voice said, 'Is everything all right?'

I attempted to merge with the wall, held my breath and prayed as Helga edged the door open. She shone the torch on the boy man's serene face and he squinted into the light as though he'd been asleep for hours.

'Sorry to bozzer you,' she said, shutting the door fast. I slid down the wall with relief. The Head Boy climbed out of bed, leaned against the wall beside me and we doubled up with secret laughter until I registered his half-nakedness.

'I have to go,' I said, standing to leave, but he held me back.

'Not yet. She could be waiting.' I felt his lips close to my ear.

'I'm sure she's gone.'

'Wait,' he said, holding my arm. 'I want to …'

'What?' I snapped, fearing the combination of his confidence and my desire. I didn't want to hear what he wanted, in case I couldn't resist. He let go of my wrist, and his hand slowly opened as he interlaced his fingers with mine. The tenderness of his touch filled my whole body and I ached with wanting. Unable to look at his face or his full mouth, I turned my eyes away, but that didn't help. The shape of his collarbone and the curve of his shoulder were painfully beautiful. I shut my eyes and in that moment of submission, he led me to his bed.

'I'll miss you,' he said.

The Head Boy was leaving after his exams, less than a week away. I was about to risk my marriage and my husband's job to make love with a boy I'd probably never see again. I was rooted to the floor.

'I can't. I'm sorry. I'm married.'

He stood still beside me, tall and gently close. 'If I give you my number,' he said, his finger sliding down to the tip of my nose to rest on my lips, 'promise you'll call me when you get the seven-year itch?'

I opened my mouth just enough for the tip of my tongue to touch the tip of his finger. He moved closer, then closer still and his mouth met mine for a long, soft kiss. And then I turned and ran out of his study, up the stone stairs to the safety of my marital bed where the lights would be out, no doubt about it.

❖

Soane House wasn't the same after the Head Boy had gone. His presence had made the boarding school bearable. Without him I was left with a predictable marriage and the drudgery of an office job. Administering companies, even for French clients, soon came down to transferring cash to avoid tax. An unexpected invitation to lunch with the Lawyer who owned the firm was the most exciting thing to happen in weeks.

'I've got a new client for you,' he said, standing in my office door as I unwrapped a sandwich. 'It's pretty straightforward. All the details are in the file.' He balanced a green manila folder on top of my computer and scrutinized my lunch. 'That doesn't look very appetizing. I've got a one o'clock reservation. Why don't you join me?'

The lunch was long and I didn't care that office gossip raged by the time we returned. The secretaries and bookkeepers had always objected to me and a working collaboration with the Lawyer appealed to me more. The cases he referred became more interesting, and as their complexity increased, so did our lunchtime meetings which fuelled supposition and jealousy. It wasn't long before I found the office as tense as the boarding school.

I begged my husband almost daily to leave the island and take me with him. But he dismissed my pleas, saying that I was nagging, and I was about to give up when a former colleague, now a headmaster in England, invited us to his new school to offer my husband a job. Fuelled by my enthusiasm, he communicated his interest and I applied to the nearest university. When I was accepted for an interview, it seemed we were about to properly start our life together.

We flew to England and drove for hours to reach the school, where the headmaster and his wife made us welcome. The following day I attended my interview, was instantly granted a place to read Law, and that evening my husband was offered the job of assistant headmaster. I had never been happier, until sitting on the aeroplane heading back to the island, my husband turned to me and said, 'It's been good for the ego, but it's not really what we want, is it?'

'It's what I want.'

'I don't think we want to leave the island.'

'I do.'

'Well, we're not going to.'

'What?'

'We're not leaving the island and that's the end of the discussion.'

And that was my husband's idea of a discussion. A fair teacher, proud to be considered a liberal among his conservative colleagues, the Schoolmaster imposed his will in our marriage like a dictator. There was no point trying to persuade him to change his mind. Like a junior boy, I was expected to respect him when he deemed a subject off limits.

Soane House rules restricted my present and, behind his benign, happy-go-lucky exterior, my husband prescribed my future. I didn't know how to tell him that unless I left the island I'd go mad. He couldn't bear confrontation and, conveniently for him, I didn't know how to confront. All I knew was how to be good, which perversely meant I also knew how to be bad. I regretted the departure of the Head Boy. If he'd been around, I could have got into trouble and been expelled from the island in record time.

Taking up my university place and going ahead with my plans alone never occurred to me. I longed to escape the confines of my marriage but couldn't imagine doing so without another man to set me free. In the absence of the Head Boy, only one other came to mind.

❖

A few weeks after the trip to England, the Lawyer and I had met by chance on a flight to France, and he had casually offered to take me to the Tour d'Argent for dinner the next time I was in Paris. The invitation was bold because it implied an overnight stay.

'I'm married, and so are you,' I mumbled, in spite of the sensation chasing to the core of my body.

'I may be married, but my wife doesn't understand me,' the Lawyer replied.

I sympathized. I couldn't resist the Lawyer's pretty lies, or my own and, assuring myself that I couldn't be a mistress because I was already a wife, accepted his offer.

The Lawyer's attention made me feel like a woman and it excited me that he drank vodka rather than milk, wore expensive clothes, drove an Aston Martin and was willing to lead me astray.

The Lawyer was a selfish hedonist and just what I needed. I soon discovered that he was very good at being bad, so good in fact he was even a bad lover.

We first made love in Paris, or more accurately the Orly Airport Hilton – not quite the same thing – where our lovemaking was as nondescript as the hotel itself. The paintings were impressions of impressionists, the sheets smelled of cigarettes and aeroplanes roared overhead like angry prehistoric birds. The following morning the Lawyer took the first flight back to the island, having convinced me it would be indiscreet for us to return to the island at the same time. I waited in the hotel room for the next flight and, without the Lawyer to occupy my thoughts, felt sad, sick and ashamed. For the first time it occurred to me that I was an adulteress. I had broken one of the Commandments yet when the Lawyer asked to see me again, I said yes simply because he told me that he wanted me and I wanted to be wanted.

Finding places to meet became an adventure I couldn't resist, but while the hotels got better the sex did not. This didn't stop me believing that because we were lovers there was love between us and our affair gained momentum. My husband never once questioned my extended absences although he did comment that I'd stopped complaining. One evening, watching television, he had pulled me on to his lap and, nuzzling my ear through my hair, said, 'I love you. You're so much happier these days. Thank God you've seen sense.'

This made me wonder for the first time, but unfortunately not the last, why the man I was with loved me more when I no longer cared.

❖

My secret affair was a few months old when the Lawyer invited me to meet some friends at an exclusive island restaurant where he often took his wife. He wanted to step out of the shadows.

'I don't care who finds out about us. I love you.'

Some part of me remembered that being found out had motivated this affair and so I decided to be reckless. That night we drank too much champagne and after dinner the Lawyer and I went to his yacht in the marina. We walked barefoot along the smooth wooden boards, holding hands, holding shoes, pleased with ourselves for being so bold. We stepped lightly onto the yacht. The Lawyer indicated the entrance to the main cabin while he went for more champagne. I tiptoed down the steps, opened the cabin door and froze. Instantly sober, I reversed silently up the steps and ran to the Lawyer.

'There's a woman — '

The Lawyer's expression did not change. 'That will be my wife,' he said, as though he'd half expected her. I wondered whether this had happened before, as she emerged from the cabin, clutching an empty bottle of wine.

The Lawyer's wife was Amazonian, twice my age and very drunk. The three of us stood in a wobbly triangle. Hoping to forestall an attack with the wine bottle, I said with great calm, 'Let's talk about this.'

To my surprise we all sat down. The Lawyer and his wife faced each other and I sat next to her. Suddenly I felt guilty. 'I'm so sorry,' I said, reaching towards her.

'Don't touch me,' she spat. 'And don't think you're so special. You're not the first.'

I looked to the Lawyer, expecting him to contradict her but he had slumped.

His wife raged on. 'Does she know you have children her age? Does she know about your other affairs? And did you tell her about your disease?'

Disease?

'Darling, do we have to go through this again?' the Lawyer said.

His wife ignored him.

'You won't be working for my husband after this. Be on the first flight off the island, or you'll be headlines in tomorrow's paper.'

'She's married,' the Lawyer said wearily, as if to redeem me from a certain kind of sin.

The Lawyer had claimed that his wife did not understand him, but I saw that she not only understood him, she loved him and would fight to keep him. It was messy, but it was a marriage, and I had no right to be there.

'I think you need to talk without me,' I said, picking up my shoes.

'Come back to the boat tomorrow. I'll know what I'm doing by then,' the Lawyer said, looking at me like a little boy who'd peed his pants.

I took a taxi back to Soane House, and crept in through the back door. I ran a hot bath and soaking in the dark, lay back and closed my eyes. The Lawyer and I had floated on champagne dreams which came back to me now; a life together in Paris, an apartment for me in London, a yacht on which we'd sail the world. These fantasies of dissatisfied middle age and dissatisfied youth had been dispelled by his wife. My head buzzed from the revelations of our meeting. Particularly the disease. What kind of disease did the Lawyer have and had I caught it? I scrubbed my skin raw then, in buttoned-up pyjamas to protect my husband from contagion, went to bed.

My husband hardly stirred as I settled my back against his. The warmth of his body and the rhythm of his breath were a comfort I appreciated now that I was leaving. I could no longer pretend that his future was mine. Listening to my husband breathing, I tried to imagine a life without him but my mind was numb. Nothing compelled me, apart from escape and in the absence of any other plan, I decided to return to the Lawyer's boat the following day.

The following morning my husband and I hardly spoke. He didn't ask about my late return home. I offered no explanation.

The thought of confessing my sin was inconceivable. I couldn't risk his forgiveness.

'Cheer up. Try to have a good day and maybe we'll go for a walk on the beach when you've finished work,' he said, kissing me lightly and leaving for school.

Walk on the beach? He'd never suggested that before. For a second I thought about staying, but there was nothing a walk on the beach could change. I wrote my husband a letter of goodbye and left it on the bed for him to find later that afternoon.

My darling

Please forgive me for not having the courage to tell you that I am leaving. Don't try to find me. You cannot change my mind.

I realize now that I was too young to be married. You have always been clear about what you want and I'm still discovering those things. All I know is that I'm not ready to settle for your island life.

You once said that I expected you to make me happy. Sometimes you did. Sometimes you made me so very happy and I shall always remember those days when a whole life with you seemed possible.

❖

I crept out of Soane House with a rucksack on my back and took a taxi to the marina for my meeting with the Lawyer. On my way to the yacht, I met his senior partner, David, and we walked together.

'Are you okay?' he asked. I nodded even though tears were welling up.

We stepped onto the boat, leaving our shoes in a line, taking care not to ruin the teak deck even as marriages were being wrecked all around. David signalled for me to go through while he waited outside. Finally the Lawyer and I were alone.

'I've decided,' he coughed, 'to stay with my wife for the moment. I can trust her to be with me when I'm old, which I couldn't reasonably expect from you.'

An image surfaced in my mind. I was wearing patent Yves St Laurent shoes, matching handbag and dark glasses. The Lawyer wore a suit and I was pushing him in a wheelchair on a cliff path, the edge ominously close …

'Darling? Are you listening?' he said.

'Yes … yes, I'm sorry. You're staying with your wife.' My voice seemed to come from far away, as though it wasn't mine at all.

'I think it's for the best. You should go back to your husband and look for another job. I'll give you severance pay.'

'I'm not staying on the island.'

'Then I'll pay the rent on an apartment in London. We'll see each other when I visit clients there. If we're meant to be together we will be.' He had it all worked out.

The Lawyer called for David to join us, and he came in with a transparent envelope stuffed with clean £20 notes.

'That's your three months' severance. And we've agreed that you should have the company car.'

He couldn't get me off his sinking ship fast enough. In a daze I took the car keys and the money and when I left, the Lawyer didn't even stand up to say goodbye. David walked me to a BMW, which was old, but still too sporty-looking for the mood I was in.

'Take care and good luck,' he said, earnestly gripping my shoulder as if he could pour courage into me.

I sat in the car, which smelled of cleaning fluid and leather, numbly staring at a grey sky as it began to rain. Through rivulets streaming down the polished windscreen I stared at the dock and the ferry from France. The horn sounded and in that moment I knew I had to be on the next crossing.

❖

Once I got to France I called an ancient great-aunt, who welcomed me to stay. And then I called my mother to break her heart. 'Your husband is a good man. You'll regret leaving him,' she said. I feared confessing my infidelity but my mother had already guessed that I was an adulteress. It would be some time before she could see me, or even speak to me, again.

I decided not to be so cavalier with the truth when I met my great-aunt, who greeted me with open arms outside her rambling manor house. She held my sobbing body against her ample bosom for a long time, smoothing my forehead, over and over reassuring me: '*Pas grave, c'est pas grave, si tu peux pas avoir des enfants.*'

The old dear thought I was crying because I couldn't have children and, grateful for any kind of sympathy, I didn't contradict her.

We sat at a yellow Formica table in her warm, dark kitchen, and I stared at the field of grazing Friesans beyond the window. The stone floor was cool, and the cream painted walls faded and cracked. The shelf above the table was cluttered with countless eggcups, a reminder that the old woman had given birth to thirteen children. Family defined her life. The last thing she expected to hear from me was that I had escaped my husband and wanted a divorce. The longer we talked, the greater my need to be honest, and slowly I wound my way round to the simple but scandalous truth. My great-aunt's response was curt, and one I should have predicted. '*Appellez le prêtre,*' she commanded.

I was not welcome in her house without the priest's absolution. Too exhausted to protest, I made the call while the suspicious great-aunt listened from the kitchen. The priest suggested a private interview, but first insisted that I attend Mass the next morning. I agreed, assuming I would be an inconspicuous presence, but there was little chance of that. The village community was tight, a newcomer in their midst a big event, and they all had a good look at me as I followed my great-aunt to her family pew at the front of the congregation. It didn't help that I was wearing a white summer dress and towered two feet above the average communicant, each and every one clad in black.

Halfway through Mass there was an unexpected twist to the order of service when the priest summoned me to the lectern. Reluctantly I stood behind the microphone, wondering what he intended to do now that a hundred pairs of eyes were on me. I had feared the humiliation of public condemnation, so was relieved when all he asked was that I recite the Lord's Prayer in English while he said it in French. It seemed a simple request, but by the time we reached 'forgive us our sins' my tears pronounced that I had strayed from the path of righteousness.

After the service I questioned the priest's compassion, and the wisdom of meeting him alone, but knew that if I refused, I would be turned from my great-aunt's house. I had no choice but to visit him that evening as had been arranged.

I was greeted by the priest's housekeeper, frail and bent as an olive tree. Wrinkled skin fell in folds from her brittle bones and she had no top teeth. But she moved quickly and indicated that I should follow her down a narrow passage towards the back of the house. We passed life-sized photographs of children and a samurai costume draped on the wall with sabres on either side. My great-aunt had proudly told me that the priest had been a missionary and the children's faces were Asian, dark-skinned and bright-eyed, but for some reason their framed faces made me feel uneasy.

I was taken to an enormous, sparsely-furnished room where, behind a Japanese silk screen, the priest was giving a trumpet lesson. The housekeeper told me to sit while she closed the shutters, slowly robbing the room of daylight until I was sitting in the dark. Finally the screeching trumpet stopped and I heard a timid young musician ask if it was time to go home.

Once his student had gone, the priest turned his attention to me. He switched on his desk lamp, angling its hot bare bulb at my face. I squinted in the bright light, which he refused to turn away.

'*La lumière est la verité*,' he said.

The priest wanted the truth and, in good faith, I gave it. After my confession, he sat for a while staring at me, rocking back and forth in a gentle rhythmic motion, then reached into his desk drawer to produce two sheets of paper.

'I created these myself,' he said proudly. In bright felt-tip pen he had drawn two graphs representing sexual pleasure. 'Graph A shows a selfish lover,' he said. The red line, which represented the man, peaked like a mountain then fell away. The yellow line, a sensationless plateau, represented the woman. 'Graph A shows sex with your husband,' suggested the priest. 'And this,' his voice rising in anticipation, 'was your lover.' Up came Graph B, its red and yellow lines peaking and falling in simultaneous, orgasmic ecstasy.

'It wasn't like that at all,' I said.

But the priest seemed not to hear. He was fixated by the graphs and wanted to discuss their implications in lascivious detail. I sat back in my chair, away from the heat of the overhead light, and closed my eyes. The last thing I needed was a highly-sexed holy man.

'You must leave these men. Come stay with me, be my *copine*.'

The bespectacled priest licked his cracked lips with the tip of his tongue and fearing he wanted me to be more than his 'friend', I jumped to my feet.

'Don't leave. You are too upset. Wait, be calm.'

I sat down again to take a breath and regain my composure, as the priest pulled a camera from beneath his chair. 'May I take your photograph?' he said, blinding me with the flash before I could answer.

I ran to my car and sped to the safety of my great-aunt. Over a cup of tea, I recounted my strange interview with her revered clergyman and suggested that she should not place so much faith in him.

'Our village priest is an honourable man, how dare you damn him?'

Such was her indignation she served nothing but lettuce from the garden for dinner, which we ate in silence before an early bed.

The following morning my great-aunt prepared a breakfast of warm brioche and café au lait, a sure sign, I thought, that things were looking up.

'My youngest daughter and son-in-law will be visiting this weekend,' she said lightheartedly, pouring me a bowl of coffee. I was about to enthuse at the prospect of meeting a distant relative, when she continued, 'And because my daughter's husband is a man who appreciates beauty – perhaps a little too keenly – I would be grateful if you would leave today.' She dipped a corner of the soft sweet roll into her coffee before popping it into her mouth.

My great-aunt had shown kindness for she had considered taking me in, but overnight I had become a stranger who threatened her world. I left that afternoon and set off on the long drive to the night ferry for England. En route I fell asleep behind the wheel so many times, I finally stopped by the roadside to rest. It was almost midnight when I reached the port and drove onto the ferry's hold, open like a whale's gaping mouth. The crew waved me on, the ramp was raised and the ferry moved off. For the first time in my life, I was free. I should have been elated but with my freedom came fear. I thanked God for my sister, the only person to whom I could turn. She had divorced her snakeman and left her childhood village. Surely she would understand how instantly unfamiliar my world seemed now that I was homeless, jobless and husbandless.

Four

The Lover and the Lord

When I felt trapped by marriage I had equated freedom with happiness, but as I negotiated my divorce and a new life in London, independence was losing its charm.

'I swore before God, and a few lesser mortals, to stay married until the day I die. Now I feel guilty to be single and alive,' I said to my sister, lying on her bed, surrounded by books on psychology and spirituality.

'You've got to have an identity,' she said.

'I wish the Lawyer would call,' I said.

'Don't rely on him. You need stability.'

My sister was practical and purposeful and not coming up with the easy solutions I wanted to hear. I was not ready for her Road Less Travelled – a copy of which was digging me in the ribs. I pulled the book out from under me and slung it to the floor. 'Why does life have to be so complicated?'

'Anna gave me that book. You should read it. The answer is to be self-'

'identified. Yes. You've said.'

My sister had talked of little else since I'd arrived at Anna's cottage. Anna, her new friend, had invited her to stay when she could no longer tolerate the humiliation of her former employer, Lady F.

'Anna's my inspiration. She manages to live life on her terms without being selfish,' said my sister.

Anna appealed to me more than her theories of empowerment. She was a maverick, with warmth and humour in equal measure. 'Divorced?' she laughed when she met me, 'you don't look old enough to be married.'

I felt welcome the minute I arrived at her rented cottage on the Duke of W's estate. It was a warm September day and the sunlit acres around the cottage looked like a film set: ancient trees, fields of long grass, insects dancing on the river in the early-evening light. Anna, a respected horse trainer, was holding a party for the riders she had trained that summer for the Olympics, a group of world-class sportsmen and women who drove Range Rovers and open-top sports cars. During the day I had helped get the party together, but once the guests arrived it didn't occur to me to join in the revelry. I watched from a distance as the equestrians prepared to race each other across the river in battered wooden rowing boats.

A fit-looking older man in a flat tweed cap stood in the back of a boat holding an oar like a gondolier. The women riders clambered into other boats, gripping both oars, competitive to the last. Halfway across the river the gondolier was winning and laughing. In fact, almost everybody was laughing by now, but not as hard as they laughed when the man in the lead began to sink. His boat was filling with water and there was nothing he could do about it.

My sister, sitting alone on the hay bales, was as removed from the merrymaking as me and looked so sad I thought I'd try to cheer her up. An ethereal-looking man in a threadbare cashmere beat me to it. My sister brightened in his company. He made her laugh, and when a strand of her auburn hair fell forward on her face, he tucked it behind her ear. I turned back to the comedy on the water.

'Who are you?' asked a voice behind me. I turned to see the gondolier, his trousers soaked up to his thighs. I gave him my name and asked his.

'Do you work for Anna?' he said, ignoring my question.

'I don't ride,' I confessed. Everything about him spelled Horseman – even his legs, which were shaped as though a horse stood between them.

'I suppose you eat chocolate cake?' he asked.

'Of course,' I said, and we went towards the queue for cake.

'Darling! You're soaking wet,' said a woman with long blonde hair and a grating laugh, standing in line. She wrapped her arm around the gondolier and sucked his cheek, gnat like, resting her hand on the back of his neck where his hair was short. Their familiarity made me move away and, after piling my plate with strawberries and cake, I went to find my sister. When I saw that she was still with the tall man, I sat in the middle of the field to eat soft berries which were so sweet they had to be the last of summer.

'Why did you disappear?' The man with no name stood above me.

'Your wife didn't like me.'

'She's not my wife. What about you – are you a wife?'

I owed him one unanswered question and, turning towards my sister, asked, 'Do you know that man?'

'I do. And do you know that girl?' he said.

'I do.'

Ten minutes later the four of us were in a Landrover, my sister in the front with her friend, Harry, and me in the back with the gondolier, who tried to reach for my hands, in a gesture at once both intimate and strangely impersonal. The bumpy road became smooth as we followed a stone drive towards the kind of ancestral house that people pay to see and take all day to walk around.

Harry led us through a side door into a dark red room where a trolley was set with every kind of drink. I would have liked champagne, but my sister asked for G and T so I did, too. The men had straight vodka and ice and were slicing up the last of the lemon when a butler glided in.

'Good evening, Your Grace,' he said to Harry, who was a most unlikely duke.

'Thanks, Rupert. We're okay. Why don't you take this evening off?'

We moved into a vast drawing room, and I sat on the fire surround, my shorts too short and grass-stained for me to recline in one of the deep armchairs. While the gondolier stuck much too close for a man who wouldn't give his name, Harry was respectful and attentive towards my sister. Between them was desire and tenderness, which created a potent atmosphere that enveloped us all. It was a rare moment of possibility which could have gone anywhere, until the hall door slammed.

'Daddy .... '

'Darling! Home from school already.' Harry stood to greet his daughter. 'We'd better get these girls back to Anna's party. Don't want to ruin their fun.' In that second, the magic was gone, but the Gondolier saved me and my sister from humiliation.

'Come on, girls,' he said clapping his hands. His face was alight with affection, humour shining from his eyes. 'There's nothing I'd like better than to escort you.'

❖

The gondolier rang the following day to thank Anna for her hospitality. He also enquired 'if one of those girls' could take dictation during one of the riding trials that afternoon.

'Yes, your one can,' said Anna, letting him know his motives were clear.

Three hours later I arrived at the training ground where the Gondolier introduced me to the dressage coach. We sat in a Range Rover parked at the short end of a rectangle as he scrutinized riders handling horses I recorded his comments. The gondolier stood outside on my side of the car, listening to our conversation.

'Do you ride?' asked the dressage expert.

'A donkey once when I was six, and a camel at the zoo.'

The gondolier took me to lunch, which was served in a converted barn beside an elegant house. He chose to eat on another table, leaving me with a few friendly equestrians but, defeated by the non-stop horse talk, I was soon ready to leave. There seemed no point in saying goodbye to the gondolier, who was busy talking to his equestrians. I was in my car, about to drive off, when he came running into the car park.

'Where are you going?'

'Back to Anna's.'

'I wanted to take you to tea with some friends. Please, say you'll come.'

I accepted, willing to be invited into his world and diverted from the muddle that was mine.

'Let's go in my car. It will give us a chance to talk,' he said, but he quickly monopolized the questions.

'Where do you live?'

'London,' I said, deliberately vague.

'Where in London?'

'Chesham Crescent.'

'Is your family from London?' he asked. He was right to be suspicious. I had one of the most expensive addresses in the city and the right kind of car, but I didn't have the shoes to match.

'We're from Shropshire,' I said.

I could see him thinking: ah, that accounts for a little something in her accent. He probably filled in the other blanks too; small public school, tennis court at home, but no ponies because she doesn't ride. As he drove, I studied his profile. He was classically good-looking.

'You still haven't told me your name,' I said.

He gave me his first name and then asked for my telephone number. I smiled, said no and we drove the rest of the way in silence.

Tea was with a famous sculptress, and we sat in her studio surrounded by marble and bronze horses waiting to be shipped around the world. A few, she said, were going to princely palaces in the Middle East and one was for 'Twinkie's place in the Bahamas'. And then her eyes lit up. 'Oh, darling, a bit of gossip, Lady F's ex-nanny's *in love* with Harry! Every time he went over to see them, the stupid nanny thought he was coming to see her. She was so besotted they had to fire her, and now they're stuck without help, and can't cope at all. What do you think? Do you think he could possibly take a shine to a nanny?'

I stood looking onto the lawn where the sculptress' children were playing cricket. I had been given a cup of tea but wasn't included in their conversation, which was just as well. The nanny they were talking about was my sister and my new friend knew it. He laughed uneasily, but said nothing, protecting us all from embarrassment. Why was it so impossible for the sculptress to imagine a single man, even if he was a duke, falling in love with my beautiful auburn-haired sister, even if she was a nanny? The gondolier steered the conversation back to the sculptress' latest commission, and I drifted off inside my head, the boys on the lawn reminding me of happy times on the island, which now seemed reassuringly familiar.

From far away I heard somebody call my name, and then again. It was the gondolier. He thrust a pair of Hunter wellies into my hand and said, 'We're taking a walk, if you'd like to come.'

The September sun was low in the sky and had lost all its

warmth as we followed a narrow path, which trailed the river and led away through the fields. I hitched up my skirt to better feel the long grass against my legs, leaving the man and the sculptress far behind, talking about people they knew. I was standing in the peace of the land and the sky, drawn to the early evening light of the golden fields, when the head of a blade of grass tickled the back of my knee. I turned to find the gondolier behind me and our shadows, side-by-side, cast long and far before us.

When we got back to the training ground, everyone had gone. I was about to drive off, when the gondolier asked, 'Are you sure you'll remember my telephone number?' and recited it a second time. I nodded but wasn't bothered whether I would or not. 'Don't forget to call me. Please.' I nodded again. 'I'll write it down,' he said, and handed me a piece of paper with neat, very legible figures. 'Put it in your pocket. Don't lose it,' he said.

❖

I moved into my basement flat in Chesham Crescent, and waited for the Lawyer to call. After a week my faith in our love lacked conviction. After two weeks it felt like a pretence. And after three I stopped worrying about love all together and started to worry about the rent. The Lawyer may have lost interest, but the landlord had not and he called daily, wanting to know when to expect the next rent cheque. My mantra was 'any day now', but there comes a time when such a day can no longer be deferred and we agreed to meet.

'You must be in some kind of trouble,' he said, seeing my anxious face. 'I don't want to make your life more difficult, but I do need the rent.' The landlord looked like a musician, or playwright, and was so sympathetic that I decided to tell him all about the Lawyer.

'He's a bastard, but you're not the first and you won't be the last to be abandoned by a married man. With your deposit you've still got a bit of time, so long as you pay the telephone bill and don't break anything before you go.' He was joking, but neither one of us laughed. He pushed his glasses up his nose and blinked. 'The thing is, I'm writing at the moment, and cash flow problems are distracting.' My landlord suddenly reminded me of Tom Stoppard and seemed so traumatized by the messy business of money, I overcame my pride and called the Lawyer's secretary.

'Who is it?' she asked.

'A friend.'

She knew it was me. 'He's in Bermuda with his wife.' It was an unnecessary clarification but one, I sensed, that she enjoyed making.

To compound my woes, my sister had called that evening to tell me that she had met a new man with whom she was in love.

'It's so exciting. I've met this amazing French man and we're going to live in his cottage, without telephone or electricity, on the west coast of France.'

'Then what?' I asked, resisting the temptation to deride her romantic enthusiasm.

'Plant vegetables and make babies.'

I tried to sound happy for her but as soon as we hung up, was so much sadder for myself. As the evening wore on, I felt worse. I needed to talk to somebody who wouldn't say I told you so. I called the gondolier after finding his number squashed in the pocket of my skirt.

'Hello.' His voice was so abrupt I almost put the receiver down.

'It's me. The girl — '

'Darling, I was about to give up on you.'

He sounded so happy to hear me, I had to bite down on my lip to stop myself from crying.

'Darling. Are you there? Let me come up and take you to Annabel's. Do you like Annabel's?'

'Not now,' I said, not knowing what, or who, Annabel was.

'Tomorrow night, let me take you tomorrow night.'

'Eh … not really,' I said.

I heard him turning the pages of his desk diary. This was getting complicated. All I had wanted was a voice at the end of the telephone. I should have called the Samaritans.

'Next Thursday, eight o'clock.' he said. I heard the creak of his desk chair as he leaned forward to write my name and address at the foot of the page. I was in his diary. We had a date.

The next day a package arrived from my sister in which she enclosed a small book called *The Prophet*, by the Lebanese philosopher Gibran. A post-it was stuck on page twenty-nine and she had underlined these words:

Then a ploughman said, Speak to us of work.
And he answered, saying:
You work that you keep pace with the earth
and the soul of the earth.

That was all very well if you're planting vegetables but how could I aspire to keep pace with the earth while living in the Tarmacked city?

'What I'm trying to say,' my sister had written, 'is that work is good and I think you'll feel a lot better once you get a job.'

She was right. I needed a focus to my day as much as I needed money because my severance pay was disappearing fast. The day before, in a narrow street at the back of Harrods, I'd groaned when I had seen the sign 'Knightsbridge Secretaries' in a window above a sandwich shop. I knew it wouldn't be long before I'd have to be back behind the typewriter.

I rang the bell and the door clicked open. A narrow staircase with winding steps led to an office the size of a shoebox and behind the desk, her back to the door and maypole straight, sat a woman with sleek dark hair and pearl earrings. In the cramped surroundings her elegance was an act of defiance. She swivelled her chair to face me, and her mouth fell open, displaying the presence of gold-capped back teeth, which hadn't been there in our convent days.

Helen had been my only friend at school, but after A Levels we had lost contact. Her father, a famous psychiatrist, had encouraged her to be 'fully expressed', and she had never been naïve. As a girl of seventeen, she'd had an older boyfriend who took her for weekends in Paris or Rome and every Monday I watched in amazement when he dropped her at the convent in his blue Aston Martin.

In those days Helen's intention had been to live in London, but running a secretarial agency above a sandwich shop ('deli, darling, we call it a deli') seemed an unlikely choice for a girl who'd been brought up to be liberated. Something must have gone wrong, but I knew better than to ask. For the daughter of a psychiatrist, Helen had always been surprisingly disinclined to share her thoughts. She shook a pack of Marlboro Light at me. I shook my head.

'Good girl. How about Mars Bars?'

One term we had eaten only Mars Bars for lunch, cutting the bar in half on the horizontal, discarding the fake nougat base in favour of the caramel top. All the pleasure, half the calories.

'I'm not eating Mars these days,' I said, which brought us to the subject of men, although I didn't mention the Lawyer and didn't dwell on my divorce. 'Work is the priority now,' I said firmly, 'because London's expensive.'

'How long did it take you to figure that out?' she said, reaching into a drawer full of forms. 'Fill this in and I'll get you a job within the week.' She gave me a multiple-choice questionnaire entitled 'A Psychological Work Profile for Women', which, I noticed, she had compiled herself.

Glancing through my questionnaire, she read out the first line of my address. 'We're neighbours,' she said, as though it were no surprise. We lived on the same crescent, ten doors apart, and agreed to meet that evening.

Helen was as good as her word. The following Monday I was secretary to a property tycoon, who, I'd been warned, couldn't keep a secretary because he made them cry. According to my 'psychological work profile', the fact that he was a bully mattered less to me than having natural daylight in the office and a view from the window. The tycoon's view was Hyde Park, and those ancient trees kept me sane. The property man paid a high salary, another key requirement from my test, and was idiosyncratic enough to be interesting. There wasn't much shorthand, and only marginally more typing, which also appealed to me. In fact, Helen's work profile concluded that I was 'unsuitable for secretarial work', a detail she withheld at the time because, as she explained later, 'finding out what you really want to do can take for ever, and you didn't have that kind of time to pay the rent'.

When I went over to Helen's flat she was full of advice about living in London: the best bars, the best health club, the best places to walk in the park, the best shop in Chelsea for second-hand clothes, 'all designer, some never worn'. Every recommendation she made was geared towards meeting a man, ideally *the* man rather than the *ideal* man, because, Helen assured me, 'the ideal man does not exist'.

'And don't get put off if you're not mad about the first man you're with because you'll meet his friends, and chances are you'll like one of them. It kind of goes like that.' She sounded weary.

'But I've met a man,' I said, surprised to find myself sounding as though a relationship with him was inevitable.

'That was quick. Who?'

I told her the gondolier's name.

'What's his family name?'

'He won't say.'

'That's strange. Where's he taken you?'

'Nowhere yet. But next week we're going to Annabel's, whatever that is.'

'It's the toffs' nightclub on Berkeley Square where the Middle East meets the middle-ages. How old is this guy by the way?'

'No idea.'

'That old?' said Helen as she pulled a plain black long-sleeved dress from the wardrobe behind her sofa. 'You can wear this, so long as you absolutely promise to get your hair done. You can't go to Annabel's with hair like that.' Helen was talking, her bottom in the air, as she searched for a handbag to match her dress. 'Take this,' she said, giving me a fine silk purse decorated with mother-of-pearl beads.

I had accepted Helen's clothes and was writing down the number of her hairdresser when the doorbell rang. A big man with an elfin face, gold-rimmed spectacles and a squinty, shy smile walked into the room. He handed Helen a book, concealed in a taped-up black plastic bag.

'Would you give this to Lydia? I promised to return it months ago.' Lydia and Helen were flatmates, though their basement wasn't much bigger than mine.

The man smiled at me. His lips were narrow, his mouth wide and he held out his hand in greeting. Helen's eyes volleyed from him to me and back again.

'Glass of wine, anyone? We were just about to open a bottle.'

'Helen, I can't, I've got to go,' I said. She stared at me, as if to say *where the hell to?* The wine may have been to prolong the man's visit for my benefit, but an impulse to run had swept through me the moment he'd walked into the room. Something about him made me nervous, and I didn't want to hang around long enough to find out what. I thanked Helen for the loan of the dress, then bolted out of her door and down the crescent. I ran, the black dress flapping, its clear plastic cover pressing like transparent skin into my legs. People on the pavement stepped out of my way and I kept running until it hurt to breathe, until all of me hurt and I had to stop. Back at my flat I took a steaming shower, put the kettle on, and was feeling almost back to normal when the telephone rang.

'He wants your number. Can I give it to him?' Helen whispered. I guessed he was still with her.

'But I've got a date with the mystery man.'

'In seven days time. This man's right here, he's young, interesting and has *loads of friends*.' Her voice dropped to a whisper. 'And apparently he's fabulous in bed.'

Fifteen minutes later the telephone rang again.

'I hope you don't mind. I got your number from Helen. Would you like to meet this evening? Have a cup of tea, a glass of wine … something simple.' He held the silence. Then, in a steady voice, 'I'd like to see you.'

The straightforward way he said that appealed to me, and I told him to come for a cup of tea. Before he arrived there was either time to wash the dishes or get out of my too-comfortable pyjamas. I chose the sink, which was a disaster zone, and had cleared away two days worth of plates by the time he buzzed the front door.

He walked down the Titian blue carpet to my basement where we drank tea, sweetened with honey, and talked. Crinkly blond hair fell to his shoulders, and his small sharp eyes framed in gold-rimmed spectacles made him look intense and bookish. Nevertheless he said he was 'a manual kind of man'. He had quit the City a year before to buy a house, which he was renovating himself and planned to sell at a great profit.

'Giving up a high-paid City career to strike out on my own cost me more than money,' he sighed. And then he began to talk about a girl called Camilla whom he had loved and lost. Even though Camilla became the focus of our conversation for the next two hours, we agreed to meet the following day. And the day after that. And the day after that. By day five he'd stopped talking about Camilla quite so much and had become my Lover. He had long limbs, long nose, long legs, long *everything*. In fact, it was all rather a shock.

❖

By the time my date at Annabel's came around, it felt like an obligation – until I saw the gondolier descend the stairs in a dark-blue suit and Gucci loafers of cracked black leather polished to a high shine. He was holding a bunch of sweet peas in delicate colours.

'From my garden,' he said, bowing slightly and giving me the flowers. He brushed his lips close to mine.

I sat wide-eyed as he drove from Knightsbridge to Mayfair, up Park Lane and around Berkeley Square. I knew so little of London I was impressed he knew the way. He parked on Berkeley Square, and handed the keys to a footman in a dark-green overcoat and top hat. Then he took my arm and led me down the steps into the nightclub where we were greeted by a gracious Italian.

'Good evening, m'lord.'

I was so surprised to learn that the gondolier was a lord, I turned immediately into the ladies' – except it wasn't. A man dressed like a butler in striped grey-and-black trousers directed me across the corridor. The cloakroom attendant, an old woman who sat on a gilded chair, took one look at me and I knew she knew everything. My dress didn't fool her. I was wearing neither coat nor shawl, so had nothing to give her apart from a polite smile. She pinned me with unfriendly eyes. I smeared on more lipstick to justify being in her cloakroom at all, and stared at my reflection. What was I doing here in a borrowed dress with an old lord? And why did he inspire so much deference? I decided right then that he was just a man to me, whoever he was, and walked back into the nightclub, relieved to find him waiting. Lord or not, he was less intimidating than that old woman on her attendant's throne.

Our table was in a corner that was so dark we could hardly see our plates, let alone across the room. The Lord put on half-moon reading glasses and drew the candle closer to read the menu. He ordered tricolore, Dover Sole and a fine bottle of white Burgundy and I went along with his choices, my mind more on him than the menu. Now that we were beside each other I tried to scrutinize his face, but there was so little light it was impossible. And that was the point of Annabel's. It was a place where men of indeterminate age engaged in dark seduction and only the staff saw clearly.

The Lord cut a slice of butter, balanced it on a corner of bread, and covered it with a layer of salt so deep I found myself worrying about his blood pressure. But when we danced together, his hand in the small of my back, his age didn't cross my mind at all.

We drove back to my flat, where he walked me to the door. We stood in the yellow ring of light that spread from the street lamp.

'Are you going to invite me in?' he asked.

'I can't.'

'Not even for a coffee?'

'No. I don't think so.'

'Darling, is that yes, or no?'

'No. But thank you for this evening.'

I had expected him to turn in a huff, but he stepped closer, rested his palm on my hip, and put his mouth on mine for a light lamplight kiss that lingered in my memory for days afterwards.

Men aren't supposed to be as intuitive as women, but I've often thought that a man can certainly sense when a woman no longer loves him which is usually the day he declares his undying devotion. Or at least puts in a call with the promise of love. Now that my time was taken up with the Lover six nights a week, and the Lord every Thursday for Annabel's or the theatre, the Lawyer only came to mind when I was worried about the rent or driving the BMW. Selling the car would put an end to the bad memories and my need for more money so I advertised it in the local newsagent. Watching the new owner drive away, I felt as though a dark part of my past was being taken with it and I no longer cared whether I spoke to the Lawyer again. Naturally, he called the very next day.

'I've missed you sweetheart. I'm in London tomorrow. I'll see you at six.' He sounded pleased with himself, and I allowed him to think that I was looking forward to his visit. I even smiled as he walked down the basement stairs, his Bermuda tan set off against a bright shirt.

We stood in my living room facing each other and he seemed like a stranger when he took my arm to lead me through to the bedroom. 'My wife's back at the hotel so we'll have to make it quick.'

'Make what quick?'

'You've changed,' he laughed, as though whatever I was, was insignificant.

'I haven't heard from you for a month. And it's so expensive to live here.'

'I should have sent the rent, but I couldn't have seen you. My wife won't let me out of her sight. She's dropped twenty pounds, looks amazing and wants sex all the time.' He drew out the words sex-all-the-time, and held up his hands as if to say what-can-I-tell-you?

The Lawyer took off his pin-striped jacket, then carefully unbuttoned his shirt, scratching the soft surface of his tanned belly, which hung over the top of his Gucci belt. He failed to notice that I was stock still with my arms folded, not a single cell in my body inclined to nakedness. In a way that would have seemed playful once, the Lawyer pushed me on to the bed and lay on top of me.

'I don't want to.' My hands came up against his shoulders.

The weight of his body was so heavy I pushed harder, screwed up my face and was about to shout stop, when he moved away as if from a bad smell. He fastened his shirt, pulled on his coat and walked to the door without a word.

'You understand, don't you?' I said, as if to console him.

'I understand,' he said with his back to me. 'And I trust you do.'

On the front step he turned to fix me with a stare then walked away, step by slow step, as though he were a dignified man.

That night my Lover came over, and we celebrated the death of the Lawyer in my life. Later, lying on my bed, the Lover watched me undress.

'When you walk around the bedroom, when you take off your clothes, you should make a man afraid,' he said.

'Why would I want to do that?'

'That's a woman's power. Don't turn away to take off your clothes. Have confidence.' He propped his head on his hand, gazing. 'Know the power you have.'

I leapt into bed and curled up beside him, my inhibitions gone once we were horizontal and naked together.

'Funny girl. Funny woman girl.'

The Lover stroked my hair, pushed back my face to find my mouth with his, wanting to make love. There wasn't a moment that he was with me that he didn't want that. After we'd made love for the third time, he promised to prepare aphrodisiac food the following evening.

'We hardly need that kind of encouragement,' I said. 'Anyway, it's Thursday. You know I'm going out.' I tried to sound casual.

'Where are you going this time?' He kept his voice in check.

'The theatre.'

'What are you seeing?' It was the safer question. The Lover had never asked who was taking me.

'*My Fair Lady.*'

'The musical?' His eyebrows fell inward. He knew it was the Lord. A musical was an older man's choice. At least I wouldn't be going to the National or the Almeida, places the Lover considered interesting, and that made him feel better.

The Lover and I rarely went out. We cooked in my flat and had sex. Although one Saturday afternoon the Lover had taken me swimming. In a quiet corner of the pool, away from the women with dimply thighs and dive-bombing boys, he had asked, 'Have you ever made love in water?' He was gathering my wet hair back from my face holding it hard in his fist and the idea that we could have sex right then in chlorinated water, surrounded by half-naked lovelies from South London, didn't seem ridiculous.

The Lover never invited me to where he lived, and whenever I asked if we could spend an evening there, he would always find an excuse. I thought he must either live in his car, or in the house he was renovating, which was why he spent most nights with me.

'Why do you see that old man?' the Lover asked, as if this abstract thought had only just occurred to him.

'I don't know. I really don't care if I never see him again.'

'Then why go to the theatre tomorrow night?'

'Because he asked me.'

'You could always say no.' This simple truth, so clearly expressed, made me cry. Try as he might to let me suffer, he soon wrapped his arms around my naked body, rocking me back and forth until I fell asleep.

Even so, it didn't occur to me to stop seeing the noble Lord. Maybe it was the way he asked me that did it. I felt instructed, not invited, and in so many ways that it shouldn't have, that suited me. For one who thought she was rebellious, obeying orders came easily. But the Lord's appeal exceeded his authoritarian manner. It was a delight to spend time with a man who knew so much about the world, it hardly seemed to matter that he didn't, and possibly never would, know me.

A few days after our evening at the theatre, the Lord called me at the office.

'Come to Ascot next Saturday and then we'll go to my estate.'

I had never been racing and said yes without thinking. I was also curious to find out what he meant by 'estate'. The Lord was so solitary, I couldn't imagine him alone in a stately home, surrounded by grounds and staff. Perhaps he was joking, playing with my great expectations, because I secretly hoped he *was* the owner of some grand estate, tumbling down from lack of funds.

'Oh, and darling, you must be on time,' he went on. 'We can't miss lunch or the first race.' His instructions were militarily precise, and I promised to catch the ten-thirty train.

The Lover came to see me on Friday and stayed the night, as always, and on Saturday morning we made love, as always. Except this Saturday, without missing a beat, he kept on. It took a while, but eventually I was at the right angle to glance at his watch.

'Fifteen minutes before the train leaves,' I cried.

The Lover kissed me all the same, which made me mad, even though his kisses were good. 'I'll take you there,' he offered. And so my Lover drove me to the Lord to spend the day with people I didn't know to watch a sport I knew nothing about. But I felt no guilt. In fact, I laughed as I ran across the gravel to the open front door of the Lord's white painted cottage – obviously he had been teasing me about his 'estate'. He lived in a romantic country pad, with rambling roses in the garden and polo sticks in the hall.

The Lord was the guest of an Eastern prince who had a box at Ascot and wore handmade shoes from Lobb. When he told me he went jogging in Hyde Park and I said, 'So do I,' the Lord scowled, later warning me that the prince was renowned for misinterpreting any sign of female friendship. I was only being polite to a man who seemed to be a parody of an Edwardian regent. The prince was so spoilt it was a relief to leave his company.

As we walked around Ascot, the Lord introduced me to his real friends, every one a Lord This or Lady That, who moved and talked in such prescribed ways they too seemed like caricatures. One Lady This half turned her face from me to drill sloe-eyes into my friend as only a lover could. The Lord winked at her but gave nothing away. Nevertheless, whenever he introduced me, I noticed that he gave both my first and second name, but gave me his friends' titles only. Later I would realize that this distinction let his friends know they should not take me too seriously. As with much in the Lord's world, racing was riddled with so-called etiquette which was little more than a way to keep each person in his place, from stable lad to duke.

The Lord and I left before the last race, and I was glad to be back at his unpretentious cottage where he took a bottle of champagne from the fridge, poured two glasses and invited me to supper. When I said, 'Yes,' he was so enthusiastic he clapped his hands and proclaimed, 'I'll put on the Jacuzzi.'

That evening we sat in the hot tub drinking cold champagne, heat bubbling at our backs, surrounded by late climbing roses bright white in moonlight. We dried ourselves on rough towels under the cold night sky and pulled on battered towelling bathrobes that had seen better days. Wrapped up in that robe, I felt happier than I had all day, than I had in a long time.

'The daily left some fish pie in the fridge,' the Lord called from the dining room where he was laying the table. Empty apart from the potato-topped pie and two bottles of champagne, the fridge light shone unobstructed into the kitchen. The 'daily', had cooked the pie in a rectangular stainless steel tray, which reminded me of my boarding house days. I boiled some peas and to complete the school food theme we had ketchup. Everything else about the evening was very grown-up.

While we ate by candlelight, the Lord asked about my marriage to the Schoolmaster and my life in the boarding school. He had been sent away to school and could imagine what the boys had thought of me, he said.

'A nineteen-year-old Matron would make sleep difficult.'

'I was more like a housemistress, although in the end I was just floating around with nothing to do.'

'Even more mysterious. Women can seem strange creatures when you're a boy away at school.'

The Lord was silent for a second, the past brought to life by some memory.

'Stay with me tonight,' he said, looking straight at me. Turning from the temptation of his perfectly still, brilliant blue eyes, I noticed the time. It was almost eleven o'clock but it didn't occur to me to stay. I had the Lover to think about, and work in the morning.

'Help. I can't miss two trains in one day. Will you drive me to the station?'

'Whatever you say, my darling.'

I rushed upstairs and pulled on the clothes I'd worn racing, which seemed less honest somehow than the old bathrobe. The Lord raced me to the station, but when we got there, the train was pulling away. But he was not about to give up, and spying the solitary guard on duty called to him: 'Guard, please. You *must* ask the train to wait for my friend at the next station.'

We drove five miles, breaking all speed limits, and to my amazement when we got there, the London train was standing on platform one. Waiting for me.

❖

The more at ease I felt with my noble friend, the more difficult it was with the Lover in the land of bed. I had assumed I loved the Lover simply because he had made me his beloved, but I was beginning to resent his constant presence in my flat. Our relationship had become as predictable as a marriage, with great sex thrown in. I should have been grateful, but was too recently divorced to see it as a blessing.

I was increasingly divided between the part of me who had fallen for the Lover and the part attracted to the Lord. I didn't know how the Lord felt, or what I really felt for him, and the drama engendered by that uncertainty was addictive. And there was another part of me, of which I was less conscious, that simply wanted to go home. I wanted, more than I could admit, to be wrapped in my mother's arms and reassured that even though my life seemed condemned to uncertainty, it wouldn't be this way forever. This benediction was so unlikely I denied that I wanted it all and carried on rushing about my life. I spent every waking second at work, or in the company of the possessive Lover, or the enigmatic Lord, never stopping to think about the web I was weaving.

Then one morning, as I ran to the office after a night with the Lover, my mind busy with thoughts of the Lord, I tripped on a paving stone. I was so surprised to find my nose pressed to grey concrete, it took a while to realize what had happened. Finally, I was no longer running. Looking around calmly, I noticed the mosaic of discarded chewed gum, flattened by feet, decorating the pavement. Who knows for how long I would have happily stared at those patterns if a passer-by in a pin-stripe suit, a bandana wrapped around his long hair, had not stopped to help me up. He got me to my feet before disappearing into the crowd.

I leaned against the newsagent's window and stared at Knightsbridge, that straight highway into the heart of London, crammed with cars, throbbing taxis and busloads of passengers resting heads on windows smeared with grease from foreheads before them. The soul of the earth seemed far away as I slowly walked to work in a daze.

Reality soon sucked me back in when my boss screamed that I was late, demanding to know who had eaten his secret stash of organic dates. I cursed myself for forgetting to replace them and ran in for dictation.

I forgot about my fall until a week later, when getting out of bed to draw the curtains, I fainted and was on the floor again. I was up in a second and on with my day, dismissing yet another sign that a fragmented life was bringing me slowly, but surely, to my knees.

❖

Warm and naked, the Lover's body was entwined with mine as we slept. But my dream was not peaceful, interspersed as it was with an alarm bell. I woke at three o'clock in the morning to the insistent sound of the telephone and extracted myself from the Lover.

'Hello?'

'It's me.'

Who is *me*? I'm wondering.

'Darling?'

Only the Lord said it quite like that. 'Are you all right?' I ask, thinking he didn't sound it.

'Yes. Well, no. They've taken my car.'

'Who?'

'The police. I need a bed for the night.' I say nothing. 'Darling?'

'Yes … '

'Good. Thank you. I'll be there in five minutes.'

'I didn't mean yes to a bed.'

'Darling. Please.' He wasn't the kind of man to beg.

'You can have the sofa,' I say.

'Oh.' He sounds as though I've slapped his face.

My Lover's eyes are closed, his arms crossed behind his head. I look at his bicep's soft full shape, the lucent skin on the inside of his arm, the hair on his broad chest turned golden from the streetlamp's light falling through my window. I whisper his name, even though I'm trying to wake him. He opens his eyes and I can tell that he heard my conversation. I press my shins into the edge of the bed cutting my skin. We both know this isn't going to be easy.

'The Lord's at the police station and he needs a bed.'

The Lover keeps his eyes on mine.

'And you're the *only* person he knows in London?'

It hadn't occurred to me that the Lord could have called other friends or gone to a hotel. He'd made me feel that only I could help him.

'You're right. I'm not thinking straight but it's too late now. He'll be here any minute,' I say as a car pulls up on the pavement above us. The door slams, no voices, no goodbye, just the sound of high heels clicking on stone. This sound in the otherwise silent night makes the Lover move. He pushes back the bed covers and his naked body extends before me on the white sheet, so perfect I now understand what he meant about beauty instilling fear. With my eyes turned down I trail his bare feet on the blue carpet as he pushes open the bathroom door and I smell the stale basement air that gets trapped in there.

The Lover returns to the bedroom, wearing familiar clothes – white shirt ripped at the collar, black cashmere, blue jeans and tweed coat from which he loosens his hair as he heads for the door. I wonder if it is a sign of devotion or indifference that he leaves like a sad but obedient dog. I follow him to the foot of the stairs. He opens the door and my mind is whirling as cold outside air hits my face. I think of calling him back to say we'll put the Lord on the sofa, send him off in the morning and then make love as we always do, but the door slams shut. The Lover has gone and I sit on the sofa, hoping that he doesn't bump into the Lord on the doorstep. But I wait in the dark for almost half an hour for the Lord to arrive, and all I can think is what I should serve him for breakfast.

❖

The Lover didn't ask about the Lord's visit when he came over the following evening but his passivity masked a growing intolerance. Something wasn't right between us, and that something was me. Meanwhile, the Lord grew bolder still. It was October, a wasteland for some between the end of the polo season and the beginning of hunting. Rather than turn out all the polo ponies, he had kept a few in the paddock and invited me to ride. He put me on the finest, fastest horses and I was terrified.

'Come on, darling! It's the end of the season, the pony's tired, he's not going to run away with you,' he'd call from the stability of his saddle. It didn't help that my fear frustrated him, but one of the horses going lame did. Now we *had* to keep my pony at a walk until his tendon had recovered. The weeks went by and my confidence grew as the pony healed. Now when the Lord invited me to his cottage, we spent perfect days riding through unspoiled country, talking, always talking, about our lives.

I had so many distractions, it was easy to forget that my Knightsbridge days were numbered but, in the back of my mind, I worried constantly about finding an affordable place to live and was paralysed with fear when it came to do something about it. My idea of London was Knightsbridge and Mayfair, hardly postal districts for a girl on my budget. So finally I bought a map and the evening newspaper, and one night over supper with the Lover, faced up to my future.

'"Clapham Junction. One bed flat. Close to amenities. Amenities?"' I read from the classifieds.

'You know, launderette, tube, that kind of stuff. You'd be close to the house I'm building.' The Lover sounded optimistic.

'Where is it?'

'Clapham, of course,' he said, indicating an area on the map south of the river with a depressing number of intercrossing railway lines. I couldn't see Chelsea, let alone Knightsbridge.

'That looks hopeful,' I said, pointing to the opposite page and an uplifting number of green squares. Perhaps I would survive the city if I could rent a flat overlooking a park.

'That's Clapham Common. You could afford to rent a room in a house there and the 137 bus stops right outside your office.'

It was a bus ride too far. I closed the map and said, 'Let's eat.' The Lover had brought smoked oysters which he flipped into a frying pan, sprinkled with herbs and turned onto to brioche toast. We drank a bottle of wine with it, followed by Belgian chocolate and some fine love-making.

In the middle of the night I woke in a sweat from a nightmare. I had been tied to a railway line by bands of gold and was struggling to break free when a train – driven by the Lover – appeared on the track. I screamed stop, but he kept on coming and I woke just before he ran through my body. A deep dull ache had taken hold in my lower back and I rolled onto my side, convinced the pain was connected to the dream and would soon pass. After an hour it had intensified and, crying like a cat, I woke the Lover. He helped me dress, carried me to his car and drove me to hospital, where I passed out waiting for a nurse in Accident and Emergency.

At six o'clock the following morning a tea trolley rattled past my bed.

'Mornin, sugar?' A woman in an overall that had once been white held out a cup of National Health tea.

'No thanks.' I was so weak I couldn't raise my head. A paper pillowcase stuck to the side of my face, sticky with cold sweat. 'Are there any other sheets?' I asked.

'Paper sheets is all we got left,' she said, wheeling her trolley on to the next 'Mornin, sugar?'

The pain in my lower back had vanished as mysteriously as it appeared, but I was kept on a drip while doctors conducted tests to find out what was wrong. The Lord was expecting me for lunch that weekend, and by the afternoon I was strong enough to wheel the drip to the pay phone to leave pathetic apologies on his answering machine. I returned to bed, too weak to think, grateful that I had no choice but to let life, and hospital food, pass by.

The Lover visited that evening with grapes and a bunch of pink tulips and sat by my bedside picking plaster from his fingertips, telling me about his day on the building site. The Lord, my only other visitor, arrived late Monday afternoon, having assured me that he was in London anyway for dinner with friends. He gave me a bottle of Chanel 19, which faced some powerful competition but made a delightful difference on the geriatric ward where my fellow patients were waiting for colostomy bags.

'I'm in London tomorrow so I'll come by again.' The Lord leaned forward and kissed me smack on the lips.

On his second visit the Lord brought me fine cotton nightshirts to counteract the coarseness of the sheets, and promised to see me the following day. And so it went for the whole week: the Lord in the afternoon, the Lover in the evening. After six days the medical men told me there was nothing wrong with me and I could go home. The trouble was I had no home to go to. There were only two days to run on the lease of the basement flat and I had yet to find a place to live.

'Why don't you get out of the Smoke, move into my cottage and commute to work for a bit?' the Lord said.

The cottage was my favourite place and I didn't have the energy or the time to trail around London to find a flat. I could accept his offer for medicinal reasons because this was the spirit in which it had been given.

The Lover, meanwhile, suggested that we 'make a serious commitment to each other' and look for a flat to share. Although

I couldn't imagine saying yes, I couldn't say no either. Both men waited for me to make up my mind and that was the one thing I couldn't do.

'So who's it to be?' asked the beady-eyed old woman in the bed opposite, who had watched the comings and goings all week. She had removed her radio headphones every afternoon, to tune in to my conversations with the Lord. Once he'd gone, the headphones went back on until the Lover arrived, when she'd lean forward again, straining to catch every word. She had so few visitors, she'd made do with mine, enjoying the intrigue without the confusion.

'I can't believe you don't know which man you want,' she persisted.

'Whenever I make up mind that it's one, I'm convinced it must be the other. Who do you think I should choose?'

'The gentleman,' she said, without hesitation. 'The one with the blue eyes.' And that's how I decided to move in with the Lord, if I can claim to have decided at all.

When I moved into the Lord's cottage from hospital, I did not expect him to ask me to share his bed. But I agreed on the understanding that he should not expect me to be his lover. He accepted this novel idea, and we went to bed happily each night, lying in the dark, continuing our suppertime conversation. And so our relationship deepened without the complications of sex, leaving me free of expectations and amorous feelings.

The Lord was so often away with friends or preoccupied with his riding team I settled easily into his cottage. One evening when I was alone, I found a copy of Shaw's Pygmalion on his bookshelf and, flicking through its pages, remembered that when we'd gone racing he had playfully called me his 'flower girl'. The following morning, I took the Lord a cup of coffee as he organized his diary and I recognized that he was humming the tune 'I've Grown Accustomed to Her Face,' from My Fair Lady. He turned to me and said, 'You haven't got the most beautiful face I've ever seen, but it's luffly, luffly.'

After I had lived with the Lord for a few weeks, we both realized that we did some things differently and we both assumed his ways were better. I discovered an incurable fondness for cashmere when I borrowed the Lord's roll-necks, and it wasn't long before I was also borrowing some of his words. He said 'stiffy' not 'erection', 'sofa' never 'settee', thought a three-piece suite was a musical term, went to the 'loo' never the 'toilet', and 'had a fall' in the unlikely event he ever fell off a horse – which was 'awf' not 'off'.

The Lord also enjoyed remarking on our similarities. We discovered that neither of us had eaten an avocado before we were fifteen or flown in an aeroplane before we were eighteen. 'You see, darling, our childhoods were quite similar. We both grew up with restricted views on life.'

'Slightly different restrictions,' I said.

'Yes, but the effect has been the same. We're curious about the world.'

And we were curious about each other which inspired long conversations during evenings that assumed a ritual. We would bath in separate bathrooms and smelling of rose geranium, put on the towelling robes to eat supper by candlelight and exchange stories.

'When did that happen?' was one of my frequent questions.

'Oh, about …' he'd pause to work it out, 'fifteen years, or more.'

'When I was seven.'

Over time, many of the differences between us diminished in my eyes, but the chasm in our ages was unbridgeable. But I consoled myself with the thought that I was not the Lord's first young female friend; young princesses, models and actresses seemed as much a part of his life as pretty horses.

I settled into the cottage and commuted to work while the Lord went to glamorous parties in London and stayed with friends in the country at weekends. To decline an invitation because of me, or to include me, wouldn't have occurred to him. Then one night over supper he admitted that these days, when he walked into a room, the girl he most wanted to see was already in his bed, which rather defeated the point of going out at all.

His comment made me smile, but I chose not to take him seriously. Our unspoken, platonic affection was enough, or so I believed. Then one evening the Lord left the cottage without saying goodbye. He was wearing black tie and disappeared in such haste, I was convinced he was meeting a woman and I was jealous.

Desperate to know who he was with, and knowing I shouldn't but doing it anyway, I looked inside the diary on his desk. That evening's entry showed a dinner at an army barracks in the middle of nowhere. Jealousy drained out of me, leaving room for curiosity. If the Lord wasn't with a woman that night, what about the other evenings he went out looking like a matinée idol? I had to find out if he had a lover. There were so many details, names and places documented in the diary, detecting the presence of a woman seemed impossible. My own name provided a clue. After the first entry, whenever we'd met, the Lord had simply written my first initial. I could find only one other initial in the diary from mid-February until June, and mine began in September. It seemed that if there was a woman in his life, it was me. I closed the diary, carefully placing the ink pen exactly where I'd found it and swore never to consult it again. But resisting was impossible. The Lord was so secretive that whenever I was alone in the cottage, I searched the diary for information. I told myself it was harmless, but as the weeks went by, I became addicted to the diary's fine white pages. Then one evening, alone again in the cottage, I went for my usual peek and the diary was gone. The Lord never mentioned my invasion of his privacy, but from then on, every time he went out, the diary went with him.

❖

My sister sent me frequent postcards from her romantic idyll in France and I imagined that she was leading the perfect life. So I was surprised when she called out of the blue, asking if she could visit me at the Lord's cottage.

'Am I going to meet the man of your life?' I asked.

'There is no man in my life,' she said flatly.

When my sister arrived the next evening I fixed two brandy champagne cocktails and we sat by the fire as she recounted the tale of love gone wrong: 'We transformed the cottage into a snug nest, I was toiling on the soil, he was working at the farmer's market. We had passionate nights and productive days. To realize perfection I just needed a few female friends. And then a distant neighbour dropped by. She was lovely and my world was complete. I thought I had it all until she said it was natural that we should get on so well, because we had 'so much in common'.

'You don't mean …'

'I do. My ideal man was also hers. He spent days with her, nights with me, with not much market gardening in between. No wonder he was tired,' she sighed. 'I should have known that he was too good to be true.'

'What now?'

'I'm heading back to reality. Nursing at Charing Cross hospital. Renting in Battersea.'

At that moment the Lord came into the sitting room dressed in black tie and our conversation stopped.

'He's gorgeous,' my sister mouthed, when he disappeared into the kitchen to find the cocktail shaker. 'What's he like in bed?'

'Talkative.'

'During sex?'

'We don't have sex.'

'What? I thought you were his mistress.'

'I can't be a mistress. He's not married.'

'I bet none of his friends know you're living here. And you don't go anywhere together.'

'We did …'

'Not any more. So, mistress. But don't worry, once you make love he'll include you in his life.'

'Do you think?'

'Absolutely.'

After my sister and the Lord went their separate ways to London, alone without the diary, I reflected on her assumption that I was the Lord's lover. It was as though I had been given permission to admit that I had wanted to make love to the Lord all along. A few hours later, when he climbed into bed beside me, I pressed my body into his and whispered, 'Make love to me.' This invitation so surprised him at first he laughed but then turned to face me. We kissed and he drew me close. For the first time I did not pull away from him as he held my face in his hands, but then just as suddenly as we had started, he stopped. He stared at me with searching eyes. 'You could be my daughter,' he said, then turned away.

We had often remarked that even if I doubled my age he would still be older, but such observations had defeated us. As I turned to sleep, I tried to accept, as the Lord had, that we would never be lovers.

The following evening the Lord was home for supper. We avoided analysing our failed attempt in the bedroom the night before. When we went to bed, I anticipated a polite kiss goodnight. But the Lord pulled me to him and we made love as though it were the most natural thing, difference and distance between us dissolving in the dark.

After that first time, the Lord was still remote during the day, but this only intensified our intimacy at night and making love seemed to unite us, body and soul. Then one night, as I lay beside the Lord, his strong arms drawing me to his adorable body, he whispered, 'I love you'.

It felt most natural to respond, 'I love you, too.'

And that was my mistake.

According to the rules of courtly love, which were the only kind the Lord knew, while he was expected to demonstrate his love for me I was not supposed to reveal mine. A knight seduces a lady who is often unavailable, because she is betrothed to another. This condition makes his love and his heroic life possible. The Lord was no exception. It was one thing for a woman to love him while she was married to another, but a different matter for her to confess her love while living in his house, sleeping in his bed. Once I had told the Lord that I loved him, he did the only thing he could do to preserve his ideal of love and of himself. He withdrew from me.

Christmas was less than three weeks away and his sixteen-year-old daughter would be returning from school. I was reminded politely that staying at the cottage had only been a temporary solution to my homelessness.

'I think you should get back to London next week,' he said.

I called my sister in a panic.

'Don't worry, it's perfect timing. You can have my flat, the city isn't for me,' she said. In less than a month, nursing and living in South London had drained her of energy and money. In a bid for a different life, she had decided to leave Battersea to be a nanny to the family of a Texas millionaire. Difference, I thought, doesn't get much bigger than that.

I inherited her single bed and her landlord, a major in the Guards, who was impressed to meet me because he'd heard about my 'boyfriend'. I told him the Lord was too remote to be considered a boyfriend. The day I moved out of the cottage he had trailed after me to make sure that I didn't leave a trace of my presence and, once I had gone, he had done an equally thorough job of removing me from his mind. Christmas came and went, New Year too, and still he didn't call. I longed for a sign that he had not forgotten me, and while I waited, my love grew more obsessive.

My bachelor landlord became my confidant and I talked to him for hours about why some men love the way they do. He advised me to be patient.

'And don't sit around doing nothing. You've got to keep busy – and confident. I guarantee he'll call, just not as soon as you would like.'

I joined the gym and went to concerts on the South Bank where grand orchestral sounds made me cry. I read copiously and went to late-night movies to delay the moment I went to bed alone. Then one cold, wet Sunday evening in the middle of January, my landlord marched down the corridor to announce, with a knowing grin, that the Lord was on the telephone.

We had dinner the following evening in an Italian restaurant in a Battersea side street (whatever happened to Annabel's?), where he told me he wanted to go back to 'the way it was'. I didn't have the courage to ask which 'way' he had in mind. Whatever he meant, I was grateful and agreed to see him that weekend when he got back from hunting.

Later my landlord and I discussed the Lord's revived interest in me.

'If you want him to want you, I think you must be more independent,' he advised.

'You're right,' I said. 'I feel like a schoolgirl when he comes to meet me from the train.'

'Could you possibly afford a car?'

'It would have to be a very cheap one.'

'A friend of mine is selling his van. Why don't you take a look at it?'

The dark-red Ford Transit van was very old, very rusty and very cheap. And by the end of the week it belonged to me.

The Lord and I spent Sunday nights together and, because I had the van, sometimes when he was home alone during the week, he'd call me last minute and invite me to supper. He still didn't introduce me to his friends, or include me in his life, and I didn't suggest that he should.

By springtime, the Sunday afternoon invitations were extended to include the mornings so that we could ride together. Then when the summer came, we'd get back from riding and dive into the pool. One such sunny Sunday, we were lying outside reading the newspapers when the telephone rang. He took the telephone inside to answer the call and returned to cast a long shadow as he stood over me.

'That was my daughter. We're going to lunch with friends and then on to the polo. She'll be here any minute so you'd better leave.'

We had made love that morning and then we'd gone riding. When our horses were walking side by side, the Lord had reached across to kiss me and I had felt so loved it didn't make sense that he was being discourteous now.

'Darling?'

'Yes?'

'Shall I put your bag in the van?'

I slung my overnight bag into the van myself and went up to the bedroom to say goodbye. I watched him zip knee-high polo boots over white breeches. To love what we cannot have is a fool's game.

'I'm going — '

'Darling, don't cry. Please don't be upset. I can't take you to lunch but I suppose you could come to the polo.'

'Dressed like this?'

'Of course,' he said, adjusting his shirt in the mirror.

The jeans I'd worn riding that morning were the perfect disguise. Nobody would guess the Lord was with a denim-clad girl when all the proper girls would be wearing their Jimmy Choos and silk for a big polo tournament on the first hot day of summer.

'If you want to come to the match, be back here by two-thirty,' he said, passing me in the doorway, heading down the stairs. I pulled a pair of shorts and a polo shirt from his cupboard and followed him out of the door.

I drove to the launderette in a nearby village, and sitting in the Lord's clothes, watched my jeans and denim shirt go through the wash and dry cycle. When I returned to the cottage, the Lord's daughter was stretched out in the chair I had occupied only a few hours before. When we were introduced, she shielded squinting eyes from the sun and glanced up from her magazine just long enough for hello. The three of us struggled for a while to find a conversation, and it was a relief when it was time to leave for the match. We went out to the Lord's car, and I was about to sit in the front when his daughter stepped up for her rightful place beside her father. I was relegated to the back seat and the journey to the polo passed in silence.

Once at the ground, the Lord led me to a table near the bar to sit with two Argentine men.

'These fellows will keep you company,' he said.

'Can't we be together?' I asked.

'You'll be all right here darling, it's not for long.'

'Who are they?'

'They're old players,' he said, as we approached.

'Look after her,' he said, promising them as much as me that he'd be back soon. I watched him disappear to the pony lines with his daughter, and then turned to my guardians, original medallion men, with tinted black hair and gold jewellry.

'Have you known him long?' one asked.

'Yes.' I tried to sound indignant.

'So either you're his daughter or his groom?' They laughed, and drained their glasses of Pimms, their gold wrist chains clinking on their gold Rolex.

❖

I was so often hurt by the Lord's impenetrable aloofness that loving him no longer made me happy. The day he left the country on essential horse business without telling me when he'd be back, I wondered why I was still with him. Work was equally frustrating, and now even my boss could make me cry. Something had to give.

'Not another mistake!' my boss exploded, checking my third attempt at a letter to his ex-wife about their daughter's around the world trip. 'It's E-Y. Monterey, California, in the United States of America. If you know where that is.'

'Of course I know, I'm going there next week,' I lied, throwing down the bundle of papers I was holding and striding out of his office.

'Stop her, don't let her leave. Tell her I'll be nice. Tell her I'll pay her more money,' he shouted at the chauffeur, as I went to the elevator and out of that office for ever.

I had to stop being a secretary. Finally I was ready for an adventure of my own.

A few weeks before, at a party hosted by a notorious socialite and friend of my landlord, I had met Brad, the son of a Hollywood film legend. He was the youngest man there and the only one not wearing a tie and I liked him immediately. He saw there was more to me than my polka-dot dress and bow-tipped shoes, and, rescuing me from some blazered boy, suggested we go clubbing.

'Which clubs do you know?' Brad asked, walking me out of the party.

'Annabel's.'

'Shit. Isn't that for really old people?' he said.

He took me to the clubs he knew and we danced until four in the morning. When we got back to his flat we were starving and ate bowls of cereal, because his fridge was empty and this was London and everywhere was closed.

'Fatburgers on Santa Monica is open twenty-four seven,' Brad said, not getting much satisfaction from his sugar puffs.

'I've never been to America,' I said.

'And I've never known a person who could say that,' he said. 'Come stay. We've got masses of room.'

❖

I was on my way. Brad met me at Los Angeles airport and when we walked through the door of his father's house, he was there to greet me.

'Mr G- to you,' the Film Legend said, 'and I suppose you're Miss Placed.'

There was no fooling the Hollywood star who was happy for me to stay in his guesthouse by the pool. Even so, I thought it would be best to keep out of the Film Legend's way, which wasn't hard because he stayed in bed until midday, taking his breakfast, taking it easy. When he heard that I had never seen his best-loved film he invited me to watch the video.

'With those legs,' he said, directing me from his bed up the step-ladder to his collection, 'you should be a movie star.'

Brad included me in his gang of friends. I was the girl 'who could come, too' – to full-moon surfing, jazz clubs, all-night parties in artists' studios and Fatburgers at dawn.

I had been living in style on Rodeo Drive for six weeks when, at the mid-week family supper, the Film Legend announced that I had been their longest staying guest. 'Not that we want you to go,' he added, wondering, I'm sure, if ever I intended to. It was time for me to get back to London and find work, but before leaving America I had to see my sister. I called her in Texas and convinced her to join me on a road trip up the Pacific Coast Highway. We went to San Francisco, but stopped off at Monterey. On the way to the beach I sent a postcard to my former employer, with Monterey correctly spelled and 'thank you'. His rage had propelled me out of his office to the most breathtaking stretches of sand anyone could imagine and, driving back along the Santa Monica mountains, my sister decided she had seen enough of flat, dry Texas. She was ready for the final frontier. She was ready for California.

❖

I meanwhile returned to the olde country and a stack of mail, neatly sorted by my landlord. Thankfully the first letter I opened was from Rebecca, a friend of a friend, who desperately needed an assistant to work in her production company. I called straight away and was offered an interview. This opportunity to earn money was fast followed by demands for rent and my share of the bills. The letter I opened last of all was from the Lord, who had also left five messages on the answering machine.

The Lord had returned to England expecting to find me pining, and had waited three weeks for me to return his calls.

When we spoke it was clear that the balance of power (or was it love?) had shifted. He asked me to drive to see him that evening but I had felt so free, so fully myself in America, I wasn't sure I wanted to return to my *Pygmalion* days.

'Please, darling. Come for the weekend,' he pleaded.

'The weekend? You mean the *whole* weekend?'

'Of course.'

It was late September and the Lord had arranged a perfect day. We cantered across fields and rode through our secret places in the park. We had supper outside and went night swimming and all the things that had helped me fall in love with him the first time helped me fall in love again. Except this time when our love affair resumed, instead of going away without me, the Lord took me with him.

For the first time the Lord invited me to meet his friends, who had grand houses in the country, apartments in London, lovers in both and fair-faced children away at school. And the more time I spent with them the more I realized that I had been initiated into the ways of a Lord rather than a Lady. The Lord's friends who had us to stay were always kind and treated me like an old friend, too. But some of their insecure female friends cared in ways the men did not that I was an anomaly in this world. I didn't talk like them, or think like them, or dress like them. But worst of all I was almost twenty years younger than them. These women preferred the Lord single, and their game was to make me feel unworthy of his company as well as theirs.

'It's a class thing,' I said to the Lord, after a particularly difficult dinner when a woman had rested her bare foot on his Gucci loafer beneath the dinner table and cut me out of the conversation.

'Don't be ridiculous. I never heard the word class until I met you,' he said.

'That's because you're all the same class,' I said.

At least he smiled. Why should they think of others? All that was best about England belonged to them, and their lives, while not necessarily happy, ran along unfettered by introspection, soothed by staff, sex and alcohol.

In a bid to join the Lord in his world and because by now I loved to ride, I trained to go out with the hunt. He had promised me a day before Christmas and as it approached, everything in my life seemed to have changed for the better. I enjoyed working for Rebecca in her production company, and the Lord was my love who included me in his life. At weekends in the country I wore pearl earrings, yellow cashmere and loafers – for which I'd gone into debt to look the part. But these happy hunting days were soon cut short: I had a fall and broke my ankle. When Christmas arrived, the Lord and his daughter went off to Scotland and it all felt too familiar as I took the train home to my mother where I lay on the sofa, waiting for my fracture to heal and the Lord to call. And while waiting, I ate. And the more I ate, the more I needed to eat and, as my ankle slowly mended my heart was slowly breaking.

The day before New Year's Eve my plaster came off and when I walked through the door, the telephone rang: it was the Lord, inviting me to a party in London the following evening. Suddenly the old year wasn't so bad, and prospects for the new one looked bright.

We spent the evening in an elegant house in Knightsbridge with the Lord's favourite Italian friends who had invited sixteen people for dinner. There were filmmakers, academics and fashion designers, and the Lord seemed to fit right in with not a taffeta bow or an equestrian in sight. I sat between a film producer and a bearded, bespectacled American who cornered the conversation, wanting to know about my relationship with the Lord.

'It seems that you reject convention,' he said.

'You think so?'

'Your partner isn't a conventional choice.'

'I suppose not.'

'You're what is called a woman in transition.'

'What does that mean?'

'You're curious about life, and want to know yourself.'

'Possibly,' I said, resisting the idea I was in transit. I wanted my life to stop right then and settle with the Lord for ever.

'Listen, if ever you're in New York, give me a call.'

I had no plans to be there anytime soon but took his card anyway and when I got home, stuck it in the frame of my mirror. It was supposed to be a memento of a glamorous and intimate evening, but those memories soon faded. Meanwhile, the old man's phrase "woman in transition", stuck in my head, acquiring unnerving potency.

By the last week of January my resolutions for a bright future were hanging by a thread. The Lord had returned to his elusive ways and Rebecca had told me that I was about to be unemployed. I had been warned at the interview that a full-time position as her production assistant was a 'remote possibility', but since my life seemed to be a succession of these, I had taken the job anyway. After three months, I had been convinced my predecessor's maternity leave had become simply leave – until she appeared at the office door. Arms linked and laughing, sisters in spirit, Mrs Maternity and Rebecca went for a lunch that lasted three hours. When Rebecca returned I could see the wine behind her eyes, hear the sentimental reminiscences that had peppered their conversation, and shouldn't have been surprised when she gave me the bad news. Her former assistant loved the husband, loved the baby, but they weren't enough. Her old job, the one I had appropriated, was the key to her complete happiness.

I wasn't ready to leave so soon. There was much I still needed to learn from Rebecca who lived life on her terms, respected by women and admired by men. A busy working life and a suitor in the wings were the facts of her life. The latest man in pursuit, an almost famous Hollywood director, had called that afternoon to say he'd arrived in London and was waiting for her in his hotel. 'Get your ass over here,' is what she said he'd said, and for an independent woman who didn't like being told what to do, she couldn't get her 'ass' over there fast enough.

'You might be interested to know,' Rebecca said as she got ready for her date, 'that Eva, one of my best friends, is looking for a secretary personal assistant thingy to share her job. The guy she works for is a millionaire.' She shot me a look, 'I mean billionaire.'

Her wide eyes emphasized the significance of billion, but I did not respond. Personal assistant thingy for a billionaire sounded a 'remote possibility' if ever there was one, a sop from the top to help me through a bad phase. I cleared my things from the desk drawer.

'You don't have to leave *right* now, *duh*.' D-u-h just about summed me up. I slumped on my swivel chair and, with one arm, swept the contents of the drawer back into it.

'We've got a month to find you a job, and I promise we will,' Rebecca said, exhaling through fine smoke as she winked at me.

Walking home from work that night, I decided things had to change. Everything in my life seemed temporary; the Lord no longer noticed that I was in love with him and the transit van was now breaking down almost every time I went for our weekly trysts.

'Keep in touch,' he'd call from the safety of his cottage doorway as I drove back to London. The journey home was an exercise in hope. Hope he'd invite me back for supper soon. Hope the van would make it. No girl needs a van that's falling apart, and a man who refuses to in the way that love requires. Deep down (and not even *that* deep) I knew that man and van would have to go.

I worked out my month's notice, once or twice asking Rebecca about the mysterious billionaire, but she was vague. He was no more than I suspected – an idea on which to hang my hopes during hard times. Resigned to travelling on the underground every day, I registered with an employment agency. Within a week I had been to fifteen interviews, six of them with the same merchant bank. Every one I knew was most impressed to think of me working in the City, but I wasn't convinced – until my landlord helpfully reminded me that the rent was three days overdue. I succumbed and signed a contract that would tie me into a life beneath office lights, working for a precocious 25-year-old American banker who called me sweetie and promised we'd be joined at the hip once I started. I could hardly wait. Now all I had to do was post the contract. Somehow, though, that envelope stuck on my desk for days. Finally the last posting day arrived. If I missed this I'd lose the job. With heavy heart I picked up the letter and was about to walk to the post when, *deus ex machina*, the telephone rang. It was Rebecca's friend Eva, the Billionaire's secretary, inviting me to an interview the following day.

Five

The Billionaire

I was through the hotel's revolving door a full ten minutes before my interview with the Billionaire and guessed the woman pacing the marble entrance hall like an exasperated schoolmistress must be Eva.

'The last to arrive,' she sighed as I approached, ticking my name in her ringbound secretarial pad.

She led me to a room where seven professional women, studies in ossified patience, sat still and stiff on a line of identical chairs waiting to meet the Billionaire. Eva had prepared a veritable secretarial smorgasbord for her boss. Some of the women were steely in a get-the-job done way, one was spectacularly pretty and one had earphones clamped to her head, practising dictation at lightning speed. All wore neat business suits, skin-tone tights and sat legs crossed, like a secretarial centipede, black court shoes slung to the right.

Eva indicated an empty chair. 'I'll stand,' I said, mistaking her instruction for an invitation. Seven pairs of secretarial eyes swivelled in my direction, until the telephone buzzed and their focus returned to Eva as she reached for the receiver, revealing a deep circle of sweat beneath her arm. The Billionaire's secretary was a perspiring jumble of nerves and no advertisement for the job we coveted.

'Hello,' she said, the corner of her right eye twitching. 'Yes, she's here now. I'll send her up.'

'Twelfth floor. Room 1200,' she said to me.

Being the first made me nervous. I rang the bell below a brass plaque which indicated that I was on the threshold of my first presidential suite. Waiting for somebody to answer, I checked my reflection in the mirror across the hall. A black cord jacket concealed the fact that during my Christmas cycle of gluttony and despondency I had filled out in all the right places, and some of the wrong ones. My white shirt strained to contain my breasts. I pulled the cord jacket together, adjusted my ponytail and tortoiseshell specs (superficial accessories intended to imply secretarial efficiency), and rang the bell again. Five minutes later nobody had answered. I walked back to the elevator.

'Are you there? Hey, come back!' called a voice down the corridor. I turned around to see a tall man waving both arms above his head. He looked friendly, if not a little mad. Things were looking up.

'We almost lost you. Come in. Thanks for waiting. Take a seat,' he said, holding the door for me.

He had an open smile, dark, severely-trimmed hair and high-waisted trousers in the style favoured by some American men. Backing into the expansive luxury of the suite, I collided with somebody in a soft green cashmere cardigan. I mumbled an apology, my focus on the main man I was determined to have as my employer.

'Drop those amendments off tonight. I'll need to go over them before tomorrow.'

'Sure thing,' said the suited man, turning out of the door. I was about to call him back, when the man behind me said, 'Sorry to keep you waiting.'

Never underestimate a man in a cardigan. I had mistaken the

Billionaire and, in embarrassment, cast my eyes down. He was wearing socks but no shoes, which made me smile, and when I looked up he was staring at me with clear green eyes.

'Come. Take a seat,' he said, falling into a big fat armchair. 'How are you?'

'Well, thank you.'

'Not nervous?'

'Not at all.'

'Good. I don't want to make you nervous.'

He spoke as if he knew me, our meeting some Pinteresque game. 'So. I need to see certificates.'

I had been warned that proof of my secretarial skills was a condition of the interview, and he scrutinized my test results from college days.

'My last secretary had the worst shorthand. I need somebody who can keep up, *cabiche*?'

As instructed by Eva, I extracted from my handbag a pen and notepad purchased for this very occasion and sat legs crossed, for all the world a woman poised to take dictation. The Billionaire opened the hotel brochure and cleared his throat. I adjusted my specs to inspire his confidence, but suddenly I was so nervous my hand was shaking and I could hardly hold my pen. The Billionaire read the history of the hotel at great speed in a strange half-European, half-American accent, which didn't help.

'Please read what you have,' he said after a few minutes.

I turned back the pages covered in scrawled symbols.

'Whenever you're ready.'

'The hotel, built in eighteen, er, eighty, on, er, Winston Crescent — '

'Wilton,' he corrected, trying to be patient.

I continued for a line or two before getting stuck again. 'Only in the last, er — '

'The last fifty years,' he sighed, scratching the back of his head, ruffling already ruffled hair. 'And?' Now he sounded irritated.

I guessed a few more sentences, incorrectly as it turned out, then dried up altogether. The Billionaire slapped the hotel brochure onto the low mahogany table between us.

'How do you think you're doing?'

'Not very well. In fact, I think I'm wasting your time.' There was some dignity in stating the obvious and I stood to leave. 'Goodbye,' I said.

'Would you like a cup of tea?'

'Tea?'

That was the last thing I expected him to say but sank back into the sofa, thinking I may as well be served tea before returning to real life – the one in which I was overdrawn and unemployed. The Billionaire called room service, pushing towards me the hardback menu on the table. I lingered over the things to eat: scones with strawberry jam and clotted cream, smoked salmon sandwiches, homemade lemon cake – it all looked good to me. I thought perhaps we could share the 'full afternoon tea' option, until I saw the price. Tea for two would cost more than my share of the gas bill.

'Hell-er,' the Billionaire imitated Inspector Clouseau. 'A pert of tea fer tooo. Sandwiches?' He looked over to me, and I nodded.

'No, we don't need sandwiches. Scones?'

I nodded again.

'No. No scones either,' he said, taking in my tight white shirt.

The tea arrived and he asked me to pour, his eyes drifting from my resumé on his lap to my straining shirt. I handed him a cup of tea with a shy smile. He was intense, but not intimidating, and our polite conversation felt relaxed. So what if I didn't have the job, in years to come I would be able to say that I had taken tea with a shoeless billionaire who had denied me smoked salmon sandwiches *and* scones. He asked me if I had enjoyed living on an island, and told me that he too lived on an island. When we finished the pot of tea, it was time for me to go.

'It's a pity you don't have the speeds because I think you would fit in,' he said, holding the door open for me, but blocking the way.

'Thank you,' I said, trying to step around him.

'Would you train to get your shorthand speed up if we don't find anybody?'

'There are seven women waiting to meet you and they all look perfect secretarial material to me,' I said.

'If we were going on looks I might even give the job to you,' he said and stepped aside.

I did not expect to hear from the Billionaire again, but the following morning, my last at the production company, Eva called with a message.

'He would like to invite you to dinner this evening.'

'Thank him very much, but I don't want dinner. I want a job.'

An hour later she called again.

'He would like to invite you on a trip.'

'What kind of trip?'

'A work trip,' she said wearily, 'to learn the secretary's role. Are you interested?'

❖

My indoctrination started on the drive to Northolt, the airport closest to London for those who prefer private air travel.

'His car goes first, and when he's with security they travel with him. You'll meet Uri when we get to Vienna,' she said. 'Never order a limousine. He's very low-key.'

At the exclusive airport we were met by polite smiles and a helpful handling agent, who guided us through Customs where no bag was checked or body searched. A comfortable car drove us across the runway to a sleek cream and white aircraft with MAVI87 painted on the tail.

'Remember that registration number. This is his favourite plane and he hates it when they get confused.'

'How many aeroplanes does he have?'

'Five.'

Low-key indeed. I followed Eva aboard. The captain, a big man with grey hair, greeted me formally, reserving 'Hiya' and a hug for Eva.

'Secretaries sit at the back. The last two seats are for the crew. He'll call you up to the front if he wants you,' said Eva.

The Billionaire was already in the cockpit going through the pre-flight check.

'He always flies the plane for take-off and landing, which gives us a break,' she said, expiring into a smooth leather seat and clicking the belt around her waist. She rested back and shut her eyes, instantly asleep. She slept deeply throughout take-off, and exactly one minute before the Billionaire emerged from the cockpit, sprang awake with radar sensitivity. She seemed to have her own automatic pilot.

'An overview of the companies, to read asap,' she said, handing me two files. 'We don't normally give so much information at this stage, but that's the way he wants to play it with you. Please sign the confidentiality agreement.'

Above the low grey sky that covers London in January, we flew into intransigent blue, not a cloud in it. When we reached our cruising altitude, the steward prepared a table at the front of the plane. Eva looked up from her stack of papers.

'No sandwiches for us today,' she said to me. 'Looks like the boss wants company for lunch. That hasn't happened for a while.'

As anticipated, the Billionaire beckoned for us to sit one on either side of him. In the same cavalier style he then called to the steward down the plane, 'Okay, Mickey, I'm starving. Let's go. Move it.'

His easy-going mood was infectious, and I joined in with the staff laughing at his jokes. It would take a while for me to realize that it was all a charade, the people who surrounded the Billionaire were willing to be what he wanted them to be. It all came down to money, and nobody but the boss could afford to be himself.

Mickey produced a plate of smoked salmon and offered wine, which the Billionaire declined – so everybody else did too. The Chablis – it would have been delicious – was returned to the fridge. The boss raised a forkful of salmon to his mouth, and from the window behind him cerulean sky encircled the delicate pink. Surreal colours at 45,000 feet promised the end of my transit van days.

'Do you know Vienna?' he asked.

'No,' I said.

'And what about the opera?'

'I've never been.'

'Eva, get extra tickets for this evening. We'll all go.'

Eva noted this in the pad attached to her as securely as a fifth limb.

'What's on tonight?'

'*La Bohème,*' she said.

'You'll have to tell me whether you're a Mimi or a Musetta,' the Billionaire said to me.

I didn't have a clue then that he was referring to *La Bohème,* the frail serious Mimi, who dies without realizing love, and the good-hearted, goodtime girl Musetta, whose pretty party dresses are paid for by old patrons. This was surely a warning to be careful – and one I failed to heed.

The Billionaire moved fast, thought faster, and in his company people snapped to attention. After he'd landed the plane, Eva summoned the necessary responses from her brutalized synapses and was standing by the door, suitcase in hand. Everything happened as she described. Mickey lowered the steps onto the runway while the Billionaire completed landing procedures. Then we were off, bounding towards the waiting cars. Beside the Billionaire's car, holding the passenger door open, was the bodyguard. Eva and I got into the limousine beside it. As the Billionaire's car edged forward, he turned to us and made a face through the window, a thumbs in ears, finger-flying moment of playfulness. Eva laughed politely before rifling through a folder marked Vienna. I grinned. The Billionaire turned away satisfied, but then looked back, as if curious to see what we really thought. I was still staring in his direction and the cars were close enough for our eyes to meet. I was thinking that he looked isolated, like a school boy in the back seat of a big black car, when I felt my tongue slide out of my mouth. It was a spontaneous response to his clown face, and it surprised us both. I blushed and slapped my hand over my mouth, and he furrowed his forehead.

'When we're in Vienna we always stay at the Sacher Hotel. He likes the Madame Butterfly suite and if that's not available, any suite overlooking the opera house. The front desk knows all this, but always check. The secretary stays on a different floor.' Eva's commentary was running. 'Always', 'never' and 'without exception' were phrases she used over and over again. The Billionaire's wealth had provided him with certain guarantees, and the secretary's job was to make sure he wasn't disappointed.

'You can trust Uri by the way, even if you mess up – which you will. We all did at the beginning, and some still do.'

Uri was the chunky American Israeli who stuck to the Billionaire's side. He had been recruited from Intelligence in the CIA, although intelligence didn't come to mind when I looked at him. He wore a radio earpiece, a gun and a blank expression. A blue Ralph Lauren blazer concealed the gun, but not much else.

When we arrived at the Sacher, Eva whizzed to the reception desk. She couldn't have moved faster on roller blades. The key to the Billionaire's suite was passed to Uri, who went ahead to check for anything life-threatening. Finding nothing more sinister than exotic fruit in a crystal bowl and a copy of the *Wall Street Journal*, he admitted the Billionaire to the suite. Eva and I were still at reception when the Billionaire and Uri walked purposefully out of the hotel.

'Where are they going?'

'We work on a need-to-know basis,' said Eva.

I took her ensuing silence as a sign of disapproval as we went up in the wood-panelled lift.

Eva disappeared into her room to work and I was sent to mine with the secret files, but didn't find the lists of addresses and personnel that inspiring. I was distracted by the ornate features of my room, which, in keeping with the rest of the hotel, was grand in the baroque style with crystal chandelier, silk-embossed wallpaper and a four-poster bed. The hotel's opulent surroundings were a reminder of Vienna's imperial past and the Billionaire's imperial presence. I lay back on the bed, promising myself that I would read the files after a short rest, when I noticed my complimentary copy of the *Wall Street Journal*. I unfolded the paper and was amazed to see a line drawing of the Billionaire illustrating a front-page article on his global empire. He had recently added an oil refinery to his list of assets, and this acquisition had prompted an analysis on the prospects for downstream oil production.

'Did you see the *Wall Street Journal*?' I asked Eva excitedly, as we stood in the hotel foyer waiting to go to the opera.

'We never talk about press,' she said adjusting a gold brooch pinned to her slim-fitting black dress. Eva had put me in my place again, which felt even more humiliating this time because she looked so elegant. I regretted more than ever that I had nothing to wear apart from my one interview outfit.

Uri emerged from the elevator, followed by the Billionaire with a girl on his arm who was blonde and thin in equal measure. Her sheer silk, floor-length dress was almost transparent in certain places and her heels were high. She whispered in the Billionaire's ear, her pale thin forearm linked through his, but it seemed that they didn't know each other at all.

The Billionaire handed each one of us a ticket for the performance and sat himself between me and the glamorous blonde girl.

'So?' he asked three hours later, as the dark red curtain fell on a dying Mimi. 'Are you a Mimi or Musetta?'

'I hope that's not my only choice.'

I had decided, however, that his date was definitely a Musetta, even though her emaciated figure and pale but interesting features were reminiscent of Mimi.

We were in Vienna for three days and before we left Eva insisted that I taste a slice of *sachertorte*, the famous cake created at the hotel which had inspired its name.

'He's at a meeting, so we've got time to relax on the terrace. See you there in ten,' she said.

The thought of seeing Eva take it easy made me more curious than the cake. I went straight to the terrace to reserve our table. While waiting, I wrote a postcard to my mother.

Darling Mummy
What a difference a day makes. We're staying in the glorious hotel pictured here. The man I hope to work for is secretive, has a quirky sense of humour and haunting eyes. I think he's half-Swiss, half-American. A strange atmosphere surrounds him because he is so rich and powerful, but in himself he is quite self-effacing and, much of the time, unobtrusive. Nobody knows how he made his money, but there's plenty of it. According to the newspaper he bought an oil refinery in America last week.

Last night we went to La Bohème. The audience was dressed elegantly, certainly not fashionably. I imagine Vienna is like England fifty years ago.

The chocolate cake here is famous, and the recipe about two hundred years old. The cake can be shipped around the world, so I will send you one, and charge it to my room. It costs a fortune, but less than a fur coat – which is what the last secretary charged to her room! That, and bad shorthand, got her fired. I don't think charging a cake will get me into trouble. So long as I keep practising my shorthand drill every night, I've got a feeling this job could be mine.

Will write or call soon.

When Eva arrived, I followed her lead and ordered a slice of *sachertorte* with cream and black coffee. I thought the plan was to sit back and watch Vienna's street life, but fuelled by sugar and a cigarette, Eva was as unwound as a loaded machine gun and fired information at me non-stop. As she drilled me on the finer details of my secretarial future, my eyes drifted to the world beyond the terrace, to the pale winter sunlight, narrow shadows on wide stone streets and Viennese women walking at a leisurely pace in spite of the cold. Eva saw none of this. Her world was dictated by the Billionaire and contained in her shorthand pad. Her only pleasure seemed to be smoking. She snatched a cigarette from her pack, holding it between her teeth as she rummaged in her handbag. Finally, I thought, a moment's peace.

'Here, I got you one of these.'

I shuddered as she pushed across the table a spiral-bound pad exactly like her own. It was an undeniable reminder of why I was there.

Suddenly Eva dropped her cigarette stubbing it out with her shoe. I turned to see Musetta walking towards our table. 'No smoking' was one of the Billionaire's rules.

'Who ees Eva?' she asked.

'I am. Would you like to join us for some *sachertorte*?'

I couldn't imagine anything that dark and rich passing this girl's lips. Ignoring the invitation, Musetta handed Eva a folded sheet of hotel notepaper.

'Here is my address. Send me an application form for the Florida flying school.'

'When are you planning to go?' asked Eva.

'As soon as possible. And organize a nice apartment near the school.'

'With a sea view and a pool?' asked Eva. I suspected irony, but to my amazement this was a serious question. Musetta was entitled to a big goody bag and Eva's job was to arrange it.

'Sea view. No pool,' Musetta said. 'Oh well. *Pourquoi pas*? Yes. Sea view *and* pool.'

This girl spoke good English but didn't say please. Eva seemed oblivious and I began to worry that being inured to the ungracious demands of others was the defining quality of an effective secretary.

Once Musetta had given Eva her wish list, she cracked a smile and glided over to the far corner of the terrace. Encased as she was in fur and above-the-knee leather boots, she sat outside without a shiver and, I couldn't believe it, ordered *sachertorte* with cream. That day, that girl had it all.

'Who is she?' I asked, shivering from the cold.

'One of the girls. There's a section for them in the address book, under "Girls", surprisingly enough. They were under "g" but I ran out of room.'

'How many are there?'

'Last count forty.'

'The forty thieves,' I said.

'Something like that,' she said.

'I thought he was married.'

'Really? What gave you that impression?' Eva looked away. I guessed right then that she loved him. 'Now,' she said, flipping to another page in her pad, 'where were we? Ah yes, the New York office.'

We flew to New York that afternoon, stopping at Shannon airport in Ireland to re-fuel. Musetta had gone on her way to Paris, first class of course. Without her the mood was easy-going and, during the hour between refuelling and take-off, the Billionaire, Eva and I wandered around the duty free shop.

'Quick, he's coming,' Eva hissed across the aisle. 'Pick something up. If he asks, tell him you like it. He'll give you the money.'

I grabbed a big boxed bottle of Coco Chanel.

'Do you like that?' the Billionaire asked, walking up behind me.

'Yes, I think so.' I had no idea. He took it from me and walked over to the cash desk. Eva stood beside me, watching the boss through squinting eyes. 'He's never done this,' she gawped. 'Normally he sticks some dollars in your hand. But look at that, he's standing in the frigging queue.'

The Billionaire casually handed me the black box of Coco Chanel. That rococo smell still reminds me of those surreal times.

Late that evening, the usual convoy drove us into Manhattan. As our Lincoln Town Car sped down Park Avenue, I was transfixed by the world outside the window. That was the moment, right then, that I fell in love with New York City. We were gliding down the Avenue, traffic lights in our favour, one smooth ride towards the PanAm building where a cross, lit up amongst the advertising, was a reminder that America is the land of the Christian free.

The lights switched to orange. Our car stopped but the Billionaire's limousine sped on through.

Eva, whose eyes had been shut, peeled open her heavy lids and checked her Rolex.

'He's keen. He never runs a light. Mind you, she has been waiting two hours.'

'She?'

'The girl. I told her to be ready for eight.'

'The one going to flying school?'

'She was yesterday.'

'There's another one?'

'Another three.'

'All at once?'

'Three girls, three nights. But hey, there's nothing to stop them getting together.'

I assumed she was joking, but she closed her eyes again. Eva was proving to be frustratingly discreet when it came to divulging details of the Billionaire's private life.

We swept past the Billionaire's elegant hotel (he had long ago disappeared inside) to be deposited four blocks from Fifth at the unpretentious 'secretaries' hotel.'

'Welcome home honey,' the receptionist said to Eva, not at all embarrassed to be dressed like a nineteenth-century soldier in a red brocade-trimmed coat. 'And is this your first time in the cidee?' he asked me.

Was it that obvious? I cringed inside.

Waiting for the elevator to our rooms on the twentieth floor, Eva and I were entertained by a slightly dishevelled woman playing a golden harp, oblivious to her audience and the red wine stain on the front of her white frilly blouse. I hummed along with her rendition of that very English ballad 'Greensleeves'. One phrase from the song kept repeating over and over in my head: 'Alas, my love, you do me wrong to cast me off discourteously.' I found myself thinking of the Lord. I had promised to 'keep in touch', as he used to say, but hadn't which made me feel guilty. I thought I might call from my bed, but when I got there was so tired that I fell straight asleep.

Very early the following morning, over a breakfast of muffins and coffee, Eva heaved a stack of papers from her briefcase. 'One of the best ways to find out what's going on,' she said, 'is to do the filing.' She flicked her eyes at the papers, which represented a task of incomprehensible tedium. And yet I, the girl who had banged her head against a filing cabinet so many times she had questioned her sanity, was happy to file. I had been flown by private jet to the finest city in the world and if filing that morning justified my presence, so be it.

After breakfast Eva and I walked a couple of blocks to a glamorous mid-town office building. It was just after seven and the Billionaire's twenty-fifth floor office was deserted as Eva showed me around. In spite of the impressive mirrored, marble entrance, once inside, the office was like any other. Unremarkable corridors lit by grey-tinged neon led to dead-end rooms with polystyrene tiled ceilings. And then we came to a solid mahogany door.

'This is Julia's room. She's worked for him for ever. She's devoted,' said Eva as we stepped inside.

A chinchilla coat and a Hermès scarf hung behind the door, and during the night, a vase of pink roses had dropped delicate petals onto Julia's desk. Original Cartier-Bresson photographs formed a horizontal line along the longest wall, and there was a painting by Vuillard above the wooden filing cabinet.

'And this,' Eva said, edging open another heavy door, 'is His office.'

The air smelled of seasoned wood and jasmine, and an expanse of cream carpet edged up to mahogany-panelled walls and the floor-to-ceiling windows. One window looked onto a skyscraper, which reflected our own glass tower back to us, and from the other window behind the desk, was the sandstone *flèche* of St Patrick's Cathedral, its Gothic Revival gargoyles so close I could see the texture of their tongues. Eva didn't waste time looking at the view.

'Now you know, when he buzzes, this is where you come,' she said, walking out. 'Okay, get that filing done as soon as you can. He'll be here at eight.' I must have looked worried. 'Don't panic,

I'll be back by then.' She disappeared, I guessed for a cigarette break.

I lingered, looking at the black-and-white photographs in Julia's room, the filing far from my mind.

'You like them?' The Billionaire stood in the doorway. He was forty-five minutes early.

'Yes, I … eh … yes, I do.' I blushed, as an unexpected feeling of desire had rushed from the pit of my stomach to burn my cheeks. The Billionaire appeared not to have noticed and in his 'let's move it' voice barked, 'Where's Eva?'

'She was here a minute ago.'

'That's no good. I want her now. How confident are you about your shorthand?'

'Okay,' I said, avoiding eye contact. Eyes reveal lies.

'Well, we'll see. Let's go.'

I followed him into the office and, right then, the gargoyles didn't interest me either. My pad was open and I was facing the test. If I did well, the job would be mine. The hotels, the planes, the places and the speed it all happened had hypnotized me. But beyond the Billionaire's superficial life was the effect of the man himself. I sensed that wherever he was, something significant happened.

Without nerves I recorded at speed the intricate details of a contract between one of the Billionaire's companies and a South American nation. When he finished he looked at me intensely. More than my job depended on this fax being transcribed and sent within the next fifteen minutes.

'Got it?'

'Yes.'

'I'll check before you send it.' And with that he walked out of his office, leaving on his desk a scrap of paper covered with names and numbers in a clear hand. All the intricate details of the dictation were there for me to find. Ten minutes later the fax was signed and once I'd sent it the Billionaire called me back to his office. I stood by his desk, waiting.

'Sit down,' he said, swinging his chair to face me. 'Don't you like clothes?'

'Yes but — '

'You can't afford them? If you work for me you can't wear the same clothes two days running,' he said, opening the drawer of his desk and handing me a white envelope with 5K typed in the centre. 'Charlotte's in New York. She'll help you find something suitable. By the way, do you have debts?'

I was dumbstruck by the implication of his question.

'Bring me a breakdown of what you owe. And don't come into work tomorrow until you've got new clothes.'

Charlotte was the Billionaire's interior designer who lived in New York. She wasn't at all surprised that I'd been given the money.

'We call it the 5K make-over,' she said, 'which means he likes you. He also likes Chanel, so be at their Madison Avenue boutique at eleven.'

After an hour with Charlotte, I walked out with a couple of outfits that cost as much as a small car. We were on our way to lunch to celebrate my transformation when Charlotte's mouth fell open and she clamped both hands to her jaw. 'Shoes, we didn't get shoes.'

'Forget about it,' I said counting the contents of the envelope. '$5.75 left.'

'We'll stick them on the company credit card. I'll tell the accountant it's approved.'

Chanel had the perfect pair of cream and black shoes that cost as much as a year's car insurance. Charlotte was not deterred and she pushed a platinum credit card along the counter. 'When you get one of these your life will really change,' she whispered. The company credit card was granted to trusted employees and was the key to a world where money flowed like oil – high grade and just a little crude.

The following day I sheepishly handed the Billionaire my list of debts, which he hardly glanced at before passing me another sealed envelope even thicker than the last. 'I think you'll find that's enough,' he said. 'We'd like you to work with Eva, one month on, one month off, and pay you £35,000 a year – if that's all right with you?'

'Thank you very much.' I restrained myself from shrieking with delight. Not only had I got the job, the Billionaire had offered to pay twice as much as I'd expected.

'We've booked you a place at the Park Lane Secretarial School for a month and a business flight back to London on Monday.'

Business class? My face glowed at this change of fortune.

'Okay. That's it.'

I had been dismissed and was almost out of the door when he called my name. I turned around.

'Your outfit, by the way, suits you. You look very pretty,' he said. His voice was flat, as though he'd stated a fact that didn't concern either of us personally.

'Thank you.' And because his compliment made me bold, I said, 'Thank you for changing my life.'

The Billionaire looked surprised for a second, then gave a short, ironic laugh. 'I'll see you in a month's time. Work hard.'

That evening, alone in my hotel room, counting out the contents of my second white envelope – 9,700 – the prospect of intense secretarial training – 9,800 – didn't do my head in – 9,900. I was sure I could be a secretary – 10,000 – and even get to like it. Ten thousand dollars. I had never seen so much money all at once.

❖

My unavailability had once again fuelled the Lord's fire for me, and he drove up to London the night after I got back to take me to Annabel's. The following evening there was a cocktail party at

Claridges, and he invited me to that too. I wore my Chanel and this time when he introduced me to the lords and ladies, it was first names all the way. I was less wide-eyed but still new, so was glad to see the couple we had stayed with the first time the Lord had taken me to the country.

'We've missed you. How was it?' asked the Lord's closest friend.

'I got the job.'

'And if you want him, you've got him too,' his wife said.

We looked across the crowded room to the Lord who was gazing at me.

'You've cracked it. He loves you.'

'He's certainly never looked at me quite like that,' I said.

It had taken a year and a half and another man's money for the Lord to recognize his love for me. I could only think it was down to a) the Chanel b) the Chanel and c) my independence.

Now I had my own life, the Lord wanted to include me in his. He even invited me to stay with the Earl of S for a family party. I had never owned a glamorous evening dress, but I knew where to find one. When I was a Knightsbridge secretary I had passed Bruce Oldfield's shop every day and gazed at his elegant dresses. Now that I could afford one, it seemed only right that I should buy one. As much as I had enjoyed being clad in Chanel, paid for by the Billionaire, to choose and buy my own dress was altogether more empowering. Within minutes I was trying on a black beaded Bruce Oldfield evening dress, which the designer himself came up from his studio to fit. 'I think it could be more snug here,' he said quietly, teasing the dress to my waist. 'And a bit more room here,' he said, smoothing the side of my hips. 'You know, I'd like to make you this dress, but one that really fits. It will be ready a week today, if that's okay?'

Okay? I was in heaven and glided out of the shop, incredulous that I had been promised a haute couture dress at a prêt-à-porter price.

The dress worked its magic. The Lord was proud and the countess suitably embarrassed that she had sat me next to her daughter at dinner and not a more illustrious guest she wished to impress. The earl's daughter was charming, but curiosity got the better of her as she posed questions, hoping to find out why she hadn't met me before.

'Where did you say you went school?' she asked for the first time. She leaned towards me, almost imperceptibly, knowing that to appear too interested was below her standing. Perhaps she anticipated a school abroad, or a rehabilitation centre for difficult teenagers.

I toyed with various answers, but trusted her enough not to lie. 'I went to a convent,' I said.

'How fascinating. I've always wondered what it would be like to be taught by nuns.'

I was about to elaborate when the earl's old butler appeared at my left holding a silver platter of asparagus. I attempted to pick up the glistening, buttery stems with the server, but ended up pushing them over the edge and onto his shiny black shoes.

'It would help if modom held the server the right way up,' he huffed, indignant that after a life in service it had come to this. My beaded cleavage didn't convince the butler, but the guests were impressed and after that night I was known as the 'girl in the long black dress'.

For a while I was convinced that I had found the place I was meant to be. During the week I studied the art of shorthand typing in preparation for the Billionaire, and at weekends I was stayed with the Lord in stately homes where the staff called me 'm'lady' to go with 'm'lord'. If the staff were putting us together, I had passed the acid test. Everything I had ever wanted was available to me now, yet something inside wouldn't let me settle. The American man's phrase 'woman in transition' had become prophecy. I didn't want to be on the move again, but it didn't feel

Moving right along from aristocracy to plutocracy, I flew to the United States where I was met by Jeff, a bodyguard whose face shone from a clean shave and protective intentions. I didn't know where we were going but knew not to ask, and throughout our two-hour journey Jeff, who was English, spoke only sport and the weather. In a world of many secrets conversations are limited.

We drove for miles through redbrick suburbs then into an industrial wasteland where a straight concrete road lined with wire fencing and enormous rust-stained vats brought us to a checkpoint. The guards waved us through and we pulled up outside a flat-roofed building. Jeff jumped out to open my car door. There was a noxious smell and grimy yellow smoke spewed from one of the processing towers, but I was instantly seduced by the power of the Billionaire's East Coast Oil Refinery.

'This way,' said the bodyguard, leading me into a cramped canteen. Hundreds of men dressed in navy overalls sat in rows of chairs while a small group of women in brightly coloured cardigans leaned against the back wall, arms folded beneath ample bosoms. They were women who served men, secretaries or canteen workers, but everyone present listened intently to the Billionaire talking about the future, '*our* future, now that *we* own the refinery.'

The Billionaire often referred to himself as 'we', which seemed strange to me because he was independent to the point of isolation. His monarchic plural, grandiose yet modest, deflected attention from the fact that he controlled so much. It also acknowledged that he did not make money without the cooperation of his employees, so when he invited them to share the fruits of his capitalism, because he was authentic, he was persuasive. At the end of his talk, everybody applauded.

Slightly over-dressed in my Chanel, but feeling like a member of the workforce nevertheless, I stood in line with the other women. I was proud to be secretary for a man who seemed elite, yet egalitarian, and was perhaps the most inspiring person I'd ever met.

After his talk the Billionaire donned a hard hat and overalls to tour the plant and returned an hour later to bid the senior managers farewell. He glanced in my direction, immediately removed his hard hat but did not acknowledge me. He then ruffled his hair the way he had the first time we met. He exchanged a strong handshake and after a quiet joke with the refinery manager, he was ready to leave.

'Ready?' The Billionaire turned to the bodyguard, who nodded and signalled to me that we were on the move. I followed the men past the refinery, which rumbled and hummed like a great beast in the cold night air, and we climbed into a sleek helicopter waiting in a circle of delicate spotlights. Once we were encased in cream leather and glass, whirling blades lifted us vertically off the ground and I watched the refinery grow smaller and smaller until it was a speck on the flat landscape and then not even that.

Within a couple of hours industrial reality was replaced by the downtown lights of Manhattan as I discovered the finest way to enter New York City. Helicopter blades made my hair fly as we ran to the waiting limousine, the bodyguard holding the door for me to slide into the back with the Billionaire. The door closed with a heavy click and we sat side by side for the drive to the Upper East Side.

'So.' The Billionaire turned to me as if seeing me for the first time that day. 'Glad to be back?'

I was. And curious too about what had happened to the separate car for the secretary.

❖

We spent a few days in the New York office, where I worked with Julia, carrying out the Billionaire's commands. One day I was looking the part in heels and a neat Prince of Wales check suit when the Billionaire commented, 'That's a great outfit. I just gave Marleena a dress in that material – only a size smaller.' After that I forsook lunch, which was exactly the response he'd hoped for.

I still wasn't sure who Marleena was and what she meant to the Billionaire. She could have been a tenacious member of the forty thieves, but she was older than those girls and the Billionaire spent most weekends with her – enough in the eyes of some men to constitute a wife. And yet he seemed to have so many female friends it was impossible to tell how much he cared for any of them. My curiosity about Marleena was piqued on my last day in the New York office when Julia took me into the mailing room, shut the door and switched on the photocopier. At first I was confused, and couldn't understand why pure white pages were being churned out of the machine apparently for nothing.

'We need to be careful,' she whispered above the noise, her eyes darting to a small bugging device. 'Have you met Marleena?'

I shook my head, too terrified to speak and thinking it would be a pity to get fired before my first pay packet.

'You'll meet her soon. So be careful. You're a nice girl and she's tough.'

My curiosity got the better of me. I couldn't resist one mouthed question: 'What *is* their relationship?'

'Nobody knows. But I think he's got his eye on you.'

I popped my eyes wide and raised my eyebrows, trying to look surprised.

'Be careful. That's all I can tell you. Be careful.'

I resented Julia's maternal advice. She was an elegant beauty in her early fifties, a Sophia Loren lookalike who, Eva confided, had received her share of attention from the boss when she was younger. But Julia had kept herself apart and her marriage intact.

Late that afternoon the Billionaire called me into his office and I stood gazing at the *flèche* of St Patrick's Cathedral. Ever since our first meeting he had made me wait like this, as if intuitively knowing that I needed to learn patience. Eventually he said, 'I've got tickets to the opera this evening if you'd like to come. And don't worry if you don't. I'm going anyway.'

'I'd love to join you,' I said, ignoring Julia's advice. Apparently a girl grown accustomed to trouble doesn't know how to be careful, no matter how many times she's told.

'Be at my hotel at seven-thirty,' the Billionaire said, turning back to the papers on his desk, as if indifferent to my response.

I was in the foyer of the Billionaire's hotel a few minutes early when he bounded down the stairs two at a time and alone. I supposed his date was waiting in the car and I felt nervous as we walked to the limousine, but there was no girl there.

We were on the dark sweeping road that cuts through Central Park to the West side when the Billionaire turned to me: 'Wagner. *Tristan and Isolde*,' he said as though he had read my mind. 'A tragedy but ultimately uplifting because it makes your own life seem like a piece of cake.'

When we took our seats in the best box at the Metropolitan Opera, I was still expecting the Billionaire's girl to show up. Only when the curtain lifted and the music began did I believe, that evening, the girl was me.

The following morning the Billionaire's limousine swept by to pick me up from my hotel and I was surprised to find him waiting for me in the back seat. Billionaires don't wait to pick up their secretaries but here he was, all rise and shine and happy to see me. By nine o'clock we were flying out of La Guardia airport to the island the Billionaire owned and called home. After take-off he beckoned me to join him at the front of the plane. I sat opposite him, pen poised, head down like a runner waiting for the gun. After a while, curious to see why he hadn't launched into full speed dictation, I slowly tilted my eyes in his direction. He was leaning back watching me.

'You're very earnest,' he said.

Was earnest good or bad? Was earnest what he wanted? Nervously I touched my top lip with the tip of my tongue.

'And very manipulative,' he said.

'I'm *not.*' I knew manipulative wasn't good.

'Then why do you play with your mouth like that?'

I withdrew my tongue, and bit my bottom lip.

'Leave your mouth alone,' he sighed, leaning back to loosen his tie.

I felt like a scolded child and feared the Billionaire had summoned me to say that he didn't want to employ me after all.

'Do you want to work for me full-time?' he asked.

'What about Eva?'

'She's leaving.'

'Why is she going?'

'That's not your business. All you need to know is whether you believe you can do the job.'

'I do.'

'Good,' he said.

It was our first deal. I stood to return to my place.

'Where are you going?'

'To my seat.'

'That's your seat,' he said, pointing to the one opposite his, 'if you want it.'

He had offered to elevate me from the back of the plane to the seat facing his. It was a promotion I couldn't resist. I sat back down and faced the boss.

'Here's looking at you, kid,' he said, signing off on my future with a wink.

A few hours later we landed on his Caribbean island, rising heat and warm wind pushing through humidity as we walked together across the runway. A group of island staff were there to greet us and when the Billionaire proudly introduced me as his new secretary, I was in the centre of his world, which made me feel ten feet tall.

'See you in the office on Monday,' he said, his hand on my shoulder as we leaned tentatively towards each other for a farewell kiss on both cheeks. Before we got that far, an open-top Mercedes pulled onto the runway. The Billionaire's hand dropped away from me. A tall blonde woman in her early forties in dark glasses emerged from the car. After encouraging identical dogs from the back seat, she led them on golden chains towards the Billionaire. Standing a good inch taller than he, she put her face nose to nose with his for a closed-mouth kiss. Their lips may not have been open, but their eyes were, knowingly. She seemed to draw in the Billionaire with a look that went beyond the surface right to – where? His heart? The seat of his pants? I couldn't tell. Then Marleena – who else could it be – turned to me. 'And you are?'

'Meet my new secretary,' said the Billionaire.

Marleena's hand wrapped easily around mine. Her grip was like metal, more a warning than a welcome.

I watched the perfect couple walk to the Mercedes, the dogs leaping into the back to sit upright like obedient children. Marleena slipped into the passenger seat and the Billionaire drove his family home, followed by a cavalcade of staff.

Alone on that runway, without the Billionaire and his entourage, the heat and unexpected isolation suddenly overwhelmed me. Not knowing what to do, or where to go, I sank down onto my suitcase. Sweat ran down between my breasts, my feet swelled from stockings and heels and hot tarmac. It was some time before I realized I was staring at a practical, polished-to-a-high-shine white Renault 5. It had 'secretary' written all over it.

Sure enough, the driver's door was open, keys were in the

ignition and the map, open on the dashboard, indicated the location of my new residence. In case I was in any doubt, 'secretary's apartment' was scrawled beside a red circle. I loaded my suitcase into the back of the car and sat at the steering wheel without the slightest desire to drive away. For a moment all I could see was the Billionaire kissing Marleena. I didn't feel jealous because quite simply I didn't feel anything. The only thing I knew for sure was that I was a secretary and being a secretary, wherever it was, whoever it was for, seemed to negate everything – including me.

The island's palm-lined beaches, azure seas and sky were incidental to the landscape of the Billionaire's office, which was modern with a casual atmosphere that masked the intensity of the work taking place there. The Billionaire had culled the best and brightest from around the world to develop his ideas for programmes to predict trends and to operate his trading room. While he employed one female analyst, the minds who ran the trading room were all male, and every move was made in millions. None of the traders bothered whether market prices went up or down; so long as they kept moving there were opportunities to make money. Forecasting the outcome of instability was an art the Billionaire had often mastered, as his vast fortune proved. Complete mastery of the markets was beyond the possibility of any man, however, and the Billionaire was captivated by this area of life beyond his control.

The Billionaire's only financial concern was how to spend the money he made. He donated countless dollars to hospitals and friends in need, and established funds for every kind of animal, for while he couldn't tolerate weak people, he treated all animals with compassion. By far the most indulged creatures were the Billionaire's dogs, who were treated as lavishly as the wife of an average multi-millionaire. A private jet flew them to the best vet in America, a bodyguard took them for a daily swim in the sea beside the Billionaire's house, and their hair was blowdried and tied with pressed scarves in toning colours. The dogs were granted respect, not only because they could be fierce, but because they were the Billionaire's most trusted friends.

He often assessed people according to the dogs' reaction: if they snarled and a person was fearful, the Billionaire was disdainful. If a person didn't flinch when faced with the hounds bounding towards them, the Billionaire was more gracious. And on the rare occasion that the dogs greeted a new person with licks and wags, the Billionaire held that person in high esteem. Licks and wags were how the dogs responded when they met me at the office – which may have accounted for my invitation to dinner that evening.

The Billionaire's house was at the opposite end of his island but still no more than a twenty-minute drive away. I gave my name at the intercom, and a white wooden gate rolled back to reveal a long driveway and an astoundingly modest house. When I arrived, a maid in a black dress and white apron offered me a glass of sweetened pressed limes, carried on a silver tray – the only sign of opulence. 'He's asked me to tell you he'll be with you in a minute, miss,' She almost curtsied then disappeared.

The Billionaire's sitting room looked out to the ocean and, apart from one bad oil painting in an impressive frame, the walls were bare. I searched for photographs of Marleena but there were none to be seen.

'Hello.' The Billionaire was right beside me in fresh clothes, presumably straight from the shower because his hair was still wet. 'I'm glad you came early. I wanted to apologize for the other day.'

'What do you mean?'

'At the airport.'

'It was nice to meet Marleena,' I lied.

He stared straight back at me. There was no fooling him. Before the other guests arrived, the Billionaire walked me around his landscaped garden that rolled to the sea.

'We eat supper outside. I hope you'll be warm enough. Let me know if you get cold,' he called as he went to answer the door to his other guests.

That evening I met the man who had run the Billionaire's head office in Europe for the last twenty years, a Japanese man who didn't speak much English and confirmed that I should add Japanese to the six languages I knew the Billionaire spoke, an Indian gentleman from Madras and a steely-eyed woman. The Billionaire had put me at the head of the table, opposite him, and between the man from Japan and the woman whose hair was cut in a bob so precise, it could have been moulded plastic.

Towards the end of dinner the chef carried in cherry cheesecake which looked so mouth-meltingly delicious it stopped conversation. In that silent appreciation, the Billionaire called to me down the table, 'Don't even think about it.' Most of the guests laughed. I blushed and declined the pudding when the waitress offered me a slice.

'Eat the cake if you want,' said the woman beside me who peered over the rim of her silver-framed spectacles. It was the first time I had heard anybody contradict the Billionaire, but I didn't dare. I knew he wanted me to be a skinny thing and to serve myself cake would have given him the wrong message: I wanted to impress him with my commitment to be the best I could be.

'What do you do?' I asked the woman, dragging my eyes from the pudding as it was carried away.

'I'm a psychiatrist. And you must be Marleena?'

'No. I'm the secretary.'

'Ah. He doesn't ... I mean, that must be interesting,' she said, abandoning more controversial observations.

'Are you his psychiatrist?' I asked behind my hand to keep my question secret.

'I'm an animal psychiatrist. I see the dogs.'

'One at a time?' I tried not to laugh.

'As a couple. And individually.' She nodded sagely. I half expected her to decline further conversation on the grounds of confidentiality, but she continued. 'One of the dogs is particularly aggressive, and I'm trying to establish if it's worth considering an alternative to the usual treatment.'

'Which is?'

'Cutting his balls off.'

I winced. This was no talking cure. 'That's brutal,' I said.

'I'm a Freudian and let me tell you, nothing hurts more than prescribing castration.' She sighed and swallowed a spoonful of bright red cherry cheesecake.

A week after that dinner, I booked the dogs on a private jet to the States for an appointment with the vet, after which one of the dogs came home a few pounds lighter. And sure enough he did become quite docile, and was never again such a discerning judge of character.

To work on the island owned by the Billionaire was to live in a cocoon. Everyone who lived there was his employee and the ground we walked on belonged to him. It took some time for me to acclimatize. The Billionaire's business affairs and travelling in private aircraft to swanky hotels didn't impress me quite so much as the Billionaire's island. On my first weekend there, standing on a rocky headland, it seemed that the land, the air, the sea mocked the notion that title deeds drafted in a Manhattan lawyer's office could confer their ownership on a mere mortal. But the Billionaire's life disproved my naïve theory: he daily demonstrated how easy it was for one man to possess so much so comprehensively.

Gradually the outside world receded. Trading reports and hourly market analyses arrived from London and New York, but these cities seemed no more significant than the names of recognizable stars in distant galaxies. Real Life took place on Planet Billionaire.

My office hours were long, the commitment expected no less than total and I began to understand why this secretarial job had previously been shared. There were compensations, however. Marleena was off the island most of the time, presumably in New York where she invested the Billionaire's money in trivial pursuits, which left the Billionaire free to invite me to dinner. At first there were always other guests present, but then I was invited alone, and one evening we had gone for a swim together in the ocean at the bottom of his garden. The air of formality between us was suffused with subtle intimations of romance which neither of us acknowledged. And later that night when I reached my own bed, the Billionaire, who occupied my every waking thought, filled my dreamtime too.

❖

We had been on the island for six weeks when the Billionaire called me into his office and said, 'We're going to Rome on Friday. Make the arrangements.'

I called the pilot, spoke to the crew, received estimated flight times and searched out the Italian file. Every country the Billionaire visited had a file divided into cities with numbers, names and notes of how things happened when he was there. Among Rome's significant details was the name and number of the last girl he'd seen in the city. Given the date Eva had pencilled beside her name, I assumed she was still current and wondered when the Billionaire would ask me to call her.

On the way to Rome the Billionaire indicated for me to take the seat opposite his. After glancing at Uri the bodyguard, who I left to sit with the crew at the back of the plane, I gave the boss a self-assured smile. We got straight to work. I received dictation and a list of meetings to arrange for the following week, but was curious when there was nothing for me to organize that weekend. It was the first time since I'd worked for the Billionaire that I didn't know where he would be and what he would be doing. Normally each day was accounted for, usually down to the last minute. I guessed he would be busy with a girl or two because there hadn't been any around since we'd got to the island. I consoled myself with thoughts of the Sistine Chapel. Visiting the Vatican would be the perfect way for a lapsed Catholic to spend her first days in Rome.

I went to the back of the plane to type up my dictation. When I'd finished that I read through the Billionaire's list of instructions for the week ahead. The last one surprised me: '*Please tell me if you want me to keep this evening free?*' was pencilled in his gently sloping script at the bottom of the page. I would like to say that I waited before responding. I did not. Without stopping to think, I deleted the first eight words so that he would know to '*keep this evening free*' ... and I returned the list at the bottom of the pile of faxes and letters he needed to sign.

As we drove into the city, Rome was turning red in the sunset, but I was miserable. We had reached our hotel without the Billionaire inviting me to dinner.

Greeted like returning royalty by the hotel staff, the Billionaire disappeared to his suite while I checked everyone into their rooms. When I finally fell back onto my bed, the soft pillows mocked my romantic expectations. The Billionaire had been cruel to tantalize me then leave me in the Eternal City with only a guidebook for company. I opened it at random, but was too bewildered to learn about Rome's ancient history. My eyelids grew heavy and I was drifting to sleep when the telephone rang.

'Come to my room,' said Billionaire, remembering to add, 'please.'

I climbed off the bed, adjusted my hair, picked up my pen and pad and went down the corridor to the presidential suite where the door was open.

'Hello?' I called. There was no response so I stepped inside. The Billionaire was standing in cool air beside an open window watching the street life below the Piazza di Spagna.

'Come here,' he said and for a while we stood in silence staring at the city. Then he turned slowly towards me. 'You won't need this,' he said, tugging the pad, which fell happily from my hand and dropped to the floor. 'Take off your shoes.' His voice was steady, almost serious. I did as I was told and we stood eye to eye. After what seemed a very long time he leaned forward and kissed me. I watched to see if he would close his eyes, and he did, instantly lost in that kiss. I closed mine to join him there.

'Don't move,' he said.

I resisted putting my hand to his face, to feel his skin, to feel him close to me. It felt unnatural to drop my arms, to stand completely still as he had commanded. Unnatural and then oddly exciting, as he kissed my neck, my mouth and rested soft lips on my closed eyelids. He breathed me in, then pushed the shirt from my shoulders and bit my nipple through my bra until it almost hurt. I cried out, and went to move away. 'I said don't move.' I stood beneath his touch as he unhooked my skirt, which fell to the floor.

The fine white curtain was carried into the room on a light breeze, playing across the surface of my body as his fingers moved inside my panties. Hazy hours later, every sensation spent, we lay together, our bodies fuzzy at the edges as though we had drifted into each other. And then, quite unexpectedly, he bit down hard into the soft muscle at the top of my arm. I shrieked and pulled away.

'Do you understand why I did that?' he asked.

'I think so,' I said, rubbing my arm, studying the indentation there.

'However close we get, it will never be enough,' he said.

He needed to consume, and to be consumed. Instinctively I needed to move away from him and got up from the bed, but by the time I had pulled on my bra and panties and stared at his naked body on the bed, I was ready to make love to him all over again. He lifted his torso from the bed on bended elbow.

'What shall we do now?' he asked.

I raised my eyebrows, half smiled. 'We could ... take a ride on a bus.' It was the last thing he had expected me to say.

'Where would we go?'

'Anywhere. When did you last take a bus?'

'I can't remember,' he said.

'Then maybe it's time.'

Nothing appealed to me more than a freewheeling bus ride with the Billionaire.

'What about security?' he said.

'A bodyguard on a bus. Are you crazy?'

We sneaked out of the hotel separately like children escaping from school, and met at the top of the Spanish Steps. We ran down the steps and jumped on the first bus that came along.

'We don't even know where we're going,' I laughed.

'If you don't know where you're going, all roads will take you there,' he said, and right then, with him beside me, that was good enough for me.

The Billionaire stood in the middle of the bus looking as happy as a man released from a ten-year prison sentence. Tired men smoking cigarettes and giggling girls in cheap clothes stood beside him as the bus swung through narrow streets. The Billionaire came to join me at the back of the bus and we sat there a while watching the people until the bus reached the city limits. Then he took my hand and we leaped off the bus to hail a cab. It was time to get back to Billionaire's world. Back to the luxury of late night shopping on the Avenue via Condotti.

Soon we were sitting outside Caffé Greco, drinking champagne, watching Roman life go by.

'Is there anything you want to buy here?'

'I've got everything,' I said.

'We're in Rome,' he said, as though I hadn't realized. 'Home of Valentino.'

It's not that I didn't know Valentino, but I already had my designer outfit and a few more besides. 'I really don't need any more clothes,' I said.

'Let's hope we've long surpassed meeting our needs. I asked if there's anything you want.'

'Okay. Just one Valentino dress,' I said, nervously biting my bottom lip.

'There you go again with your mouth,' he said. 'But I still love you.' It took a second to register his words. I stopped chewing my lip. The Billionaire folded his arms across his chest and sat back from the marble top table between us. I grinned.

The Billionaire loves me and we're going to Valentino. Careful didn't cross my mind.

In the white boutique the Billionaire sat on the glass table beside a vase of lilies and, swinging his legs like a boy, watched me walk back and forth in first one, and then every dress the shop possessed. Each one was as incredible as the last and I was beginning to worry that I'd never be able to decide when I heard the Billionaire tell the sales assistant to wrap them all up and deliver them to the hotel. 'But leave that one out,' he added.

I came out of the dressing room to see that he had selected the bright green, body-hugging dress, 'with those shoes and that hand bag', for me to wear straight away.

'I like you in Valentino,' he said, as we walked back up the Spanish Steps, his little finger hooked in mine.

I was his girl. In fact, I was *the* girl. I reassured myself that I couldn't be one of the forty thieves because he said he loved me and the extravagant clothes were a reflection of this love. It was the beginning of an insidious metamorphosis. Slowly I was learning to confuse what money can buy with love itself, simply because that was what the Billionaire was able to give. And if one day I'd suffer like Mimi for this man, I was at first his Musetta.

On our last night in Rome the Billionaire took me to an exclusive club. We danced slow and close and he whispered, 'when I'm with you I feel like an 18 year old falling in love for the first time.'

His confession made me bold. 'I want to do a trade with you,' I said.

'Trading's a dangerous game,' he said.

'I'll risk it,' I said, but hesitated.

'So what do you want to trade?' he asked.

'Would you trade the forty thieves for me?' It was an audacious move.

'The who?'

'The girls in your book.'

'What? I've got the telephone numbers of forty girls?'

'Forty, plus Marleena.'

'I'll trade the forty for you. But Marleena's not part of the deal.'

'Why?'

'She's been around too long. I can't tell her to go. But if you stick it out, she'll leave eventually.'

With words like that I determined to be patient and wait for the Billionaire to be free.

Finding himself dealing in a new commodity that he called 'Love of a Sublime Kind', the Billionaire did what traders do – he tested his market. But this commodity required an emotional investment that made him nervous. Volatility was no longer a required condition for market entry: when it came to dealing in Love the Billionaire demanded constancy, which he considered my responsibility to provide. I was expected to be steadfast, my mood unaffected by his. Whether he was intimate and caring, or dismissive and aggressive, my role was to spring back like a punchball, adoration in my eyes. No longer a stranger to strange games, I submitted to the challenge. And the Billionaire did what traders do and hedged his bets, so that while loving me, he also held on to his position with Marleena.

We returned from Rome, to stay on the island and I was hurt when after several weeks of romance, the Billionaire became suddenly remote. It was as if there was no love between us. I struggled to keep my mood in check, but was rewarded when, at the end of a long working day, he called, 'Don't move' after I'd handed him a stack of letters to sign.

All I had to do was receive his affection without revealing a trace of resentment for the way he had ignored me. I remembered Rome, dropped my pad and welcomed his kiss. Anybody could have interrupted this moment, but that danger was part of the pleasure and we knew it.

'Kiss me, hold me, tell me that you love me,' he whispered.

I tried to concentrate and forget that Marleena had charged into his office the day before without waiting to be announced.

'Relax. I've measured it out. Nobody can see us here,' he said.

'But anyone could come in.'

'Let them,' he said, his hand between my legs. Potential interruptions fell out of my mind. His intimate attention made me bold enough to ask what I should do when he was so brutal it made me freeze.

'Do what you're doing now. Take me in your arms, tell me that you love me.'

It sounded simple enough but was not. I found it terrible to be in his presence when his mood was so bad. I hardly had the courage to enter his office then, let alone to reach out in the way he claimed he wanted. Too often the Billionaire's love seemed to depend on my performance: my secretarial efficiency, whether I was thin enough, how I'd done my hair, my clothes, how I spoke to other employees. In fact, some of the Billionaire's demands were so pedantic, it was possible for me to offend him without realizing how I'd done it. There was, however, one subject I knew to avoid, and it drew me like a tongue to a wobbly tooth.

'Will you ever leave Marleena?' I asked the Billionaire, for the third time that week.

'If she wants to leave, I won't stop her, but don't expect me to kick her out,' he said. With an aeroplane at her disposal, crew, staff, and houses throughout the world, I knew Marleena wasn't going anywhere. Yet he expected me to wait and go on waiting. But the more I wanted him, the harder it was to have faith that he would one day be free. Increasingly I saw the Billionaire and Marleena as the jejune Jack and Jill of the children's book series, held together by habit and hard cash in an indestructible bond that allowed for predictable outcomes. 'Jack and Jill Go Shopping' (for an island); 'Jack and Jill Go to the Beach' (in their thirteen-crew yacht).

Meanwhile our Sublime Love suffered the consequences of subliminal insecurities. The less time he spent with me, the more I tested the Billionaire to find out whether he loved me at all.

'Would you like to see me this evening?' I asked, knowing that Marleena was on the island.

'Where shall we meet?' he asked.

'Wherever you want.'

'Let's have dinner at your flat.' I hadn't anticipated this response.

'What would you like to eat?' I panicked.

'I don't care. I'll be there at seven.'

My flat was a mess, the fridge was empty. 'Can you make it eight?' Desperate to create the Perfect Love Scene, I obsessed on the quality of my housekeeping and forgot that lovers don't eat, or only eat after loving.

My hesitation killed the Billionaire's spontaneity and, sensing my insecurity, he picked up his briefcase. 'It's sounding complicated. Let's leave it,' he said.

'You mean you aren't coming over?'

'No.'

'But I miss you. I want to see you.'

'Stop making demands,' he said, and walked out.

❖

My darling sister

My island life sounds like paradise but can be bloody hell. Count yourself lucky to be living in Beverly Hills, even if you occasionally feel like a slave. We're all slaves to something, and there are worse masters than wealthy Californians …

I know you told me not to, but I couldn't help it: I've fallen in love with my boss and, as you predicted, things have become complicated. This man is quite something and when we're together there is no doubt that he loves me. When we're apart, I'm not so sure. He doesn't call and often ignores me all day at the office. I suppose it's because he's got another woman around – a not-so-minor detail I kept from you.

The whole thing is very messy and I'm so nervous I've started to make terrible mistakes in the office. Yesterday he shouted, 'Bring me a pot of tea' through his closed door, but I was grateful. It was the first time he'd spoken to me in <u>three</u> days. Determined to take him the best tea he'd ever tasted, I put the kettle on the stove, then went through the rigamarole of covering the tray with *the linen napkin, setting out the silver spoon etc. Trouble was I went back to my office to do some filing while the water boiled and promptly forgot all about it. Half an hour later the Billionaire bellowed 'KETTLE' so loudly my knees banged together. The whole office stank of smoke for the rest of the day, which hovered on the ceiling, even in the trading room. Almost setting the kitchen on fire was nothing to the mistake I made that afternoon. The Billionaire had told me to book a plane for Marleena and the dogs for a last-minute appointment with the New York shrink. (That castrated dog is now so fat and passive the local vet has recommended assertiveness training or testosterone shots – and they wanted the shrink's opinion.)*

There's nothing I hate quite so much as making arrangements for Marleena, particularly booking her a private jet when the Billionaire is being cruel to me. I think it's one of his weapons when he wants to hurt me.

When it came to calling the pilots I couldn't find them. Of course this didn't mean Marleena would be flying commercial – that'll be the day. My job was to get her a plane that afternoon and with no planes or pilots on the island, I called one of the spare planes down from New York – only to discover an hour later there was a plane on the island after all.

It's my job to make sure that all the planes and pilots are properly coordinated. Booking an unnecessary round trip to New York was a $50,000 slip-up and, terrified the Billionaire would find out about it, I decided to tell him myself. I was convinced he would fire me, but he just looked up from some mathematical formula he was inventing for his trading system and said, 'We all make mistakes.' I turned to go but he told me to wait, put down his pen and walked over to me. Then he kissed me and asked me to dinner. Can you believe it?

I'd better sign off because I'm meant to be at his house in an hour. He told me to bring my toothbrush – his way of inviting me to spend the night. I'll let you know how it goes.

Love you, and please, don't tell Mummy about these latest developments.

❖

Eventually the Billionaire and I agreed that the quotidian requirements of office life were not for me. I was terrible at dictation and filing. I was finally allowed to acknowledge what I had always known: I wasn't cut out to be a secretary. The Billionaire and I had been lying on his bed after hours of love-making when he said, 'You don't need to be my secretary. You're my woman,' and I liked the sound of that more than anything I'd heard in a long time.

Yet for some reason I protested. 'But I don't want to stop working.'

'You don't have to. I need a record of commodity prices linked to fundamentals. Do you think you could put that together?'

'Of course.'

'Just remember kiss. Keep it simple stupid,' he said, kissing me. 'Who knows, you may end up becoming an analyst and I'll have to get another secretary while you're at Harvard.'

Going to Harvard was one of my secret dreams. The Billionaire was so matter-of-fact about the possibility, he made it sound inevitable.

'Let's talk about it tomorrow. Can you come over tomorrow night?'

'Eh … I'll need to check my diary,' I mocked.

'Why not bring all your things with you?'

'What, for dinner?'

'I'm asking you to stay here, if you'd like to.'

I arrived the next day with suitcases of clothes, somewhat nervous that the staff would judge me for moving in while Marleena was away. I needn't have worried. If I was what the Billionaire wanted, they wanted me, too – in his kitchen, on his tennis court, at his breakfast table, or in his bed. I was the welcome guest. But my guilt was fuelled by Marleena's big bras in the dressing room, and her slim-fitting trousers in the wardrobe. The Billionaire expected me to disregard such reminders of my rival. 'She's not here today, and unlikely to be here tomorrow. So where's the problem?' Gradually I relaxed. As long as Marleena was in the Billionaire's St. Tropez mansion I was happy.

The summer days turned into weeks, and the Billionaire and I discovered a rare thing: Sublime Love of a stable kind. He was, when he chose to be, a man who understood the value of living simply, one day at a time. Our days were disciplined and focused, following a routine balanced between work, physical exercise and loving pleasures. Now that I had a research project, and my secretarial days were numbered, I enjoyed the office. When we wanted to escape the staff and the constant calls from the outside world, we would retreat to the Billionaire's bedroom, a magical place at the top of the house, facing west to the sea and its clear horizon. The room was empty, apart from a wide, deep bed, a hand-carved chest from India and a single shelf stacked with books on psychology, philosophy and chemistry. One evening I picked up a book by Jung.

'"If a man knows more than others, he becomes lonely,"' I quoted. 'Do you agree?'

'Yes,' he said, as I moved to the bed where he was reading. I curled around his body and knew that in many ways the Billionaire was a lonely man.

'What made you the way you are?' I asked.

'I know and that's enough,' he said.

'Did you ever see a psychiatrist?'

'You know I've employed them – and not just for the dogs.'

'Did you ever talk to one?'

'I don't need to talk, but some people find it helpful. It gets things off their chest.' He removed his half-rimmed spectacles, set down his book.

'Why didn't you marry Marleena?'

'Because I didn't want to marry Marleena,' he said.

'One day I'll make sense of my life, have it all together,' I said, as if to convince him that I could be worthy of him.

'When you finally reach the place where everything in life adds up, that's the day you die,' he said flatly.

'That's a terrible way to think.'

'It's the way it is. We are imperfect beings – which doesn't mean we can't be good. I want you to be good and I know you can be,' he said, smoothing my hair back from my face.

'What's your motivation?' I asked.

'What keeps me competitive? Is that what you mean?'

I nodded, but he didn't respond and I waited, listening to his breathing, his arm tucked beneath my head, cradling me against his shoulder, his fingers caressing the soft skin behind my ear. Then finally he said, 'I know what it is that makes me the way I am. I just don't want to say.'

That's how he was – self-reliant and remote. Sometimes though, without words of explanation, he let me see beyond his defences. Those moments were sacred to me and kept me hypnotized, so that for longer than I should have, through situations that I shouldn't have, I loved him.

❖

It was September 15th 8.21 a.m.

'Marleena's back tomorrow,' the Billionaire said, spreading homemade apricot jam on to his homemade croissant. For a second I was sure I had misheard him. I had effectively convinced myself that Marleena was no longer a threat and it took a few seconds to understand what the Billionaire had said. When I did, my breakfast turned to a block of ice in my stomach.

'Marleena's coming back here?'

'Yes.'

'Then I'd better pack.'

'Stay. She'll have to get used to it.' He sipped his tea and I can still hear those words. *Stay. She'll have to get used to it.* The idea of us all living beneath one roof was surreal. My first thought was what if Marleena attacked me in the middle of the night? Too shocked to pose reasonable questions and introduce some kind of reality to the notion of communal living, I tried to joke about it instead. 'Marleena's nearly six foot and a black belt in karate. I don't think I'll be the one to kick her out.' The Billionaire smiled and sliced his croissant into six even portions, fed one to each dog and ate the rest. He wiped his mouth with a thick white napkin, golden flakes falling to his empty plate, and then he pushed back his chair.

'I'll pack my bags, then,' I said, hoping the Billionaire would contradict me. He left the table without a word.

Marleena, so patrician when dressed in expensive clothes, was beneath all grit and no grace. Apparently, ten years ago she had single handedly moved the possessions of the Billionaire's wife out of their marital home and installed her things in their stead. And all this while the Billionaire's wife had been abroad, working for peace in the Middle East. The Billionaire had let it happen, for while he willingly waged battle in business with prime ministers and industrialists, he wouldn't confront Marleena. By suggesting that I stay for her return, the Billionaire was asking me to fight his fight with her. It was his ultimate test of my love and the one I failed because I was not convinced that it was my responsibility to tell Marleena that she was out and I was in.

And it wasn't the karate chop that worried me, as much as the man: the Billionaire was one of the most powerful businessmen in the world, but what good was that if he was a coward when it came to his heart?

❖

My darling sister

I'm back in the secretary's flat where the Billionaire visits hardly at all. To complete my torture, Marleena drops by the office every afternoon just to remind me who's boss. My only consolation is her bad dress sense. When she's not in designer clothes and tries freestyle dressing, she always gets it wrong. This morning it was white short shorts, hair in bunches, and a pink jacket. Her legs are long but they ain't that shapely and her thighs are dimpled with cellulitic patches of no small significance and I can't tell you how happy that makes me. Oh, God forgive me …

It is time to take your advice and get out of the Billionaire's life and back to my own – whatever that is. As if in answer to my prayers about where to go next I received a postcard from the Lord. He's longing to see me, loves me still and says he'll always be my friend. It's a pity that he posted this declaration to the office in an open postcard, which, for some reason, the man in the mail room decided to put on the Billionaire's desk rather than mine. When the Billionaire handed me the card he scowled and didn't say a word, but I knew he felt betrayed, as though I'd been carrying on a secret hedge of my own.

I was going to tell you that we agreed I should fly back to England – but actually the Billionaire told me to go. There was no point in protesting. He'd made up his mind. When I was booking my flight, I could hear him on the other line calling the pale blonde he put through that Florida flying school. Apparently she has just graduated and he's sending his latest aeroplane to pick her up and bring her to the island. She arrives the day I leave …

This has been a horrible day. I'll write to you from England.

With all my love,

❖

When I landed in England, the Lord was at the airport to welcome me home. He knew of my affair with the Billionaire, and his courtly devotion thrived in the presence of a rival. What's more, the Lord was patient and told me he was willing to wait for me. But he was too late. I was obsessed with the Billionaire, who kept me on the pay roll and did not request the return of the company credit card. I clung to the belief that these financial hooks signified hope for our future.

It was six months before I heard from the Billionaire: his new secretary called me at the Lord's cottage and when I was put through to him, he greeted me formally as though we had never shared a single intimacy. Then he asked me whether the dossier on certain commodity prices was ready. I had researched diligently, collecting every detail in more than twenty files, and that week had completed my task. 'Then please come to Paris tomorrow with the research and I'll book you a room at the Ritz.'

❖

'We've missed you,' said the receptionist whose smile was reassuring. She had not forgotten me, but then her professionally serene expression faltered.

'Don't I have a reservation?'

'Yes, but we rarely give this room to guests. We're full, you see.' Her head angled apologetically as she passed me the key.

My rooftop room resembled a student's garret, with a sloped ceiling and skylight window. Within any other building in the heart of Paris it would have been a romantic hide-away, but in this luxurious hotel its minimalism was harsh and a sign of changing times. Pushed beneath the door was a note, written in the Billionaire's hand: '*Come straight to Room 1200.*' I brushed my hair, pulled on one of the Valentino dresses and rushed down to his suite. I rang the bell, heart pounding, hoping he'd keep me waiting long enough for me to calm down, but this time the Billionaire was at the door immediately.

'How have you been?' he asked, falling back into a deep armchair, so in control it was impossible to detect how he felt. He ruffled his hair. I was unable to match his cool performance and sat with legs crossed, then nervously uncrossed, a blush rising to the surface of my cheeks.

'I always liked you in that dress,' he said.

'Thank you,' I said.

'Would you like a cup of tea?' he said.

The first time he had offered me tea I had been an overweight, optimistic girl who had dared to stare him in the eye. Now love, anxiety and desire had made me lean and unable to look at him. The tea duly arrived. He asked me to pour. I reached for the pot.

'I've thought of you every day. I still want you,' he said.

We made love right there on the floor and never drank that cup of tea.

Later, resting in the deep comfort of his gilded four-poster bed, he whispers I love you. I tell him that I love him too. Nothing has changed. We are just like before.

When we took a shower I angled: 'When we're not together, our relationship exists inside my head.'

'That's the best place for it,' he said, soaping his legs and refusing to bite.

'But I want to see you more.'

He scrubbed his arms and chest vigorously, soap streaming down his body. 'Nobody can make demands on my time.'

'That means you'd rather not see me.'

'That's what my wife used to say. Those were good days. I always think the past is better than the future.'

'Than now?'

'No, not better than right now.'

We got out of the shower and he wrapped me up in a thick

white towel, and then I lay on the bed and watched him dress for dinner.

'I've got thirty people to entertain this evening. So get dressed, go to your room and I'll call you when I get back.'

I did as he requested. As I kissed him goodbye, he whispered, 'Just remember. You'll never be alone.'

After the luxury of his suite my garret room felt like a pink box. I settled back on the bed to read and wait for the Billionaire's return, but as the hours passed, waves of drowsiness broke over me. By midnight, desperate to stay awake, I was standing on the desk chair, leaning out of the skylight to breathe cooler air. I watched people in the cobblestone square below and the hard rain falling in yellow lamplight which made the street shine. At the hotel's entrance, black limousines formed a glistening line and chauffeurs opened doors for elegant passengers who glided beneath an ark of umbrellas, held by staff getting soaked. By quarter to one there was still no sign of the Billionaire. To take the edge off my uncertainty that he was coming back for me, I ordered a sandwich and a glass of champagne and promptly fell asleep.

When the telephone rang, my head shot off the pillow and I caught sight of the red digital figures on my bedside clock: ten minutes past two.

'Hello,' I said.

'Asleep?'

'No,' I said, sounding sleepy.

'Did I wake you?'

'Not really,' I said, but he could tell.

'Goodnight,' he said, hanging up on me.

I didn't hear from the Billionaire the following day. It seemed that the punishment for succumbing to sleep was excommunication. I needed to convince him that I wanted him, so spent four days cooped up in the pink room, ordering room service and reading, in case he called. Every night a waiter brought me the finest food and wine on a perfect table set for one and every night I thought how sad it was to drink alone and sleep alone in a single bed in the heart of Paris or anywhere. In the evening I dared to venture to the hotel spa, to swim in the deserted Grecian style pool, with its Doric columns, fresco walls and classical music playing beneath the water. Such anodyne luxury did not sedate my loneliness and longing. I started leaving messages for the Billionaire, and finally, on the fifth day at eleven o'clock in the morning, he called. 'How are you?' I said, trying to sound cheerful.

'Very busy.'

'I've got the research you wanted.'

'Ah, ze research,' he put on that Clouseau accent, which didn't sound funny any more.

'If we have dinner this evening you can give it to me then. I'll call you later.' He hung up.

Now that I had a date, I headed out of the hotel, into the rain and low cloud of a melancholy afternoon. Walking down the Avenue des Champs-Elysées I noticed a retrospective of Titian's work was showing at the Grand Palais. It was the middle of a week day and the exhibition rooms were almost empty. I drifted into Titian's blue, gazing at his Madonna and sensual Venus, wondering at the ways men love women and then at the ways men had loved me. I began to think that no man I'd loved had seen me beyond those parts that served him best and, looking at Venus, there was little doubt about what those parts were. For the first time it occurred to me that if I wanted a man to see me beyond the superficial surface, it was my responsibility to show him.

I began to run towards the hotel, through its revolving doors and up the marble stairs, around and around, up to the

Billionaire's suite, rehearsing my confrontation around and around in my head. With each step I was finding the courage to challenge him, to tell him that I wanted to be with him, not in glamorous locations for secret moments, but for days and nights that would add up to our idea of a normal life.

I knocked on his door and waited. Then I rang the bell, at first politely, but soon constantly. There was no reply. I noticed five white envelopes from the hotel reception tucked beneath his double doors and, feeling entitled to any means available, eyed the messages. I would allow myself to read just one. I glanced up and down the corridor and waited for a maid pushing a linen trolley to pass. We exchanged half-formed smiles and I rang the Billionaire's doorbell again as if for the first time, to justify my presence there. Once the maid was out of sight, I carefully unhooked the fold of pure white to read a single typewritten line: *'Mlle Albertine will be at the hotel this evening at 8.00 p.m.'*

My hand shook as I returned the message to its position beneath the door. I rushed back to the safety of my room, praying I wouldn't meet anyone I knew, not even the maid, and once inside, crumpled to the floor in tears. I crawled to the bed and sobbed mascara-stained tears into the pure white pillowcase. After an hour of crying I drank a jug of water, took a long hot shower and felt ready to confront the Billionaire. I returned to his suite and was surprised to find the doors open. Calling his name, I stepped inside, ignoring the 'Do Not Disturb' Sign. Grapes wilted in a silver fruit dish and a bottle of champagne languished, almost untouched, in a bucket of melted ice. Clearly the Billionaire hadn't been disturbed for days. The only bright point in the room was the desk where pristine white documents piled high reflected light from the window. I glanced through the papers, which made up a contract between the Billionaire and two nations, guaranteeing him payment of a million dollars *every* day. For the first time I saw how he was able to generate infinite amounts of cash.

Turning into the room, I jumped with fright to see a figure sitting in the shadows, watching me. 'I wondered when I'd see you again,' it said.

I gasped with relief when I realized it was Jeff, the English security man. 'Hello.' I arched my eyebrows in nervous acknowledgment that I'd been snooping.

'I didn't know you were around,' he said.

'These days I wonder why I am.'

'We've all got our reasons for being here.'

I sank into the chair opposite him, sensing Jeff was about to continue the conversation that Julia had started in the New York office when she'd cautioned me to be careful.

'I heard you left him because you couldn't be bought,' he said.

'Is that what they said?'

'Yes, and good for you because he's bought me. By his own admission he doesn't need me for anti-terrorism. All I do is run around after his girls.'

'Really?'

'We've got five here — '

'Including Mademoiselle Albertine?'

'She's new but no different — another girl he's picked up and will leave to me to look after. They're just a bunch of shopaholics. I tell you, I wish I was a skinny six-foot chick. I'd do him for every penny.'

'He can afford to give money away.'

'Look, he'll be back in a minute and I don't think he'll be alone.'

This was my cue to leave and I returned to my room. In the end there was no dinner invitation from the Billionaire that night so I lingered in the hotel reception, hidden beneath a hat and long coat, to spy on his date. At precisely eight o'clock a beanpole girl stalked into the hotel. She was outrageously glamorous, even for Paris. Her black evening dress, gathered at her tiny waist, cascaded in a trail to the floor, and her blonde hair was cut severely short to flatter her swan neck. She was chaperoned by a woman in her early fifties and they spoke to each other in French, discussing arrangements at the reception that even I could hear.

'You don't have to spend the night. Just have dinner if that's what you want,' the older woman said.

'But I want to spend the night,' the tall girl said.

Her fate was sealed. I could predict her future more certainly than my own. Unable to face an evening imprisoned in the pink box, I walked out into another rainy evening to eat *croque monsieur* in an anonymous café and wander along the Seine where I decided that Paris was the perfect place for suicide.

The Billionaire called me the following morning at nine-thirty.

'Have I woken you?' he said, feigning concern.

'I've just had breakfast.' So had he, I imagined, with his mademoiselle, having fed her one of those 5K envelopes.

'Come to my room with the research. I'm leaving in ten minutes,' he said.

The drama of the markets, the stories behind the stories that affected commodity prices, mattered not at all if I wasn't going to work for the Billionaire. The reality of becoming an analyst no longer inspired me and the information I had compiled with pride, seemed insignificant now. I carried the research down to the Billionaire's suite where the doors were open.

'Sit down,' he said, without looking up.

I sat in a hard back chair beside the desk while he loaded the documents on his desk into his massive briefcase.

'Thanks for the research. The crew will pick it up later. Now, in memory of what we had …' he began.

He had consigned to memory.

'… I'd like to pay for you to go to university.'

I turned my eyes to the floor to hide the shame and delight and hurt that hit me all at once. I knew immediately that I would accept his gift of a paid education, even if taking his money without expecting his love would transform me into one of the forty thieves. My corruption was complete.

Inspired by thoughts of attending Oxford, I didn't linger on that observation. La Sorbonne was the next university to come to mind followed by Philadelphia's Wharton School and Harvard. And then I wondered why? Why this sudden change in the Billionaire's affections? Mademoiselle Albertine was pretty, but not that pretty. Were happiness and pleasure so unrelated in the hearts of some men? Then, for some reason, I remembered my first limousine ride down Park Avenue.

'Can I study in New York?' I asked.

'Keep the credit card, go wherever you like,' the Billionaire said, nestling the knot of his dark-blue tie into the smooth cradle of his white collar and for a second I believed that he really wouldn't have cared if I'd wanted to study on the moon. 'Keep in touch. Let me know what you need.' He picked up his brief case and headed for the door. This was a familiar scene, except this time the Billionaire set down his case and returned to bestow a chaste kiss.

'This is your chance to be good, don't waste it,' he said. To hear him say this, his voice soft and close, reminded me of the perfect days we'd spent together. Suddenly I found myself in tears, a display of emotion which sent the Billionaire running for the door. 'There's something for you in the desk,' he said, and then was gone.

I opened the desk drawer to find four 5K envelopes – the Billionaire's consolation for leaving me alone in Paris and possibly for ever. The $20,000 conveniently packaged, slipped easily into my bag and I was about to leave the room, bemused and confused by my conflicting emotions, when the maid with the linen trolley appeared. '*Je peux faire le lit*?' She was attractive, my age, or less. In heels and the right clothes, she could easily have passed for one of the forty thieves. Perhaps she was resigned to her fate and that grace gave her dignity. Her life may have been 9 to 5, but at least it was her own. We glanced at each other and she smiled. In that moment she reminded me of the girl I had been before being refined by the Lord and bought by the Billionaire. I told her I needed to be alone and asked her to return in a minute. She nodded, left her trolley in the doorway and disappeared.

I drifted into the Billionaire's bedroom to stand at the foot of the unmade Louis XVI bed. Without his presence the luxury seemed as fake as a stage set, although the unmade bed was real enough. I took two of my white envelopes and scrawled across them '*pour la femme de chambre*' and stuck them between the pillows.

Six

No Man's Land

I flew to JFK and checked into the Plaza Hotel, determined to be a summer school student by the end of the week. It was a vain hope. Recorded messages at New York University and Columbia announced that all courses were full. Resigned to waiting a few months, I called Fall term admissions.

'Applicants for next year …' an efficient voice said. Next year? So much for New York bringing immediate order to my life. The only order that seemed possible now was room service but, when the table set for one arrived, instead of providing solace, it compounded my loneliness. The expansive double bed, the his-and-hers wash basins, two towelling bathrobes and two pairs of slippers all proved that in a city so good they named it twice, making it on my own would be difficult.

I longed to talk to somebody. I dismissed the idea of calling Julia, who was the only person I knew in the city. Being lonely was better than shamefully confessing that I had accepted the Billionaire's charity and still wanted him to want me back.

I lay on a big bed in a big room in a big hotel with big dreams fast amounting to nothing more than a big bill on the Billionaire's credit card. My hopes for the future had evaporated, leaving a void even a slab of New York cheesecake couldn't fill. With $10,000 and a company credit card in my bag, I was an overfed refugee from my own life, unsure of where I belonged, or where I should be. I was a woman in transition. The flip phrase that had rolled off the tongue of the old man had cursed me. And then I remembered his parting words were to call if ever I was in New York. So I did know somebody else in the city after all. I found his number in my book, that narcotic Hope seeping back into my veins as I dialled.

'New York University,' said an efficient voice on the other end of the line.

'Sorry. I think I've got the wrong number.'

'Who you after?'

'Harry Shiffer.'

'Professor Shiffer. Please hold.'

It turned out the Professor was Head of Cultural Studies and had travelled to tribal cultures in Africa and societies in industrialized Asia to analyse what he called 'women's new ways of seeing'.

'You fit right into my area of specialization,' he said, and suggested that taking the cross-town bus to meet a prospective subject for his study presented no problem at all. I was encouraged when he offered to meet for breakfast, 'but not at the Plaza,' he said. 'That gilt interior makes me nervous.'

The Professor had recommended a Third Avenue diner for our rendez-vous, where I waited at a Formica counter watching short-order cooks prepare breakfasts for workers on the run. The place was crammed and steamy, and when the Professor arrived, his forehead shimmered from the morning heat. He was smaller than I remembered, almost pixie-like.

'Welcome to New York. No better place for a woman in transition,' he beamed, taking my hand in his soft broad palm, which was delightfully cool.

'I hate that phrase.'

'Why? It describes you perfectly.'

'It feels like a curse.'

'Transition is a phase, part of discovering who you are.' He placed his hand on my shoulder and squeezed.

I didn't like the way the Professor's hand stuck like a parrot to my shoulder. I leaned dramatically towards my corn muffin and off it flew.

'What are you going to study?' he asked, folding his hands into his lap.

I mumbled evasively, 'Economics or English or French literature.'

'Don't worry. Confusion is part of the process,' he said, guiding me out of the café on to the downtown bus towards Washington Square where a drunk, draped over a bench, called out, 'Have a good day,' as the Professor and I went past. I ignored the tramp who shouted after me, 'Hey, lady, take the cork outta your ass, you're in New York City.' The Professor raised the wry eyebrow. I appeared to be not simply a woman in transition, but an uptight one too. This wasn't turning out to be such a great morning.

We toured the NYU campus and then went up to look around Columbia, but even a respected scholar who knew the system, couldn't help me circumvent the bureaucracy. I was too late to register for any course that year at NYU or Columbia. The Professor took me for a consoling cup of tea in the heart of academia, the Columbia canteen. 'I think you should try one more university, an old Ivy League girls' college, famous for liberal arts — '

'What kind of arts?'

'Humanities, languages, literature. The Fine Arts. Not ideal if you want to be an economist. It's also a train ride out of the city and very expensive. Perhaps you could try for a scholarship.'

'Money is the one thing that isn't a problem,' I said, believing I had devised for myself an exclusive kind of scholarship.

Once the Professor had made an appointment for me to meet the head of the adult education centre at the University of Liberal Arts, he accompanied me back to the Plaza on the cross-town bus, giving me the number of a real estate agent on the way. I was silently blessing his unexpected presence in my life, when I found his roving hand resting on my knee.

'Excuse me,' I said, picking up his hand and returning it to his lap. 'I think you may need this.'

He chuckled and I thought perhaps I had misjudged him until, one stop from the Plaza, the Professor looked me steadily in the eye. 'I'd like to suggest an idea which you may find unusual ...' I waited, open to the wisdom he was about to impart. 'I would like to offer you the opportunity to sleep with me, no strings attached. Just something to think about.'

I declined to tell the professor that an old man wanting unconditional sex with a young woman didn't seem that unusual to me. What was unusual, however, was the way he presented the idea as though it were an act of philanthropy for my benefit. I ran off the bus without saying goodbye and never called him again.

My immediate reaction was to ditch the professor's real estate agent, but realizing I was in no position to throw out a lead, I retrieved her card from the waste bin and dialled her number.

'Do you have flats on the East Side?'

'East, West, up, down, it's all my kinda town. Where are you?'

'The Plaza.'

'I'll be right over,' she said, sensing the possibility of making a fast buck.

Twenty minutes later she appeared in the hotel foyer, pert and laser-eyed, dressed to impress in gold jewellery, a bright red jacket and tight pencil skirt. She was perfect for the Plaza, blending with the wallpaper and 'all that glitters'.

'You're younger than I thought,' she said, shaking my hand. 'Are you sure you want the East Side? It can be a little high-priced, not to mention uptight.' Uptight? So perhaps I'd fit right in? The agent fired me another question, getting straight to the point. 'What's your budget?'

I had no idea about rents and Manhattan real estate or what the Billionaire was willing to pay. The budget for the wife of a billionaire is one thing, his ex-wife another, but what about a billionaire's ex-lover? The Billionaire was not extravagant on his abodes and, not wanting to be so myself, I settled on a monthly rent of $3,000 – an amount he distributed freely to almost perfect strangers.

The agent spun around, her face glowing. 'Upper East side here we come,' she cried, commanding the driver to take us to 92nd and Madison.

'Isn't that Harlem?' I panicked.

'Trust me. I'm taking you to a proper neighbourhood, real European, boutiques and everything. One block from Central Park, near the subway, everyone friendly. Even the local panhandler's a good-lookin' guy. You're gonna love it.'

Carnegie Hill was that rare thing: a blend of British and French, tacked on at the top of Madison Avenue before it becomes Harlem. There was a French restaurant with real French waiters, and the grocer's, Le Grand Bouffe, was run by an Irish man who sold hand-made designer deli food to go and Heinz baked beans. Fifth Avenue was one block away and the International Center of Photography down the street.

'A doorman building honey, cos safe is better than sorry,' the agent said, taking me up thirty flights to a one-bedroom apartment. There were two vast, unfurnished rooms with wooden floors and windows from floor to ceiling with sky-scraping views. The concrete asphalt mass that is Harlem, and the Bronx beyond, sprawled to the north, while to the west the sight was postcard perfect: Central Park, the reservoir and the twin towers of the Dakota Building. The agent leaned against the window, cooled by air conditioning, and for a moment stopped trying to sell. 'John Lennon,' she sighed. 'God bless. Think of him every time I see that building.'

The agent reminisced, leaving me the space to see clearly. 'I'd like to rent *this* place,' I said with a conviction that surprised us both. I had rarely felt so sure of anything my whole life.

The agent's eyes rolled like a cash register at the prospect of so much commission so easily earned. 'Had you down as an uptown girl the minute I heard that accent,' she smiled.

We returned to the Plaza lounge to work through the small print of the tenancy agreement, which I signed on the dotted line before handing over two months' rent in advance.

'Gotta celebrate,' she said, thrusting my fresh dollar bills into her possibly Chanel handbag. She snapped her fingers to attract a passing waiter. 'Kir royale. Make that two, right hon?'

I had one champagne cocktail to the agent's three, by which time she was over the edge. 'Gotta go,' she said, waving for the waiter. 'Isn't he adorable? Have you seen those buns,' she breathed as a fine young man walked towards us with the check. 'Charge to room … 511 right hon?'

I signed and led the agent to a waiting cab. I watched her clamber into the back seat, splitting her skirt on the way. 'Oh fock,' she said, relaxing into a Brooklyn accent under the influence of a sealed deal and too much champagne.

The following day I took the train to my University interview. The adult education centre accepted mature students without a standard aptitude test and I was accepted for summer school straightaway. My Liberal Arts education – a gloriously expensive route to bohemia – had begun. One thousand dollars per credit to study 'Urban Lives' was a high price to pay, but at the end of the summer I'd have five credits towards the 120 that would make up my degree. If 'Urban Lives' was a diffuse subject, the Professor was impressive enough to compensate. Professor Maya was to spend four weeks leading us through research papers and reference books detailing the strata of inner city life, from the upper to the 'under class' – those who survive on charity or money earned illegally. The college faculty had me down as upper class (an English accent in America does it every time), but my hope was that living in New York and going to university would liberate me from such labels. My intention was to be autonomous and independent, but with every step into my brave new world, my financial dependence on the Billionaire deepened.

Receiving money for nothing filled me with guilt, which eased only as the money disappeared. And so I spent. Easy come, easy go, the money the Billionaire had given me in Paris was disappearing on furniture, deposits and college fees and I was worried I'd be panhandling myself if he didn't make an urgent cash transfer. The most important thing for me to do was open a bank account – at least then I'd be able to receive money if it was offered – and forever the optimist, the following morning I went to the local bank with my last $1,000.

'I'd like to open an account,' I said to the man standing in the bank's entrance, his belly straining the buttons of his jacket. I guessed he was about thirty, and he shook my hand, all enthusiastic to be looking at new business and it not yet five past nine. We sat at his desk, which was bare apart from a red telephone, a computer terminal and the *New York Post*.

'Okay, ID,' he said.

I produced my passport.

'I mean ID. This isn't certifiable.'

I produced my student card.

'I'm thinking Con Edison,' he said, as if talking to an idiot.

'You're thinking what?'

'You don't got no electricity bill? No utilities?' He scratched his head with his pen, his amiable expression fading.

'I've only just arrived in the city.'

He sighed, heaved himself out of his chair, headed for the vending machine and returned to stand over me, sucking coffee from a white plastic cup. 'Trouble is no ID, no business.' He placed his cup down, lifted his trousers to get the crease comfortable, and sat heavily. 'Social Security number? Sure you've got one of them.' He sounded positive, the caffeine fuelling a short-lived revival, but he slumped when he realized a British passport was all I had. 'With respect,' he said sliding it back across the table to me, 'this ain't worth Jack.'

I furrowed my forehead.

'Jack shit,' he whispered. He leaned back in his chair and drained the rest of his coffee, our meeting over so far as he was concerned.

'I need an account,' I said, staring him right in the eye.

He sighed again and punched my name into the computer using his index finger. 'Nothing's coming up. No records means we can't open no account.' He was ready for his *New York Post*, but I wasn't about to give up. I had a young, honest face, blonde hair and $1,000 in fresh bills. It was a delicate combination but with enough determination I was confident I could persuade somebody to bend the rules.

'Please can I see your supervisor.'

'You ain't foolin' nobody with no ID.'

'*Please.*'

The reluctant man disappeared behind the scenes to return a few minutes later with a woman in gold-rimmed spectacles, cradling in her right arm a 'new business' file. Two hours and fifteen telephone calls later, I walked out of the bank with a temporary cheque book, a cash card and an identity graciously granted by Citibank. Finally I existed.

❖

My fellow students guessed what my accent confirmed – I was a WASP. What's more, an English WASP. Maya's students sat around an oval table; two black women, both single mothers working in the university admin department to pay their fees, a number of married white women each with grown children and a Mercedes, and our token male, Christian Acre the Fifth. He spent the class resting on the back legs of his chair, his pink polo shirt, Ralph Lauren jeans and worn cowboy boots hinting at pursuits far from academic.

I appeared upper class to the New Yorkers, but this young man was a blue-blooded aristocrat of the American variety. He was the youngest heir to the biggest fortune in the United States, his name familiar thanks to a national chain of superstores, the source of his family's wealth for over a century. Mr C. Acre shot migratory birds on his estate in Florida, rode $100,000 horses and his girlfriend's father was America's most famous film director. Christian Acre V embodied the all-American dream, and was quite a dreamer himself, spending most of our three-hour class gazing at my breasts.

The Breast Gazer wasn't a natural fit in a room of budding feminists. Neither was a tiny woman who wore shoes tipped with fake leopard skin and perfect make-up. She looked like a doll - which was also her favourite word: 'Hey, doll', or 'Be a doll', or 'Doll, don't suppose you gotta cigarette?'

As the course went on, the Breast Gazer was the only student interested in becoming my friend, and he often drove me back to Manhattan in his four-wheel drive monster truck for lunch at Pig Heaven, a modest Chinese restaurant on 1st Avenue. In spite of his millions, Christian's tastes were as basic as his prejudices and for all his reticence in class, the Breast Gazer turned out to be quite a talker.

'That girl,' he said, his mouth full of pork dumpling.

'Which one?' I sat opposite him, fumbling with my chopsticks, yet to get a good bite of anything.

'You know, the one you sit next to sometimes.'

'Erinoula.'

'She's weird. All that make-up and stuff. And her shoes. She's got to be Jewish.'

'Greek actually, but not Orthodox.'

'Watch her. She's into rich people.'

'Well, I've run out of money,' I said.

Christian's jaw dropped, as though I'd told him I'd got a terminal illness. 'You're kidding, right?' That somebody could run out of money was beyond his comprehension.

'A transfer hasn't arrived,' I said, trying to sound casual, smiling to hide the horrible truth that the Billionaire hadn't returned my calls and my bank balance was close to zero.

'Banks tell you transfers get lost, but they hold onto them deliberately.' Accustomed to receiving big bucks on the wire, he spoke about transfers with a familiarity I found reassuring.

After lunch the all-American dream boy went for a meeting at his father's office downtown, not at all fazed that he had yet to think of a subject for our final paper due the next day. This paper had made me quite neurotic because it would determine our course grade and if mine were good enough, I'd be able to graduate from the adult education centre and move up to the main campus for the Fall term.

The significance of the paper had made me so anxious, I hadn't drafted even one page of it, which left me no choice but to sit down and write twenty-five pages straight off. I read through my research notes (again), and by four o'clock had the paper's premise, problems and solutions in my head, where they spiralled into a confusion that went forever downward.

By eight o'clock I had written 2,000 words and had fourteen hours to write 13,000 more. My mind was numb, my eyes ached, the fridge was empty. I walked to the deli on the corner, hoping to be inspired by the food counter. But on that short walk, my inability to transform thought to text magnified every doubtful aspect of my life. I wondered whether the Billionaire would call, and asked myself yet again why I had been so willing to believe that he would pay for my school fees and three years' rent.

A few hours later, my doubts allayed by a generous portion of honey covered chicken wings, I was approaching my 4,000th word when the telephone rang.

'Hello.'

'How amazing …' I said.

'Why? I'm not on another planet,' said the Billionaire.

'You may as well be. But you sound close now,' I said, trying to discover if he was in the city.

'Sorry I haven't called, I've been busy. How's university?'

'I love it. I'm writing my final paper right now.'

'And how's the money?' Money was indeed our third person, no less a bond than a child connecting parents long after divorce.

'It's terrible, the money's almost gone.'

'Give me your bank details. I'll send some more.' The Billionaire never judged the rate at which his dollars disappeared. 'In the meantime, are you home tomorrow afternoon?'

'I'll be wherever you want me,' I said, ever ready to drop my life to fit in with his.

'We'll send the driver over with an envelope to tide you over.'

'Thank you. Do you want to see my new apartment?'

'It's a one bedroom?'

'Yes.'

'In a doorman building?'

'Yes.'

'I can picture it,' he said. 'Keep going with that paper, and don't forget – kiss.'

'Right, kiss … When can I see you?'

'I told you I'm busy. Okay?'

'Okay.' Mine was a hollow okay, because I wasn't. I desperately needed the Billionaire's money, but I wanted him.

Keep It Simple Stupid was the advice I needed. I returned to my paper and simplified ideas flowed miraculously onto the page. By three o'clock, while eating wild rice with sultanas and tomato salad, I'd written 14,000 words. I carried on working long after I'd worked through the food and was writing still when pink and orange melted through the surface of the night sky. I switched off my desk lamp to watch dawn light transform my white-walled apartment. Three hours and 1,000 words to go.

At nine-thirty, my paper finished, I ran for the Madison Avenue bus clutching five $1 bills – all the money I had until the Billionaire's chauffeur dropped off the cash. It was enough for a return train fare from the station at 125th Street where I often caught the overland train, because it was quicker than travelling from Grand Central on 45th. But Harlem made me uneasy. Once a cab driver had refused to take me there and I was always the only white girl on the street. I'd walk with a steady pace, my heart beating fast, everybody staring, every time.

That morning I stood in the ticket queue and a tall thin man in a long wool overcoat stood so close I could smell the nature of his life. I stared ahead, but he was determined to be noticed. He stepped in front of me holding a piece of paper beneath his chin, daring me to read: 'Rozes is red, vilits is blue, honee is sweet, an I wanna fuck you.'

I stepped closer to the ticket desk as the line went down, but the man stepped too, reciting his poem in a monotone, followed by a sinister, 'Sister, can you spare a dime?'

'I don't have a dime,' I said, 'Sorry.'

I felt instantly safer when I reached the ticket counter, even though I was on the wrong side of its opaque bulletproof glass, scratched as skated ice.

'Return, please.'

'$4.80,' said a muffled voice belonging to a person I couldn't see.

Fumbling for my precious one-dollar bills, I dropped one and bending to pick it up was shocked to find at my feet a figure wrapped head to toe in dirty white bandages. He had raced across the floor, in spite of an amputated leg and one arm in a sling, and held his prize – my dollar bill – in his dark full mouth. It was impossible to tell whether he was man or boy, but either way, he should have been in hospital. Through the holes in the bandages that encased his face his frightened eyes hypnotized mine until he scuttled off like a crab on broken claws, back to his blanket beneath the pay phone. I bought a one way ticket.

After that morning's class, summer school was over and I walked up the hill towards the library. I had been counting on the American heir for a ride back to the city, but he had not turned up to class – presumably his way of dealing with an unfinished final paper – and borrowing a few dollars from the librarian was my only hope.

'Hey, doll, hold up.' I turned to see Erinoula, and waited while she lit a cigarette. 'Can I have your number? We can go for coffee when I'm in the city.' She said cawfee and held her cigarette in red painted lips as she hunted for a pen. 'I'm going into Manhattan if you want a ride.'

Erinoula chatted nervously as we walked to the car park, 'I used to have a BMW. Can't believe I own this Ford. It's a shit car,' she said, opening the passenger door for me.

I wasn't bothered about the make of Erinoula's car, so long as I got back in time to pick up the Billionaire's special delivery. I negotiated my way under the automatic seat belt, shut the door, and was clicked into place. It was at least 120 degrees inside the car and I felt like a trussed chicken on a slow roast as we drove down the freeway into a long line of traffic heading south.

We stopped at a set of lights and bare-chested boys appeared with rags and bottles of water, threatening to clean the windows.

'No. I said NO!' Erinoula shouted. 'No change, guys,' she said, putting on the windscreen wipers, shaking her head, holding up her palms as they squirted the glass anyway. Defeated, Erinoula switched off the wipers. The expressionless boys worked vigorously, polishing and squirting, and when they finished, the light was still red. They wanted their money. Erinoula pushed twenty-five cents through a crack in the window, careful not to touch the black kid, as he tried to reach his bony fingers into the car.

'Thanks a lot for nothing. No means no, guys,' she said. But the boys didn't move. They wanted more money. 'Here, give them this,' I gave her my last dollar, which she threaded through the window as we drove off.

'Crazy, paying them to piss on your windscreen. Cos that's what it is. It's not water in those bottles. It's pure piss.'

Erinoula took the traffic, the street kids and the heat personally, and as much as I wanted to belong, I felt no more than an observer on the sidelines of her city. It would take more than a month at summer school and a fancy address for me to become a New Yorker.

'I can't believe the AC's packed up in August. Why not January?' Erinoula whined on, then slapped her steering wheel and squawked. 'Gahd, I'm a miserable bitch. I mean, go on, tell me I'm a miserable fuckin' bitch.' I chuckled but didn't have the guts to agree, and anyway, since joking about it, her moaning wasn't so bad. She gave up fiddling with the air conditioning, lit another cigarette and pushed a Julio Iglesias tape into the cassette player.

'I mean, this guy, he looks adorable, but listen to those words. "Of all the girls I loved before." Could be my ex-husband. He couldn't keep his hands off the girls.'

'You were married?'

'Stupid me, right, believing in happy ever after.'

'I did.'

'Gahd, you must have been a child bride. At least you escaped with a fat divorce settlement to put you through school.'

'There was no settlement.' Immediately I regretted not going along with her notion of a settlement, which would have been much easier than trying to explain the awful truth.

'So who's paying for your life?'

'A friend,' I said evasively, but my concealment didn't fool her.

'Good girl. So you got yourself a sugar daddy.'

'Rich men don't make you happy.'

'Men don't make women happy full stop. But their money does.'

'That's not true.'

'Then you haven't had a rich man.'

'You don't know the men I've had.'

'You mean there *is* a rich guy?'

I said nothing, relieved that we were at the top of my street. Erinoula pulled the car over. 'Hey, doll, before you go, what are the three most important words in the English language.'

I kept quiet. Somehow I knew not to say, 'I love you.'

'Send the cheque,' she said. 'And the two most beautiful words are "cheque enclosed".' She repeated 'cheque enclosed', punctuating the air with her index finger. We laughed. 'So, did he send the cheque?'

'He doesn't have to. It's going on standing order.'

'Standing order,' she whispered as though repeating a sacred mantra for the first time. 'Forget "cheque enclosed". "Standing order": they're the ones. No more waiting for Mr Postman.' She mimed a furtive hunt in an empty envelope.

'He spends money but no time and that makes me sad.'

'Baby doll, I'm sorry. I know what it's like when you love and there's no love coming back. I've done that. Watch out for that cynical Mr Snake squirming right now in the pit of your stomach, because if you feed him, he'll wrap around your heart strong as a python, and what chance will love have then? See, doll, I've prayed for love, and sometimes I got it, but in the end, the only thing that never let me down was money.'

While running for my cash delivery, I dismissed Erinoula's words because she seemed bitter. Love may have let her down, but I still had faith that if I waited patiently, the Billionaire would realize he loved me and come to find me. Until that day, I would accept his money.

I prayed that if I had missed the chauffeur, he would have left the package in my absence. When I saw the doorman on duty was the eccentric Italian American who plucked his eyebrows and often had traces of red nail varnish beneath his cuticles, I panicked. He could easily have turned my package away. I said hello, but he was busy, head down and miles away. I peered over the counter. He had covered tiny pieces of paper with black biro cubes, traced and retraced, each line repeated and within each box was writing, 'I must, I must, I must.'

'Did a packet arrive for me?'

He settled his eyes above my head so that he was seeing but not looking at me, 'Somebody came by.'

'Did they leave anything for me?'

'Sure, miss, sure they did.' He disappeared to the storeroom behind the desk and returned holding a padded A4 envelope.

I waited until I was in the elevator, then tore open the envelope. A sales brochure for the latest Gulfstream jet had been used to conceal a smaller envelope containing $10,000. I fanned through the glossy pages searching for a note, for the words that would make sense of it all, but found nothing. The Billionaire had been too busy to send more than money. Once again I was rich, but that evening, with no homework, no deadlines and three weeks before the start of the Fall term, I was lonely.

❖

'I didn't expect you to stick it out,' said the Lord.

'Why?'

'New York in August is unbearable … and I'm missing you

terribly, darling.' There was silence on the line. I didn't want to encourage him. 'So I'm coming to see you.'

'When?'

'Wednesday.'

'*This* Wednesday?'

'Yes, my flight gets in around seven.'

'You can't stay with me.'

'I've arranged to stay with a friend,' he said, his counter-attack in place. 'Darling, promise you'll see me,' he said softly, his voice falling away. 'Darling, are you there? Tell me you'll see me. I need to see you.'

'Of course I'll see you,' I said, trying not to cry.

'Good. Now I'll be able to sleep.'

The Lord's plan to see me may have helped his night's sleep, but it disturbed mine. He had always found it easy to love me when we were apart, and then lose sight of me once we were together. Now I understood that this sad state seemed to correlate directly with my ability to lose sight of myself whenever I was in love with him, or any man.

As the day of the Lord's arrival approached, I feared his visit would loosen the tenuous roots I had put down in the city. Forging my own life in New York was tougher than falling in line with the life of another. I imagined a sweet future with the Lord in which I bore his name, possibly his child, and accepted the identity bestowed upon me as his Lady.

The Lord called me the minute he arrived at the Park Avenue apartment of his friend, a French comtesse and ex-lover he had known longer than I had been alive. She was elegant, still beautiful and more than happy to have him as her guest. In his honour she held a dinner to which she invited her most entertaining New York friends – and me. The comtesse understood that winning me back was the purpose of the Lord's visit, but while she appeared to go along with his plan, she did not abandon her own. She was determined to have the Lord for herself and during the dinner she placed him on her right, and me out of his sight between two distractingly eligible men. One was fair, cerebral and good-looking in an intense, masculine way. The other had darker features, with the body of a Greek statue and unfortunately the brains of one too. It was The Cerebral Mr X who captivated me and, when he discreetly asked for my telephone number, I couldn't resist giving it to him.

The Lord spent every waking hour of his stay in the city with me but I had no difficulty in keeping my distance because The Cerebral Mr X was on my mind. He didn't call that week, or the week after that, but the possibility that he would gave me reason to hope. I took perverse pleasure in the Lord's company now that I no longer needed him to love me, and my confidence grew as I showed him around Manhattan, feeling the strength of his desire without succumbing to it. My independence and unavailability convinced the Lord that I was his true love and standing in the queue to enter the Statue of Liberty, he whispered, 'Marry me.'

Although I had prepared for this proposal and my rejection of it, when I heard the Lord say those words I was surprisingly moved and not at all sure how to react. That evening, on the steps of my building, beneath the gaze of my inquisitive doormen, I relented to more lingering than I had previously allowed when kissing the Lord goodbye.

All this was very unsettling, and as soon as I got back to my apartment I called Erinoula, asking her to meet me the following morning.

'Go on, marry him. So what he's older?' she said, ordering her third black coffee.

'I thought my feelings for him were over long ago,' I said.

'He still gets to you. You look nervous when you say his name.'

'Do I? But that doesn't mean I love him, does it?'

'I don't know what it means. One thing's fer sure, if you didn't like him, you'd have told him to fuck off, and this proposal would never have happened.'

'I did want to marry him once.'

'That's typical. A woman waits years for a man to say marry me and the moment she no longer wants him, he's incontinent, pissing proposals left, right and centre.'

'It's such a mess.'

'Sure is, because he's the one isn't he? The one who pays. That's why you've got no choice baby doll, not if you want to keep your apartment. I mean the thirtieth floor? You weren't exactly working to a tight budget. Nobody in your building earns less than half a million dollars after tax. So tell this Lord you'll marry him but don't fix a date.' She lit another cigarette. 'And if you don't want to be Lady Ladida call it off once you graduate.'

'He doesn't pay for anything.'

Erinoula puffed in silence for a thoughtful second. 'Let me get this straight. The old Lord doesn't pay.'

'No.'

'And you don't want to see him?'

'Not in the way he wants.'

'Then, honey, you've got a whole different set of problems. Forget this guy. Therapy's what you need. But he's a real lord, you say?' She looked at my half-eaten slice of carrot cake. 'Are you going to eat that?' I pushed the plate in her direction, and she dipped her fork into the cream cheese.

'That he's a lord is not the point. He is an extraordinary person who has proved that it is possible for a man to change. Perhaps I should marry him.'

'Thank you, my lord,' Erinoula mimicked my English accent. 'Thank you for having me.'

'We haven't had sex for ages!'

'If you say so, but be prepared with prophylactics because his lordship didn't fly three thousand miles just to see the Statue of Liberty.'

For the rest of his trip the Lord appeared to have forgotten that he had asked to marry me – until it was time for our goodbye.

The comtesse's chauffeur watched his rear view mirror as the Lord walked towards me with open arms. 'So this is it,' he said. 'You don't want me.'

'If only I could believe –' He didn't let me finish.

'Things change,' he said, 'but my love never will.'

Seven

The Director and The Actor

In New York City, sooner or later, talk comes down to money, and because accounting for mine was complicated, I avoided the other residents in my building. But my self-imposed solitary confinement was brought to an abrupt end the day I met my neighbours in the elevator.

'You're new here, right?' asked the woman, whose perfect pale skin was flattered by black glossy hair, and black fitted everything else.

'About six months,' I said, admiring her Birkin bag.

'And we haven't spoken. This is incredible,' said her husband, in an accent from no known country. He was small and fat and somehow shy, while she was whippet thin and direct. Neither was drawn to conversation, which was a relief. The elevator doors opened, we walked to our respective doors and I thought I'd escaped, when the woman called over her shoulder. 'Come to dinner sometime.'

'Why not tonight?' said her husband.

Unable to come up with a fast enough reason not to, half an hour later I was in their penthouse admiring 1920s furniture and exclusive views of Madison Avenue.

'So what do you do?' asked Max, reclining on the sofa beneath a line-up of paintings by Gaugin, Monet and Modigliani.

'I'm a student.'

'Studying what?' he asked, hoovering up a bowl of cashews.

'Today film.'

'Carla, did you hear that? She's a film-maker.'

'No kidding. What? Directing? Producing?' asked Carla, walking in with three champagne flutes and a bottle of Cristal. 'Max? Cashews! Two hundred calories per ounce.' She faced me, rolled her eyes at her husband and said, 'Sorry. Did you say acting? My God. Max, don't you think she looks like an actress?'

'I'm a student. I just sat through Torelli's four-hour masterpiece,' I said.

'So you know Vincenzo Laborio?' asked Carla.

'Torelli's cameraman who shot the epic?'

'Exactly. He's shooting a film here. Max, let's get him over for dinner.'

Incredibly Carla summoned one of the world's greatest cinematographers, who duly arrived for dinner carrying a bag of take-out from the 2-star Japanese restaurant across the street.

'I know how you love their salmon fishcakes with caviar,' he said, searching for cutlery, at home in Carla's kitchen.

'He also knows I don't cook,' said Carla, winking at me.

'Don't believe it. She's a fantastic cook. She simply won't,' said Max, placing the food on the finest Italian plates.

Vincenzo was dishevelled-looking with a wide smile and mischievous eyes. He may have looked like an old man but he was youthfully enthusiastic about camera angles in Torelli's work – the subject of my film paper that week.

After dinner, while Carla prepared jasmine tea she told me

about the film Vincenzo was shooting for a famous director who just happened to be her brother. She seemed almost excited (this being the Upper East Side where exuberance was restrained) at the prospect of introducing me. 'Vincenzo adores you. You should go watch him work, and meet his director.'

'Won't the director mind?'

'Mind? Are you kidding? I'll tell him to expect you.'

Carla turned out to be a woman of formidable influence. Within twenty-four hours she had arranged for me to enter the almost impenetrable set of the one of the world's most significant movie directors. I found myself standing on a roof-top in mid-town Manhattan watching a late-night love scene between a couple who couldn't live together, couldn't live apart and had returned to the site of their first kiss to say goodbye.

'Take twenty-six,' said the weary clapper boy.

'And ... action,' enthused the assistant director, as if to convince the actors, but for the next five takes even I could see they lacked vigour. The actress, Felicity Manners, famous for her marriage to the famous director, reproduced exactly the same flat performance each time.

'Let's break,' said a quiet voice close by, his words repeated by the assistant director for all to hear. The set dissolved and, turning to the tall, gently spoken man beside me, I found myself face to face with Ms Manners' husband. I was struck, but not star struck, because while half the Western world could quote from this director's movies, I hadn't seen a single one. The Director had shaved dark hair threaded with grey, almond shaped eyes and a drip on the end of his nose, which he wiped with a yellow handkerchief.

'Remind me, no night shoots in my next film. I forget they give me a cold,' he said, turning up his coat collar and sneezing. An assistant appeared with three cups of steaming tea, and I stood between Vincenzo and the Director, watched by suspicious members of the crew, jealous as courtiers around their sovereign.

The Director was keen to talk nevertheless and led me away from prying eyes to the concrete stairwell where we warmed our hands on an old radiator.

'I brought my wife here for our first date and warned her we were going somewhere cold and quiet – she thought I was taking her to a morgue. I laughed. He smiled, then his face was expressionless again. 'I hear you're a student.'

'Yes. I'm studying film and philosophy.'

'Forget university. If you want to study film I'll teach you. You're welcome any time to watch us work.' Which is what I did every week from then on, and gradually the crew accepted that I was a feature of the Director's set.

While the Director was an imposing physical presence, towering above everyone else, he was fundamentally shy and this helped to preserve a formality and politeness between us. Unfortunately this did not convince Ms Manners who, as I was to later understand, had always doubted that my motives were purely filmic. She tolerated me through the making of one movie, but when I was there for another, it was more than she could do to contain her resentment. Loyal members of the crew waited with anticipation, counting down the days when Ms Manners would finally explode.

❖

My darling sister

Your letter arrived this morning. Don't worry, I understand that you've decided not to come to New York. My loss is your boyfriend's gain, and of course you must go with him to Hawaii.

I had hoped to take you on the set when you were here, but that's probably no longer a prospect even for me. Ms Manners screeched at me this morning in front of everyone. I turned up as usual to watch them shooting and she was preparing for her close up. In the scene she had to talk to her therapist on a diamond-encrusted telephone while soaking in the bath, so the key members of the crew – and me – crammed into a bathroom in a luxurious apartment on Park Avenue. It may have been a big bathroom, but it was a tiny set. Vincenzo had designed the most flattering light, make-up and hair were outdoing themselves, doting on Ms Manners, and while her husband waited, he told me to look through the camera. I was at the viewfinder when he whispered, 'I can't think about my work today. The colours you're wearing, everything about you is perfect for one of my movies.'

He made me feel quite the muse, which was odd because I was only wearing an old grey skirt, green roll-neck and black boots, while his wife was semi-naked and at her most glorious in the tub, with bubbles strategically placed. She had a lot on her mind, with a page of dialogue to deliver, but her antennae were up and she understood that if ever she was going to act, now was the time. She screeched, loud enough for the whole of Park Avenue to hear, 'Get that girl out of my eye-line. Close the set.'

From now on I'm going to avoid the set if she's around, and stick to the edit suite for my film education. I love going there. Sometimes the Director is curious to know what I think of a cut, but most of the time I watch in silence and we talk later, walking up town. He is certainly strange-looking, almost a giant who either whispers or shouts – but I like him.

When we talk together it can be intimidating, and not just because I do kind of fancy him. Yesterday he told me it was time to decide whether I wanted to write, act or direct. 'I think I'd like to act,' I mumbled. I felt self-conscious having a what-do-you-want-to-do-in-film talk with such a famous film-maker. He was very straightforward about it all and said writing me into a film was the easy part. I can't believe its going to be that *easy, but who knows, perhaps I will be in his next movie. He gave me a Big Tip about acting, telling me to know my limitations and never try too hard. 'Never more than this,' he said, passing his hand back and forth between us, as if to say, never more effort than a conversation in real life. His office called me this morning and gave me the telephone number of his favourite acting coach. Classes are on every week, and anybody can show up. I'll let you know how it goes.*

All my love, California girl.

❖

It took me a while to find the right door on 42nd street, because there seemed to be plenty of grey doors without numbers, and by the time I got to the acting class I was ten minutes late. The enteric groans the other side of the classroom door almost sent me running but, determined to show the Director I was serious about being an actress, I stepped inside. About twenty people had set up individual spaces and were either talking to themselves or sitting in chairs, rolling their heads and moaning, some with tortuous intensity. It looked like a scene from *One Flew Over the Cuckoo's Nest.* A woman in her mid-fifties, dressed in a red shellsuit and sling-backs, scrutinized the class through heavy, black-rimmed spectacles, apparently oblivious to the young man beside her taking off his trousers.

'A private moment,' she said, catching my bug eyes as I walked towards her. The man, now stark naked apart from cowboy boots, began to sing a lullaby, swaying side to side. My mouth dropped open and I was about to laugh when the coach snapped, 'Who sent you?'

I gave the Director's name.

'Really,' she said flatly, her eyebrows quivering nevertheless. 'I've taught most of his actresses. Do you know the Method?' I shook my head.

'The first step is relaxation,' she said, then proceeded to tell me how. It sounded simple enough, although what it had to do with acting wasn't so obvious. I took a fold-up wooden chair to the furthest corner of the room, closed my eyes to shut out the people around me and tried to relax. After ten minutes I was lost in a world of my own when somebody grabbed my knee. I screamed and opened my eyes to discover the coach shaking my leg.

'Let go of the tension. Stop holding on,' she urged, until finally I did and my floppy foot was gently returned to the floor. My neck, arms, and hands were given similar treatment, and then I received my first exercise.

'Pass an imaginary warm cup over your entire body,' she said.

'With my clothes on?' I panicked.

'What do you think?' she said without a smile and stomped off.

I held the fictitious cup, passing it over my body again and again, checking my watch every few minutes, desperate for the session to end. After twenty minutes it was a relief when the teacher called her students to sit in a circle. There were a few monosyllabic models, and a brilliant nebbish guy, a waiter, who amused the class with observations on the wasteland that had been his private moment. Then it was my turn.

'How was it?' the teacher asked.

'Fine …' I began, containing an urge to run from the room, sitting stone still, monosyllabic myself.

'I said pass the cup over your body. I want to see you use the whole instrument, pass the cup everywhere, between your legs, across your breasts. Stop playing safe.'

My body no longer felt part of me and I wondered whether this had always been so. Or perhaps it was just a consequence of the teacher's insistence that my body was 'an instrument', which made it seem like some kind of kitchen utensil. By the time the teacher had critiqued her students' private moments, the idea of learning to act seemed ridiculous. But as much as I wanted to leave, I didn't. How could I expect the Director to take me seriously if I hadn't been able to stick out one acting class with a tutor he had recommended. Begrudgingly I sat at the back of the class and watched students perform scenes, or improvise – hardly noticing two hours pass by. Everyone who worked was energized and committed and I understood that if I was prepared to be dedicated, this was where I too could learn to act.

I began to live for the Monday evening acting class, as educational as any of my university courses, but my passion for acting confused my friend Erinoula.

'The Method, or whatever you call it, sounds like it taps into the unconscious, which is powerful, possibly harmful stuff. I don't get why you love it so much. You'd be better off going to therapy,' she said.

'Well, I don't understand your obsession with nineteenth-century thinkers and mental illness, when you could be reading Plato *in Greek*,' I said to Erinoula.

'I hate the Greeks. All that baklava. They're disgusting.'

'I'm talking Ancient Greeks, they're the ones.'

'They're all the same – a bunch of misogynistic pederasts.'

I didn't push Erinoula to explain, but a week later her reason for rejecting her forefathers became clear when I received a dawn call.

'I need to talk,' said Erinoula, choking back tears. 'Can you be at the café at seven?'

She stirred her steamy American coffee at our usual table, her eyes red from crying.

'My stepdad's a Greek tragedy. Last night he came into my bedroom at three o'clock to give me this.'

She pushed a scrap of paper across the table.

'I luv you, golden girl. I want sex with you, my honey,' he had written with a blunt pencil that had scratched a hole in the page.

'I'd like to tell him to go to hell, but God's arranged that. He's got testicular cancer. The jerk. Can't he see a sign from the good Lord when it's given? I mean my poor mom. Every night I go home, he's hanging around like a lovesick puppy. It sucks.'

The image of Erinoula's step father creeping around her bed in the middle of the night made me feel ill and heard myself say, 'You can stay with me for a while if you like.' Erinoula looked wide-eyed. 'Sleep in my sitting room.'

'I gave up a good salary for my city apartment to study for my degree. Going home wasn't meant to be this hard.'

'I mean it. Move in until things calm down.'

'That will be the day he dies. But perhaps it would do for me to stay a few weeks.'

Erinoula made herself at home with ominous ease. She filled my fridge with feta, olives and, on Fridays, a box of the infamous baklava. She bought a coffee-maker for black American on tap, smoked Virginia Slims, 'just the one, doll, twice a day', and scrutinized my life from my dining table.

When Felix, an actor from class, came by to rehearse, he received instant censure.

'What are you doing with a guy like that?' she said, when he disappeared to the bathroom.

'We're doing a scene together.'

'What kind of scene would that be?'

'Most scenes are love scenes of some sort,' I said.

'Right.' She laughed, her mouth twisting.

'Anyway, I like Felix.'

'Yeah, cos he looks like Jimmy Dean.'

'And he can act?

'Yeah, cos he's psychotic. I wouldn't rehearse alone with him if I were you.'

'We usually rehearse here and it's fine. But don't worry, we'll go to the café tonight.'

'Thanks. I couldn't bear to watch you two "doing a scene",' she said, her laugh catching like a cough in the back of her throat.

Felix was equally condemning of Erinoula, 'up there on her fat ass, living in your flat, criticizing your life.' He said 'flat' in a flat imitation of my English.

'She's in a bit of trouble,' I said.

'So will you be if you're not careful,' he said, holding the door for me as we walked into the intimate café.

He played a love-struck boarding schoolboy to my housemaster's wife who keeps her affection for him secret. I admired Felix's intuition for suggesting we play this scene from *Tea and Sympathy*, but never revealed it could have been one from my own life.

'You should be with a girl your own age,' I said in character.

'But I want you. You're the only one I want,' he said, touching my fingers, tears in his eyes. Our characters were virtuously restrained, but in the back of my mind I had bad thoughts about my acting partner that made me feel good.

'Need the table if you're not eating.' A waitress stood over us and kicked us out of the café back to reality just in time.

'That felt real enough to me,' said Felix, getting onto his motorbike. 'If we can produce that in class, we'll blow them away.' He winked at me, pulled on his helmet and screeched down Madison – the one-way avenue heading uptown. Driving into oncoming traffic was Felix's idea of fun.

I returned to my flat to find Erinoula eating olives, puffing on a cigarette, blowing smoke out of the three-inch crack that was my open window – we were so high up that a wide-open window would have been an invitation to suicide. She was studying one of her psychology texts, so for a while we didn't speak, until, apropos of nothing, she said, 'While you were with that punk improvising love Daddy Warbucks phoned.'

'Daddy Warbucks?'

'Yeah, Mr Standing Order.'

'Did you speak to him?'

'No. He's on the machine – best place for him if you ask me. He sounds like a robot.'

'I can't believe I missed him.'

'If you had real love for a real man, you'd know that improvising in cafés with poverty stricken lover boys was for the birds. I bet you paid for his double cappuccino.'

Too irritated to ask how she'd guessed that, I hit the play button. 'I'm in Paris. Come to the hotel this weekend. I'll book you a room.' I re-played the Billionaire's message, searching for hidden emotion. There wasn't any.

'Paris. Ooh la la,' laughed Erinoula. 'And which hotel would that be?'

'The Ritz.'

'How come he's so rich?'

'He's dedicated to making money.'

I picked up the receiver to dial British Airways, but stopped. Felix and I were meant to perform our scene in class that Monday, the Director had a Saturday screening of a rough cut of his latest movie, and my neighbours and Vincenzo had invited me to lunch on Sunday. With pounding heart I called the Billionaire's hotel to tell him that I couldn't make Paris because —

'Never explain, you know that,' he interrupted. 'Here's my direct line in case you change your mind.'

As soon as we hung up I was full of remorse and, hastily dialled his number. The line was busy. I tried again. And again – for the next hour. Every time his telephone was engaged. Finally I went to bed, despondent and rejected.

It wasn't until the following morning, over an uplifting cup of coffee, that I realized that if anyone felt rejected it was the Billionaire. Suddenly I feared the consequences of my blunt refusal to join him. He paid for my liberty and I had put everything in my life at risk for one rebellious moment. My thoughts spiralled obsessively as I imagined my allowance being cut off, leaving me without money for rent, let alone the $30,000 a year for my university fees. In the end the Billionaire's punishment was meted out more subtly. For months, perhaps even a year, every time my telephone rang, somewhere in the back of my mind, I would want it to be him. But the Billionaire never called me again with love, or the prospect of it, on his mind, and eventually I understood that there was nothing more than a standing order between us.

My regrets about not going to Paris were eased when Felix and I impressed our acting teacher. She had kept us working on the same scene for months. At last I wasn't performing it, it was performing me, as though I were no longer 'acting'.

'Excellent, both of you. Fantastic. Now, get on with something else,' she said.

Felix was keen to work on another part of the play, but once we'd finished I was aware of how emotional it had been for me to work on that scene, mixing as it did my past and present feelings into a cocktail of confusion. Unsure that I could face a love scene with Felix, or anyone, I decided to work on my private moment with the imaginary cup. It seemed safer. Felix was popular in class I was sure he'd start work straight away with another student. But the weeks went by and he didn't rehearse and then he started to miss class. I saw him one midnight when he came by my apartment building, drunk on his motorbike. I had gone down to meet him because Erinoula was sleeping – and I had almost invited him up, but the friendly doorman on duty had shaken his finger behind Felix's head as if to say 'don't even think about it'. A few weeks later Felix played the whole of 'Ventura Highway' on his guitar, singing the words on to my answer machine. Erinoula enjoyed analysing that one. 'Yeah, I bet a free wind blows right through his head. In one ear and out the other.'

Erinoula convinced me that it was time to 'set a boundary', and on the way to class, I rehearsed her line about Felix's 'inappropriate use of the phone'. I planned to skip the umbilical cord analogy and tell him, even though she'd warned me not to, that I liked his song and hadn't deleted it.

But Felix didn't saunter into class that night with his cheeky half-smile and I was thinking it never felt quite right when he wasn't there, when the teacher said, 'Felix is dead. He shot himself last night.' The room fell into deep silence.

I left class early, unable to face actors acting, and walked all the way home, grateful that I didn't live alone in New York City and that Erinoula was in my flat on her fat ass, reading and smoking. I was even grateful for her running commentary on my life.

'Here, listen to this,' she said as I walked in. 'Freud wrote: "Psychoanalytic therapy", blah, blah, blah, "consists in the liberation of the human being from his neurotic symptoms, inhibitions and abnormalities of character." Liberation, baby doll. You won't get that from acting, let me tell you.'

Too tired to contradict her and also to avoid her self-righteous conversation, I turned into the kitchen in search of consoling food. I opened the fridge (more like a Greek deli each passing day) and with my back to Erinoula said, 'Felix killed himself.'

'Hate to say this, but no big surprise, right? His behaviour was symptomatic. Gahd, there we were setting boundaries when we should have been getting him committed. Do you know how he did it?'

I found her professional interest ghoulish, without a trace of compassion.

'So, how did he do it? Don't say you don't know.' Erinoula was up from her book, standing in the kitchen with her cigarette. I brushed past her, going to bed without even saying goodnight, surprised at the perverse pleasure it gave me to deny her details she would have loved to analyse. Because Felix had shot himself in the mouth, lying on his childhood bed, leaving his brains splattered across the wall for his mother to discover.

I curled up into a ball, covering my whole body with the blankets, and I wept. Then I lay awake the whole night wondering what I could have done to save him.

❖

'So you like older men,' said the Director coolly, after I'd turned up at a screening holding hands with Vincenzo. After the death of Felix and a cooling of my friendship with Erinoula, I had spent more time with the master cinematographer. Our conversations were in French – to overcome Vincenzo's bad English and my bad Italian – and film was our favourite subject. Our times together were edifying and always fun. I could not think of him as old and told the Director so.

'He's *sixty-three*,' the Director protested.

'He told me fifty-three,' I said, instantly embarrassed to have been so easily fooled.

'Even if he wasn't lying, that's not young for a woman your age. Are you looking for a father figure?'

'If I am, it hasn't worked.'

'Why don't you date younger guys?'

'What for? What would I learn?'

'How to be yourself. But I've heard you go for men in mid-life crises. Surely relationships are complicated enough.'

The Director then went on to suggest spectacular men for me, all of whom he knew and could have introduced to me. It took some time for me to realize it was my reaction to these men that interested him rather than the reality of helping me become the first Mrs Hugh Grant, or Mrs Vigo Mortensen or better still, Mrs Johnny Depp. Just thinking about these men was enough to convince me that the Director was right. And as soon as I was ready to date a man the sunny side of forty-five, with divine timing, the perfect candidate appeared.

I had been sitting in the circle at my acting class no longer than a minute when I sensed a different presence and, glancing up, found a tall slim man staring at me. He had Marlon Brando eyes, brushed his dark hair casually back and was, I guessed, my age or even younger. He wore jeans, white T-shirt, black boots – the classic clothes for Method actors since the fifties – and was at that moment the most beautiful man I had ever seen. The whole class was captivated when he spoke. He smiled when he told the teacher he had acted in theatres across America, and he seemed proud when he said he was from California. And I could feel the difference that made. He didn't have the hard edge of the city in him.

When the teacher told him to pair up for a scene, I turned away; there were so many pretty actresses in our class I didn't want to see who she would put him with. 'Start on a scene the two of you,' she said. There was silence until my neighbour nudged me. I looked up. 'Yes, you two. Pair up for some Chekhov. *Uncle Vanya.* Improvise for next week.'

After class the young man from California and I stood on 42nd Street. 'Let's meet at your place first,' I said, wanting to delay Erinoula's scrutiny and the Actor's questions about my luxury East Side life.

'You don't mind coming to Hell's Kitchen?' he said. I was looking up at him, in effect holding my mouth up to his, and the thought of a kiss flickered through me. 'Is that okay?' he said.

'I'm sorry. What did you say?'

'Hell's Kitchen. It's where I live.'

❖

When my taxi reached the Actor's part of town I regretted my burberry mac's bright whiteness, which insulted the grim reality of Hell's Kitchen. The cab pulled up outside the Actor's brownstone. Leaning against the wall in a sliver of sun on the opposite side of the street were twenty or so people of various shapes and sizes doing nothing but staring. Looking more carefully, I noticed the sign about their heads: 'New York's Home for the Mentally Impaired (1952)'. The residents were catching a few rays and some of them waved and smiled as I ran from the cab to ring the Actor's doorbell.

I took the stairs to the Actor's apartment two at a time, passing doors that had been axed, boarded up, then axed again, side-stepping a young woman with fine greasy hair, slumped and sleepy on the stairs who half smiled and said, 'I'm waitin', waitin' on a friend.' And all the time the Actor watched me wind my way to the top.

'A white girl in a white coat. Not the best look for this part of town,' he said, taking the mac from me and hanging it behind his front door.

The apartment was long and one room wide. A tiny kitchen at the back had a sash window that opened onto a fire escape on which the Actor had set a circular table. The sitting room was bare apart from a television, a battered chaise longue balanced on bricks and a pink plastic seat with attached hooded hair-dryer.

'What did you do, raid a fifties hair salon?'

'It's all from the street,' he said, leading me up onto the roof where we decided to rehearse because it was hot and there was so little air inside.

We sat on the edge of the roof, on the ledge, reading lines from *Uncle Vanya* back and forth until we got beyond the words. Hours went by until we realized that we hadn't eaten all day. Starving hungry, we ran down for a Chinese $1 take-out and returned to the roof to eat and talk; his brother, my sister, England, California, the plays he'd done, and my desire to act in one of the Director's films. We talked through dusk and the fading day. We talked as the Manhattan lights came up, until one in the morning when a light rain began to fall.

'I'd better go home,' I said. We were standing in his kitchen and something about that enclosed space made me suddenly self-conscious and quite nervous.

'You'll get mugged round here looking for a cab in that coat,' he laughed, thankfully more relaxed than I. 'I've got a spare room if you want to stay.'

A few minutes later I was lying in the Actor's spare bed, having borrowed one of his spare cotton shirts. 'Goodnight,' he called as he passed the door, heading for his own bedroom at the front of the house.

Although Method acting requires intimacy and trust, it was a rule that none of the actors in class had affairs. Kisses, no matter how passionate the scene, were strictly without tongues and I kept telling myself that my body, and the Actor's divine body come to that, were merely 'instruments'. I believed these phlegmatic reflections would induce sleep. They did not. I imagined telling the Director that he had been right to recommend younger men. I mused back and forth for hours until finally I lay in bed, nothing going on, particularly not sleep.

At six o'clock I crept into the kitchen, sat at the table and from a stack of poetry books picked the *Four Quartets* to read aloud, my attention sometimes drawn to bedraggled city birds clamouring at the feeder outside the window.

Go, said the bird, for the leaves were full of children,
Hidden excitedly, containing laughter.
Go, go, go, said the bird: human kind
Cannot bear very much reality.

'I love that part,' the Actor said, leaning in the doorway.

Embarrassed that he'd caught me in a world of my own whispering the words, I jumped up, pulling his shirt down to cover my bare thighs. 'I'd better be going,' I said.

'Don't you want breakfast?'

We took a long good walk to 17th and I left the white mac behind because finally it was time for me to fit in. In a café, drinking the smoothest coffee, the Actor said, 'Knowing you were in bed next door did my head in. I couldn't sleep.'

'Neither could I.'

'I'm glad it's not just me.' His eyes met mine over the top of the menu.

On the way back up town we passed a gallery and looked at photographs by Man Ray and André Kertész. Then the Actor took me to his local secondhand bookstore and picked up a collection of Neruda poems, which he read to me in Spanish when we got back to his apartment.

We agreed to meet the following evening and, once again, rehearsed on the roof. When it was time to eat, the Actor cooked. Midnight came and went and he handed me the shirt I'd worn the night before. We smiled at a ritual repeated and disappeared to our separate beds. Half an hour later I was still staring at the ceiling.

'Come and talk to me if you're awake,' he said from the other side of the wall, his voice not so loud to wake me if I had been asleep.

His double bed almost filled the room, and candlelit shadows played on the white pillows. 'If we can't sleep,' he said from the bed, 'we may as well talk.'

Nervous as a schoolgirl, I was glad to see a piano beneath the window. I asked the Actor to play for me and as he played, the electric storm which had been building up all day broke overhead.

'"Don't get me wrong,"' he sang, competing with the thunder, '"if I'm acting so distracted, I'm thinking about the fireworks that go off when you smile."' He sang on, flashes of white light filling the room every few seconds, until he reached the part about thunder and rain. 'I can't compete with this,' he said, pushing back his piano stool to stand. Then he was beside me, resting his hands on my hips, drawing me too him. 'Is this too much?' he whispered into my hair. He waited, but I didn't answer, and as if he'd read my mind he kissed me on the mouth.

I lay beside him on the bed. We kissed again. Talked a little. Then another kiss. The storm moved away from Manhattan. The telephone rang at the other end of the flat. 'There's nothing I want that's not right here,' he said, and we fell asleep, delaying the day we would become lovers.

❖

'Wow! How can you afford this?' the Actor said.

I wanted to say 'my parents', the way his helped him out with a few hundred dollars each month for his apartment, but he deserved the truth, even though I knew he wasn't going to like it.

'So you're his mistress?' he scowled, trying to make sense of my arrangement with the Billionaire.

'No. But he sends me money,' I winced.

'For nothing?'

'Yes. Or for what we had, or something like that.'

It was not an easy conversation and we agreed to end it and start rehearsing Chekhov – but we couldn't escape our feelings. The Actor was sulking and I was angry because he'd made me feel ashamed. 'It's not working today,' he said, stopping in the middle of the scene. We gave up pretending and gave in to our own drama. For a while we lay on the floor in silence, watching threads of cloud high in the clear blue sky.

'The doctor and Helena's relationship is about obstacles to love, particularly her old husband,' he said. 'How old's the guy paying for this place?'

'Twice my age, but he's not my husband, and I'll never be his wife.'

I said it with conviction, certain that I no longer loved the

Billionaire. 'I'm sorry this is what I come with,' I said softly.

'Why don't we forget it.'

'What? Rehearsing, or each other?' Stung I turned away from him, curling up on my side. Seconds later I felt his hand beneath my hair and I rolled onto my back.

'Let's get out of the city. We could drive to Woodstock. My car's a wreck, but it should get us there,' he said.

That afternoon we drove into the green, wide-rivered country. The day was hot and we parked by a river and took off our shoes and waded to a smooth boulder in the middle of the current. The Actor sat on the warm rock, and I hitched up my skirt to sit astride his lap. Cool water bathed our bare feet as he held my waist. My arms were around his shoulders, and he was strong and hard inside me. Once in a while a car drove by, but only one guessed our secret, the driver whistling from his window as he passed.

Later we drove into Woodstock to walk arm in arm down the high street. We should have known better than to smile at a broad- beamed woman sitting on a porch beneath a sign that said 'bric-a-brac'.

'Come in,' she insisted. 'Nothing I like more than newly-weds.' She led us through her cluttered treasure house, proposing objects for our new home, and we played along with the idea we were just married. But nothing tempted us until she held up a photograph of a young woman in a white dress sitting on the steps of a white wooden house.

'Give him this,' the bric-a-brac lady said, passing me the framed picture of the bare-toed beauty. The Actor wiped dust from the surface of the glass and I could tell he liked it.

'Six dollars,' she said, and I agreed it was a bargain. The frame was wrapped in newspaper, and when she handed it to me, the woman whispered, 'Hold onto him, they don't make 'em like that any more. Your man's a throwback, and don't you forget it.'

She should know, I thought: she's in the throwback business.

The Actor hung the photograph above his bed, where we spent many hours in those amorous days. He was the first man with whom I felt completely confident while naked. He even got me dancing around his apartment with no clothes on, and one sweltering summer's day we floated between the bed, the fridge and a cold shower without getting dressed at all.

Lovemaking filled our days and nights, until for no apparent reason, a stabbing pain rose up between my legs. I didn't tell the Actor and rationalized that it was nothing more serious than a consequence of having a boyfriend with a generously proportioned penis. But as the weeks went by, and the pain became more frequent, I secretly visited a gynaecologist. The doctor inspected me with a light strapped to his forehead, earnest as a miner at the coal face. When he had finished his investigation he announced, 'There is absolutely nothing wrong with you. You're a picture of health – you don't need to look so downhearted.'

'I was hoping you'd tell me what was wrong.'

'Do you know the most important sex organ?' he sighed.

I hesitated, feeling sure that I should.

'It's the brain. Sex is all in the mind. The best prescription for you would be a psychiatrist.'

By the end of that week I had found a Park Avenue Freudian analyst who listened with a serene expression as I described my stabbing pain. At the end of the session she gently suggested if my ailment had no physical foundation, perhaps analysis could help me uncover why my body appeared to be resisting the idea of having sex.

'Sex isn't a problem,' I insisted. 'I like having sex with the Actor, I really do.'

'But *do* you?' she smiled, enigmatically.

I chose not to see the psychiatrist again in the belief that living with the pain would be easier. And once I'd made that decision, it miraculously disappeared. Perhaps this also had something to do with my return to my own apartment. The bitter New York winter was setting in and Hell's Kitchen wasn't much fun in the cold.

I was keen to get back to the Upper East Side not simply because my apartment was warm. It was also free of cockroaches, mice – and Erinoula.

Erinoula had met the Actor and tried to turn me against him, at first with cynicism and, when that failed, by appealing to my insecurity. 'Thing is, doll, a woman should never date a guy who's more gorgeous than her. You walk in a room, he's the one they'll be lookin' at, and that's not good.'

I knew the Actor amounted to more than looks, and Erinoula could not convince me to leave him, just as I could not convince her to leave me. Every time I tried to suggest that she should find another home in the city, she did not respond. Her books stayed stacked up on the window sill, her bedding folded by the futon, her make-up bag in my bathroom, her opinions wall-to-wall 24/7. Erinoula was entrenched.

But this standoff in our relationship shifted on a freezing night when, safely tucked up in my warm apartment, the Actor called to say goodnight. When he told me he had been without hot water in his building for three days, I insisted that he spend the night with me.

'Are you alone?'

'No.' I looked over at Erinoula watching the television. 'But don't let that put you off. She'll just have to get used to it,' I said.

When the Actor arrived he picked me up and hugged me. 'God, it's hot in here,' he laughed, the snow on his coat melting instantly.

Erinoula stood frozen in the middle of the living room. 'You could have warned me you had company. I'd have made other plans.'

'It's okay. We're going straight to bed. We won't get in your way.'

'Thanks, but no thanks. I'd rather be in New Jersey than stuck here with you love birds.' She gathered up her books, and stuffed them into her bag.

'Be careful, it's a blizzard out there,' the Actor said.

Some part of me felt guilty and wanted Erinoula to stay, but a bigger part felt relieved as I watched her edge out of my life, back to her own.

'Take care,' I said, as she walked to the door.

'Don't worry about me,' she muttered.

The next day when I got back from university, I noticed Erinoula's coffee-maker was missing. When I couldn't find her Tiffany's ashtray, I knew for sure that she had gone. She had dropped off my keys with the doorman, but there was no note of explanation. Erinoula left without goodbye and although our paths crossed at university a few times, we never spoke again, not even on our graduation day.

❖

With Erinoula out of the way, I tried to persuade the Actor to move in with me, but he struggled to accept comforts paid for by my mysterious billionaire. But where I failed, the New York weather triumphed. In the middle of December, the most severe snowstorm on record hit the city and the heating went down once again in the Actor's building. That same day he found the heroin addict from the floor below curled up dead on his doorstep. He had scooped her up and carried her frail cold body to her unmade bed, and called the police. And then he had called me.

'There's only so much reality I can take. I'm from California, for God's sake,' he said, unpacking his suitcase and hanging his clothes in my closet.

Finally he was ready to experience the alternative reality of the Upper East Side where we had doormen, maids in the laundry room, black nannies pushing pramloads of white babies and exotic flowers delivered on the hour. Everybody in the building smiled to see me with such a fine young man and nobody guessed that when he left with his keyboard he was heading to the subway to busk on 96th street where he could earn $50 on a good day. I didn't care that he wasn't rich. My studies continued, along with the standing order. These were happy days when I had money and believed in our love.

I remember the Actor's hands on my body every morning and every night. I remember poetry at breakfast with pancakes and maple syrup, American football in the Park, flying a red kite, finding a kitten in Strawberry Fields, washing our bodies with cleanser and cotton wool when his building was without water. I remember cooking Christmas dinner just the two of us, ice-skating at night at Rockefeller Center and meeting his mother who cried and I still don't know why. I remember the way he closed his eyes when he hit the high notes singing, and the audition I went to with him where all the men wore the same and almost looked the same. And I remember the day he gave me a flower on the street and said, 'I love you' and I couldn't say it back.

Even though the Actor had moved in, I assumed that we would carry on our lives much as before. The first resentment surfaced when I returned later than expected from a dinner with Vincenzo. I promised I'd be home earlier next time, but soon gave up on these dinners altogether because they upset my boyfriend too much. And our weekends weren't the same if I spent any time in the cutting room with the Director, and slowly I saw less of him too. Life was simpler when I devoted it to the Actor, so when The Cerebral Mr X called, some two years after getting my number, I turned down his invitation to the ballet. His wit and intelligence oozed down the phone and God knows I was tempted, but just in time I remembered that I had my date guaranteed Monday through Sunday. I wasn't about to dupe the Actor for a charming man who called once every seven hundred days.

While I appreciated the Actor's availability, it wasn't long before the familiarity between us felt tiresome and life seemed predictable. One afternoon, sitting at his keyboard staring out of the window, I asked the Actor what he was thinking and he said nothing.

'You mean you're not thinking *anything*?' This was the biggest surprise I'd had in days. 'I don't like to think much,' he said.

'What about all your poetry books?'

'It's the sound of the words, the rhythms, that I love,' he said.

I worried for the rest of the day that I was with an Adonis on to whom I had projected a carapace of intelligence. Eventually I calmed down. Perhaps not thinking was a Californian thing, or an art I had yet to master, and I resolved to stop thinking about the Actor not thinking. But our insecurities surfaced again early the following morning.

We were still in bed, drifting a bit before getting up. 'I had a dream last night,' he said, 'which I hardly ever do.'

My spirits lifted. Surely dreams were a sign of a reflective unconscious?

'What did you dream?' I asked, snuggling up to his warm naked body.

'Dream? It was more like a nightmare. One of the Billionaire's bodyguards was following me and I ran to my apartment to escape, except it was full of European girls like you. A man with a gun told me I'd entered the Billionaire's palace. The penalty was death. He cocked the trigger and was about to kill me, when I woke up.'

'So you didn't die?'

'No. But I would have if I hadn't woken up. You know what this means?'

'You think somebody's going to burst in here and kill you.'

'Absolutely. And that *is* something I think about – a lot. It would mean nothing for him to finish off an unknown New York actor.'

I laughed. 'The Billionaire doesn't do that kind of thing.'

I kissed the Actor to reassure him, but he pulled away. 'Did you dream?' he asked.

'I did.'

'And?'

I took a deep breath. 'We were in bed, you and I.' I took another breath, resisting the full reveal. 'With the Billionaire —'

'What was he doing here?'

'I guess he was pretty busy last night.' I tried to make light of it, but the Actor was serious. 'What happened?'

'The Billionaire was between us. And there wasn't enough room in the bed …'

'And?'

'We were a bit squashed is what I'm trying to say, and one of you had to go.'

'Don't tell me.' The Actor's expression fell, his early morning hardness with it.

'I told the Billionaire to go,' I added hastily.

'You did? And he left us alone?'

'Yes.'

'He left you lying in bed with me?'

'Yes, I said, and closed my eyes to hide the lie because in my dream it was the Actor I had asked to leave and, when he had refused, I had resorted to force and pushed the beautiful man who loved me out of the window.

❖

However much I wanted to, some part of me could not settle with the Actor. So when one dull March day The Cerebral Mr X called to invite me to a secret wedding in the Colorado mountains, I didn't take much persuading to join him. 'I know we've hardly met,' he said, 'but I need a friend here, and I can't think of anybody more perfect than you.' I was on a plane first thing the next day.

The Actor was in Los Angeles at an audition for a soap, which meant I could slip in a conversation with a thinking man and get back before my lover's return – except it didn't work out like that. The Cerebral Mr X wanted to be a lover himself, as well as a thinker. And a talker. I enjoyed the thinking and the talking and asked if we could wait on the loving. Meanwhile we consumed champagne and caviar at a mountain-top wedding where snow was the only white and everybody wore black.

Even though the wedding mood was fashionably melancholy, that weekend I felt more alive than I had in a long time. I didn't even remember to feel guilty. The only time I put in a prayer was on Monday morning, standing in line at the airport waiting for a cab back to the city. Having got away with my secret trip, the last thing I needed was to bump into my boyfriend coming back from Los Angeles. My prayer was to get back to the apartment before him, which I did – with half an hour to spare.

When the Actor walked through the door he looked so irresistible I was convinced that my commitment to him was intact, so couldn't understand why he turned away when I reached to kiss him. 'I thought this might interest you,' he said in a level voice, unfolding that day's *New York Post.* He opened the newspaper at the gossip page. I winced at the small black-and-white photograph of a supposedly clandestine wedding of an unlikely couple surrounded by a small group dressed in black. Only The Cerebral Mr X's beaming face, leaning towards mine, destroyed the impression that this was a funeral.

'How do you know these people? And who's that guy?'

'A friend.'

'He looks pretty pleased with himself.'

'Nothing happened.'

'You expect me to believe that?'

'Please believe me. I promise nothing happened.'

The Actor picked up his bag and walked to the door.

'Please …' I began.

'What? You've had your little trip and now you know you want me?'

The Actor waited at the door, half in, half out, waiting for my response. I stared back at him, words forming in my head, not a sound coming out of my mouth.

I didn't hear from the Actor for a few weeks and told myself it was proof that he was not for me. I resumed the familiar routine of dinner with my neighbours, film sessions with the Director and Sundays with Vincenzo. I even devoted extra hours to my academic studies. And in my daydreams The Cerebral Mr X played the lead.

I couldn't face the complications of a proper goodbye with the Actor. It was easier for me to cut him out of my life. My commitment was to the path of least resistance, and nothing could change that. Not even the Actor's letter, which arrived one month to the day since we'd last seen each other.

My darling
In the past weeks I've been trying to write a letter that expresses my love, friendship and admiration. I have the words you wrote me on Valentine's Day and I think, 'I must make this good; I must make it right,' because I have never shared as much, or as deeply, with anyone before. This scares me, but I don't want to lose you.

I've been insecure, and know in my heart the way through this is courage, respect and honesty, rather than trying to restrict you, and your ambitions. I can't control you, and don't want to. I don't want you to withhold your dreams and ideas from me just in case I might throw a fit. The double standards by which I have operated astounds me. I want to be your lover and friend, and not get too emotional about your relationships. Please be patient. I'm unearthing uncharted ground here.

I miss you very much. When I'm not by your side, I lie in bed and think of you in your pink pyjamas, and I feel close to you. I long for your lips, your body, your arms, your hands, your legs, your feet, your eyes. I long for your heart, no other.

The Actor's letter was a gift I wasn't ready to receive and, marooned by my idealized notions of the Perfect Man, I missed the authentic love he was offering me. In his willingness to own his part about the difficulties in our relationship, the Actor had admitted his imperfections, which, I told myself, was why I could not commit to him. All my life I had been certain that my destiny was to be with a perfect man and, as luck would have it, finally I had found him.

Since the Colorado wedding, The Cerebral Mr X had been on my mind most of the time particularly because he had not contacted me which was not at all consistent with his advances while we'd been away. Demonstrating restraint, I waited for his call. When six weeks had gone by, I couldn't hold out any longer. I called him on a Sunday evening – it would have been a social disgrace to call on a Saturday or worse still a Friday night. I dialled the number, the tone droned on and I was about to hang up when he answered with a sharp hello.

'Hi, it's me,' I said.

'Oh, yeah, hi. That's funny. I was just thinking about you. How are you?' His voice softened. I thought he sounded pleased to hear me.

'Very well — '

'Listen, I'm in the shower. Can I ring you when I get out?'

Some shower. He didn't call for six days, but his invitation to a glamorous downtown party almost made up for that.

Over the following months my love-life floundered, sustained by occasional but always passionate interludes with The Cerebral Mr X. He invited me to the most lavish parties, and late at night we would return to his apartment to make love by an instant fire with fake logs, but real flames. On fur rugs we lay beside each other, shadows and firelight playing on our creamy skin. Sometimes we'd open another bottle of wine, sometimes we'd talk. But making love was what we did best. This was the Real Thing, I was sure. The very centre of my heart opened to him. It wasn't possible, I reasoned with myself, for the body to lie. It wasn't possible for me to have such feelings in isolation. He had to feel the same way … but, if he did, The Cerebral Mr X did not let me know. We still had exhilarating times, we still had fun and because I was grateful for his occasional attention and his time, I settled for his silence. A letter from my sister changed all that. Her boyfriend had proposed, she had accepted and there is nothing quite like a sister's wedding to bring the thoughts of her single sister into perspective.

Overnight my hip city life lost its lustre. It was time for me to take note of the choices that had transformed my sister's life and, before flying to Los Angeles, I purchased a book in which to record her healthy habits. I was optimistic that if I could adopt her ways, I too could achieve stability.

A few days before the wedding I moved into the guestroom of her employer's colonial style house. I watched in awe as she ran the family while putting in place the final plans for her wedding. '*Organisation, discipline, hard work*' went down in my notebook.

Breakfast ('*healthy home cooking*') was one of the most chaotic times of the day, as everybody converged on the kitchen with their demands.

'Which sweater shall I wear today?' asked the man of the house, holding up two patterned cashmeres for my sister's consideration. My sister was scrambling eggs, helping the son with his homework and stopping the puppy from chewing the wife's latest Chanel sandals, but still gave her attention: 'You can't go wrong with the Ballyentine,' she said (*'patience, diplomacy'*).

The man disappeared, only to walk into the kitchen moments later in the cashmere my sister hadn't recommended. 'Which car do you think I should take to the dentist?' he asked.

'The Rolls. You know you prefer it.'

He picked up a set of keys and walked out.

'He's cute,' I said to my sister later that morning as we drove down Rodeo Drive in the Rolls-Royce.

'You think so?'

'Yes. Tall, intelligent-looking — '

'So intelligent he can't make up his own mind. He always asks for advice, then does the opposite of whatever people say. How smart's that?'

'The sweater he ended up wearing — '

'Was the one I thought he should wear. Same thing with the car. If I'd told him to take the BMW we wouldn't have had the Rolls for our errands, which is so much more fun for us.'

Her logic was undeniably effective. And the Rolls-Royce was vintage with red seats and a soft top, which my sister opened with the press of a button to expose us to spring sunshine and the envious gaze of passers-by. My sister had come a long way.

'Isn't it risky, counting on his contrariness?' I asked.

'Not when he's consistently contrary. They've got so much money and time, without their daily dramas they'd glide through life without touching the sides. Tension about anything, say the massage therapist being late or not having the right wine for dinner, validates their existence. They become so traumatized by high-class problems they end up on Prozac to smooth things out, because God forbid anybody should actually *feel* anything.' The pitch of my sister's voice had escalated, as if the strains of the family had invaded her vocal chords.

'How do they get through a day?'

'For the daily things, I decide. For everything else they go to an analyst – three times a week.'

My sister ran the house for these perpetually indecisive people like a ship, ordering its occupants as a captain would a crew. Yet what impressed me most of all was that even though she was paid less than their monthly florist's bill, in one year she had saved thousands of dollars. Over the same period I had received many more thousands of dollars and saved precisely nothing.

My sister married her California man in a simple ceremony attended by a few friends, her husband's family, my mother and me. My sister was serene, radiating beauty and her husband was steadfast. As they walked down the aisle he stopped to kiss her when she least expected it. My mother and I stood side by side, holding hands, squeezing tightly as if to somehow stop the tears welling up and rolling down our cheeks.

On the flight back to New York I fished out my notebook. In addition to the character traits that had impressed me, I added '*faith, trust, love, spontaneity?*' Then I wrote '*California Man*', and found myself thinking (not for the first time that weekend), of another good man from California. As I settled down in hope of sleep in my cramped economy seat, I wondered if it was too late to make the Actor mine.

❖

As soon as I got back to the city, I called the Actor. A machine message said he was touring with a theatre company and would be away until Fall. Suddenly all the uncertainties of my life were crushingly apparent. I wasn't married, didn't even have a proper boyfriend and I wasn't an actress. I had no plans beyond my graduation – less than three months away – when my student visa would expire. Six months after that I would be an illegal alien. The Director could save me from becoming a social outcast by casting me in one of his movies, but this seemed less and less likely. He had made three movies since we'd met and intimated that I was perfect for a part, but had never invited me to audition.

I couldn't afford to wait for the Director's Big Break and set about rehearsing an audition piece to present to acting agents. I was willing to be just another wannabe actresses trailing the New York streets in search of film work.

In preparation for my headshot, I trained with another wannabe actor, a diehard New Yorker and one-time lightweight boxing champion of the State, who still wore the gold gloves around his neck to prove it. His style of dress was suitably feisty (black leather-fronted Levis, diamond earring, heavy gold jewellery) and he was a youthful Robert de Niro lookalike. With wit and wisdom in equal measure, there was nothing I loved more than to hear him tawk. The physical training had been his idea after he'd watched me improvise a scene, interrupted by our acting teacher telling me to remove my dress. 'Start the scene from the top and this time, *be more vulnerable*,' she'd said. In white knickers I'd stood before my peers, a totem to vulnerability.

'Next time she tells you to strip in front of thirty people, your body's gotta blow them away,' Elvis said to me a week into our training schedule. We met every day for sessions that included covering my body with Vaseline and a bin liner before running around the reservoir three times.

A month later Elvis declared I was ready for my headshot. The hard work paid off when the Director's set photographer agreed to take my picture. The night before the shoot I was ready to stun the world with my toned body and English Roseness, when the photographer called.

'I've been asked not to take your picture,' he said bluntly.

'Who by?'

'The Director's wife. She's asked me not to do it as a sign of our friendship.'

'But that's crazy,' I said, gulping back angry tears.

'Doesn't mean I can't come over to see you. I could show you my work and give you the numbers of other photographers.'

The photographer duly came over with his book and stood by the window admiring my view while I looked through his pictures, which included famous actresses, many of whom were topless.

'Is that the kind of shot you'd let me take of you?' he asked, watching me scrutinize the breasts of one of America's leading ladies.

'Eh, not really,' I mumbled, hastily turning the page and dislodging a loose photograph which fell to the floor. Bending to pick it up, I found myself holding the photographer's self-portrait. He was standing in front of a lace curtain with no clothes on, a beam of light bouncing off his horse-sized penis. 'See anything there you like?' he asked straight-faced.

'No. But thanks for coming over,' I said, showing him the door.

If the Director's wife didn't want the photographer taking my picture, it was unlikely that she would allow her husband to cast me. But I couldn't let go of my great expectations because I was still very much part of the Director's entourage. I found another photographer, paid a few hundred dollars for my head shot and asked the Director to help me choose from the contact sheets. I rehearsed scenes from plays he recommended, continued to watch him work, attended his screenings with Carla and Max, and always joined them for dinner afterwards.

Being invited to the first private screening of the Director's latest movie was always a sign that somebody was among the chosen few. But this time, watching with the elite audience, resentment soon took place of my pride. Not only had he cast an English actress, but she was saying my lines, making my mistakes and talking with her film professor the way I had talked to the Director. The only departure from reality came when the English girl in the movie shared a cab with her film professor and made a pass at him.

'I must say,' I said later, trying to conceal my indignation while sitting next to the Director over dinner, 'that English girl in your movie has a life very like mine.'

'You think so?'

'I really do. Especially when her professor tells her to stop mixing with the mid-life crisis set and date a young man.'

'It's a story, and that's all it is. That film student represents the life of any number of females.' Unfazed, the Director sliced into his veal escalope and declined the steamed spinach offered by a passing waiter.

'Her life felt so familiar, it was uncanny.'

'Film isn't reality,' he said. 'Even documentary is necessarily some kind of fiction.'

'And fiction documents some kind of truth?'

'Yes, but whose truth?'

He was inscrutable. There was no point in responding because finally I understood that the Director was a master dissembler. His interest in me was motivated by his compulsive need to tell stories and make movies – which was how he made sense of his life.

Perhaps the nature of our conversation put the Director off his food, but that evening he was ready to head home before Max and Carla had finished their Dover sole. 'I'm taking a cab across town, if anyone wants a ride,' he said. With their chauffeur-driven limousine waiting outside, Max and Carla weren't about to share his cab fare.

'I'll go with you,' I said. Every head swivelled in our direction as I followed the Director out of the restaurant.

We sat in the back of the cab, preserving the cautious distance there had always been between us. This was the moment to take my lead from the actress in his film, to slide up to the Director and give him that kiss. The thought ran through my head, but no action followed. The scene had been played out in the movie and didn't need to happen now in reality. So we sat, the Director and I, chaste to the end, our slightly stilted conversation the only reflection of our latent attraction. I climbed out of the cab with a polite goodnight and knew that I would never be the Director's latest acting sensation.

As soon as I decided to face up to my reality it arrived all at once. Graduation was only a few weeks away, and none of the agents who had received my headshot had responded. I was gloomy. Even The Cerebral Mr X, a presence on the periphery of my life, had not called for two weeks. And so I did what I swore I would never again do. I contacted the Billionaire.

'Congratulations. Once you graduate you'll be able to start your life,' he said, heartened by my news.

'Except I'll be an illegal alien. I'll have to leave America.'

'Do you want to do a Ph.D.? If you do we could come to some arrangement.'

'And if I don't?'

'We'll send you three months' money and then you're on your own, kid.'

A Ph.D. suddenly sounded a superb idea. But then there was the prospect of three more years of financial dependence on the Billionaire.

'Thank you,' I said. 'You're always so generous, but what I want more than anything is to be an actress.'

'Acting is a very crowded profession. You've got as much chance of being an actress as I have of flying from the window sill,' the

Billionaire said, bringing our conversation to a brutal end.

Soon I would no longer be able to rely on the Billionaire for his monthly standing order, or the rent. My graduation, the long-awaited achievement of my life, marked my fall from grace. I donned black robes to receive my degree, a sombre garb that foreshadowed my mood later that afternoon when I registered with a flat-sharing agency in Grand Central Station. By the time I got home there was a message waiting from a prospective landlord. Her voice was spiky and she sounded demanding, but I was grateful.

Elizabeth Strickland worked in Sotheby's auction house and was keen to come by to pass a critical eye over my apartment. 'I can't abide clumpy furniture,' she said, striding into my sitting room on sturdy calves. Elizabeth was tall and thin from the knees up. She was far younger than I had expected. Her twinset and pearls were at odds with messy blonde hair and her 'look' was Sloane Ranger meets Cabbage Patch Doll.

'Very Bloomies,' she said, turning up her nose at my pine desk. 'What a pity you can't bring your view. Anyway, love your accent.'

I overlooked the likelihood of Elizabeth's neuroses and signed a six-month agreement to share her tiny two-bedroom apartment on the second floor above a dogs' home on 1st Avenue and 61st. My room overlooked the eternally noisy 1st Avenue side and each night as I tried to sleep I appreciated the many luxuries I had taken for granted in my doorman days. Silence in the city was the first, security the second. Tossing and turning in my single bed, I tried to forget that bullet holes punctuated the door of the building across the street.

Still, my life was not all doom. I saved enough from the Billionaire for a few months rent and had the occasional date with The Cerebral Mr X, and above all, I had my acting class and my friendship with Elvis. Elvis' funny take on life made him the perfect guide for my new Manhattan. He had hustled the city for the last five years, training boxers and coaching major movie stars and knew all about ducking and diving to make ends meet. When Elvis told me to find a cash job, I kept my eyes open and while dining with The Cerebral Mr X at a French restaurant, noticed a discreet advertisement: 'Coat check girl required'. It was May. New York was hotting up. Coats were scarce but I didn't care. I called the restaurant the next morning and by lunchtime was standing in a kiosk beneath a sign that read: '$1 a coat'. Evidently not all customers could read; after a group of four had spent $500 on lunch and left me a $3 tip for their coats, I summoned the courage to chase the extra buck. 'Sorry, sir, it's a dollar a coat.'

'I've given you enough for what you've done for me,' the cigar-smoking man replied.

Only a few months before I had spent what was now the equivalent of a year's salary on a Ralph Lauren outfit. I was the best-dressed coat check girl in the whole of Manhattan, and quite likely the poorest.

My average weekly income was $50, while the waiters earned at least $1,500 from their tips. They were cash rich and exhausted, so eventually I convinced them to train me to work on the floor. But their gratitude for another pair of hands didn't survive sharing the tips. We renegotiated and I agreed to receive only the tips given directly to me. It was a perfect arrangement and for a while the restaurant became the centre of my life. I felt part of a family, eating with the chef and the waiters, food more deliciously simple than anything served to the customers. We relaxed before each shift, like a troupe of performers, while the owner took reservations at the front of house and checked each table was perfectly set before putting the show on the road.

The French chef was backstage producing nouvelle cuisine dishes presented by waiters who impressed elegant New Yorkers with their efficient service. I did my best to keep up. After a sticky start, I became too successful for my own good and was soon earning $500 a week. The other waiters started to race me, beating me to tables and taking cocktails to customers who had ordered from me. It wasn't long before their speed on the restaurant floor had sliced me out of a job and I was consigned to the coat check and five dollars a day.

Summer in the city was not the same without air conditioning and life with the Sloane Cabbage Patch Doll was increasingly miserable. One evening I came home to find her wearing my clothes, getting ready for a blind date with a man she'd picked up from the *Harvard Review* singles section. I think that was the only time I shouted at her, but she was tough and went out anyway in my dress. My days were spent at the restaurant, most evenings too, which allowed me to avoid my roommate. I resisted the notion of falling in love with the chef, deciding it was safer to dream of a romantic boyfriend who would take me to the wide rivered country. The Cerebral Mr X continued to be my favourite after-dinner date but he was too anxious about my declining fortune even to talk about it. While there was no doubt about the attraction between us, his preference for successful, established, unavailable women was a problem. I was a wannabe actress, a failed waitress and about to become an Illegal Alien. 'Available' may as well have been stamped across my forehead.

❖

My darling sister
Congratulations on getting pregnant so quickly. Your life is going so well. I wish I could say the same.

My acting teacher has put me up for a few auditions with agents who are willing to work with 'new' talent. I hope to dazzle them with my monologue from Educating Rita. Will let you know how it goes.

Sorry for the delay in posting this to you. The auditions were no surprise. There I was preparing Rita's climactic moment and the agent was on the telephone discussing where to go to dinner, and whether she should have Marinara or Bolognese on her pasta. When she hung up, she looked at me and yawned. 'It's been a long day, but you're here now, so start whenever you're ready.'

Then I saw another West Side diva, an overweight lesbian who wore her telephone as a headphone set, and didn't get up from her computer or stop talking to a producer in Los Angeles when I walked in. All she wanted to know was whether I was willing to do nude scenes, and didn't even smile when she said going naked was the bottom line. I'm desperate to act, but not that desperate.

Last night I went to a film première with a man who works for the biggest agency in the world. I'd met him earlier in the week, and he was courteous in a tired, grey-suited way, and didn't talk about nudity, which was something. Mind you, he didn't ask to see my monologue either. He simply said I'd 'got it' and that if I lost ten pounds and learned an American accent I could be the next Geena Davis. I said, 'Why would I want to be the second Geena Davis when I could be the first me?' He laughed but I was serious.

I only went to the première because you never know who you might meet at those gala nights. And sure enough, among the New York 'A' list, sitting in a sea of blonde and cigarette smoke, was The Cerebral Mr X. I didn't get close enough for a conversation. Thank God. The agent had just spilled his white wine down my dress, after he'd nervously let it spill that he was divorced and was ready for a new relationship – with me!

I came to New York with such dreams, but nothing happens to sustain them.This is probably the best city in the world, (although I do love Paris and London's pretty good), and I wanted to make it as an actress here. It breaks my heart to say this, but nothing keeps me in New York now apart from hope, and I'm almost out of that. I'm running on empty and fear that I will soon admit defeat.

Love to you.

Eight

The One

Within a month of writing to my sister, I had returned to London, rented a bedsit on the Goldbourne Road and found a job as a waitress. I worked in a minimalist restaurant in Notting Hill with a stark interior that reflected my own as I tried to settle back into a different city. In between shifts, I went in search of an acting agent and finally it happened: an agent signed me.

My agent – I still love those words – was of the old-time theatrical kind and her first question wasn't about my willingness to do nude scenes. She encouraged me to be serious about acting, but was also a realist, and sent me on auditions for cat food and toothpaste commercials. 'You never know where or when the break will come, so keep on keeping on,' she'd say whenever we spoke.

It felt like a punishment to live at a slower pace within my means. Facing up to reality I realized why I'd avoided it. I mourned the loss of big dreams and grand passions and prayed for the strength to present an optimistic front to the world.

'It's always darkest before dawn,' my agent would say, which cheered me because surely these were the darkest days. Acting roles were scarce and when they came along they were for low-budget independent productions that didn't pay enough to cover my rent.

Then, on a whim, a casting agent, producer, director, advertising executive *and* client all agreed that I should be paid £8,000 to be in a television commercial for instant coffee. I could afford to stop being a waitress. I could also afford to audition for plays so far from the fringe they didn't even get reviewed in *Time Out.*

My conception of money had undergone a dramatic change since my slide from New York's Upper East Side. I now considered myself wealthy if I could earn in three months what the Billionaire used to give me in one white envelope. But for some reason the little money I earned lasted longer.

I forgot about the Madison Avenue boutiques. I discovered flea markets where I bought fantastic dresses for £20 and decided that the haute couture I had loved so much was too haughty for me now. My Valentino was donated to Oxfam.

It was a relief no longer to work as a waitress, but without the restaurant I lived an unpeopled life. I hadn't been in London long enough to have made any real friends, and auditions were solitary exercises.

My agent invited me to Sunday lunch to introduce me to 'a nice London crowd', where I met her niece, Phoebe – the married woman who was extraordinary for many reasons, not least because she befriended single members of her sex. Phoebe was the one to invite me to the party at Eaton Square where I met the Virgin. At the end of that affair I was once again single but also pregnant by an irretrievable male.

I didn't doubt for a second that I would keep the baby. I wouldn't be the first single mother and as much as my own would disapprove, once she saw her grandchild I knew I'd be able to count on her.

My biggest dilemma was over the child's father. I couldn't decide whether I should tell the Virgin the baby was his before I gave birth or after. In the end I was so confused about the right thing to do, I didn't do anything. His only contribution had been my accidental insemination, and as I was the one left holding the baby, I felt justified in keeping the child a secret.

But after two months the deceit became too distressing. Genes are not distributed according to parental effort and, compared to the mother, any father's role during pregnancy is negligible. It was irrelevant that the Virgin wasn't contributing to the foetus growing inside me – no father could do that. I had to accept that biologically the child was his and my emotions were irrelevant. I started to write him a letter, but email seemed more suitable. At least he'd be sitting down when he got the news.

'Subject: Congratulations'.

This wasn't the time for irony.

'Subject: You're about to be a father ...'

That wasn't right either.

'Subject: Preg – '

Forget that.

'Subject: Fatherhood'.

Wrong again.

To acknowledge his role was asking for trouble. I worried he had the right to demand that we raise 'his' child together. No Contact Whatsoever was the best course of action. I couldn't face having a cup of tea with the Virgin, let alone the responsibility for another human being, and so I prayed that when the time came, I would be prepared for single motherhood.

What I wasn't prepared for was the blood and the pain when, three months into the pregnancy, I found myself hyperventilating, going through contractions and finally miscarrying my baby. Recovering from the physical shock was easier than recovering from the emptiness left by a foetus no bigger than a pencil tip, which had contained all the elements for life except for life itself. For weeks after I felt exhausted, bereaved, a failure.

❖

It was Christmas and time to go home for Midnight Mass, carols and my loving mother. There would also be seasonal television, too much food, and Harold and Phyllis – ornery neighbours in their eighties who had hijacked my mother for Christmas ever since my sister and I had left home.

During the day, Harold sat in the big armchair, reading the paper, rolling false teeth between his gums and slugging homemade sloe gin straight from the bottle, backwashing so he wouldn't have to share it. The old man was mean, his wife burdened with resentment and together they devoured my mother's generous spirit.

On a mild Christmas day we had the gas fire turned up for Phyllis who felt the cold and, in stifling, tropical heat, ate a turkey lunch. Unable to face any more food or television, I retired to my bedroom and sat in the dark by the open window, breathing clear air, staring at the bare chestnut tree, when the telephone rang.

'Happy Christmas. I thought you were in America.' I recognized his voice immediately.

'I'm in London now.'

'I miss …'

While he paused, I found myself hoping he was going to say 'you'.

'I really miss your mother's cooking,' he said. My heart sank.

'Where are you?'

'Nearby, at my parents'. I was thinking of you – of you all – and about coming over.'

'Come at any time,' I said with enthusiasm that surprised me.

'Tomorrow morning then.' He was the first to hang up.

I returned to the bedroom, lay on my single bed in the dark and remembered the night I met my ex-husband. For the first time I considered the humiliation I had caused him when I had fled the island, leaving him to face his colleagues and pupils. Perhaps time had healed the past? Perhaps after all these years I was ready to be his wife, the magnetism of an unlived life no longer able to distract me.

Later that evening, while my mother made more mince pies, I tried to sound casual when I told her that my ex-husband would be visiting. But his name caught in the back of my throat and my mother stopped, spoon suspended. 'He's coming here?'

'Yes, to see me. To see us.'

'Oh, darling,' she said, and gave me an enfolding hug.

❖

When he knocked at the door, I answered with the same anticipation I'd felt as a seventeen-year-old. And as before, he stood back from the step onto the gravel path as if to take a better look at me. For a second I missed all that had been straightforward about myself in those early days. I missed my youthful conviction. Then, with adult eye, I scrutinized my ex-husband. He was no less attractive, his face was still open, his smile wide, but somehow he seemed simply . . . less.

I led him into the sitting room where we sat on the sofa side by side. Harold and Phyllis turned their armchairs away from the television towards us, as though we were the alternative entertainment. I didn't care. Between my ex-husband and me there was an ease and intimacy that comes from having loved. He still felt part of my family and my life. It wasn't long before I was thinking that he was the best Christmas present.

'When did you come back to England?' he asked as I appreciated the shape of his mouth as if for the first time.

'Almost two years ago.'

'And you got your degree?'

'I certainly did.' I felt proud. His academic colleagues couldn't intimidate me now.

'What are you doing in London?'

'These days nothing but auditions. But I am up for a play.'

'What, the West End?'

'Hardly. A theatre above a pub in Islington.'

'Acting's a dodgy business. Forget it. Start a family. You'd be a great mother.' I looked to the floor. Not even my own mother knew that I had been pregnant a few months before.

'I can't metamorphose into an instant family,' I said, biting my bottom lip. 'Making babies takes two. Mind you, just because we've been married before doesn't ... ' I stopped. Words were tumbling out of my mouth before I'd had a chance to think them.

'That's why I'm here ... ' The thought that he was about to propose in front of Harold and Phyllis made me straighten my spine and lift my chest as if to accept a prize.

'Any more coffee?' my mother asked on her way through the sitting room.

'That would be great,' my ex-husband said warmly and, looking at him right then, I was ready to say I do.

'In fact, I wanted to let you know,' my husband said to my mother before she vanished to the kitchen. 'I wanted to let you know,' he said again, turning to me. This was it, I thought, this is my redemption scene. 'I'm getting married.'

I choked: 'When?'

'Tomorrow.'

I sunk my teeth into my bottom lip, drawing blood. 'How wonderful,' I squeaked.

'I think it will be. It will be okay. I mean, we'll be okay. She's pregnant, you see, and it just seemed the best thing, you know, to get married.'

I smiled, trying to hide the effect of his glad tidings, and my very ex-husband was polite enough not to notice that I was crying. He kept his focus on the mince pies and a whole plate later said he really had to get back to his parents. We walked out to his car. It was raining and from the apple tree a blackbird called into the monotone winter's day.

'Sorry about my ridiculous blubbering,' I said.

My ex-husband put his arms around my waist and hugged me hard, drawing my face into his shoulder where I smelled the freshness of his skin. 'Don't wait,' he said. 'Just choose a decent man and start your life.'

I waved him goodbye, standing in the street long after he had gone, delaying my return to the kitchen. My mother was weeping and stirring gravy – vegetables boiling, steam rising, lunch almost ready, no one hungry.

'Somebody else is having your baby,' she said, staring blankly out of the window, anaesthetized by the day.

❖

Escape had always been at the forefront of my mind, but now there was nowhere else to run. I had to stop. And once I stopped, I cried. I cried for the end of my marriage, for my miscarriage, for disappointments and unrealized dreams. Once the tears dried up they were replaced by untapped reserves of anger and indignation. I couldn't believe my husband had urged me to give up acting, the one pleasure of my life and greatest passion, to accept the proposal of the first 'decent' man who came along, thus heralding the start of my life. It sounded like the advice given by an ancient aunt in an eighteenth-century novel and made me all the more angry because it was a romantic ideal I had only just outgrown myself. I may have attended one of the most progressive universities in America, but it had taken more than liberal arts to wean me off slushy romanticism onto more substantial ideals. I now understood that the hope of finding an intelligent, sensitive, sexy, solvent man with a sense of humour was not simply indulgent, but futile. World peace was more likely.

I knew the answer was to be at one with myself, and not feel a failure because I hadn't found my 'significant other'. And so I focused on one day at a time, resisting fears about the future, praying for gratitude for my life exactly as it was.

❖

'Darling, congratulations. You're the new face of Baby Bots,' my agent rasped in her fifty-a-day voice.

'Is that good?'

'Absolutely it's good. You're about to be famous.'

'For baby wipes. Is this a good career move?'

'Darling, what career?

After three years of auditioning, I had to accept that I was never going to escape from the fringe.

'They want an answer today. I say we say yes.'

'Okay … '

'Is that yes?'

'Yes.'

'Darling, I will cut you the best deal I've ever made. You're going to be rich.'

My agent was as good as her word. The commercial for baby wipes was about to make me more money than I had ever earned. All I had to do was smile to camera, hold a baby in one hand, a wipe in the other and say, 'We both have the smoothest cheeks.' Cut to baby's bottom caressed with a wet wipe, then a close-up of my face with a wet wipe, as I recite 'See how smooth we are.' In this Elysium everything was pure white and my glossy hair flew in the breeze of an open window. It was for all the world an advert for single motherhood, but Baby Bots were so impressed they took the campaign global. Posters of me holding a perfect child appeared on buses and billboards throughout the world.

I signed a three year contract with Baby Bots and moved from the Goldbourne Road to my own place on Stanley Crescent overlooking the garden square. I settled into fringe theatre, accepting that I would be there forever, and started to teach drama at Holloway Prison. I even wrote a one-act play. Almost imperceptibly my preoccupations shifted from seeking a social life to building an inner life. I no longer noticed how much time I spent alone. Then one Friday evening, on the walk home from a service at my local church, I realised this was my idea of a night out.

I had mastered the art of solitude and my life was under control, and yet there were moments I almost envied my drama student prisoners locked up together, companionship guaranteed. My biggest test seemed to be maintaining the peace I found alone while simultaneously relating to others – particularly a significant male other. Sometimes I felt ready to try again.

But even with the best intentions, I couldn't be sure that I wouldn't make the same mistakes. My aphrodisiac had been a man's unavailability and, on the rare occasion that pattern changed with the man prepared to step up to the plate, I had responded like an unavailable male myself. Deciding that I still couldn't trust my judgment to fall for a different kind of man, or to behave differently when I did, I settled for seclusion. I dedicated myself to prayer to cleanse my soul and a wise psychoanalytical therapist to sort out my head. One day, nobody could tell me when, I wanted to break the cycle that had prevailed in my relationships with men.

My dearest sister
Tomorrow I'm going shopping for the girls and will put this in with their birthday package.

Strange to be back in London after almost a month. If I didn't have to work tomorrow, I would have stayed longer in Marrakech and the High Atlas. I'm lucky to be able to come and go whenever I feel like it. The other day I wondered if my whole life had been predicated on an unconscious need to preserve my freedom. This didn't seem so bad until I heard 'freedom is just another word for nothing left to lose.'

I am tiring of the inward quest. Who said the unexamined life wasn't worth living? Well, I've examined the life out of mine. All that enquiry and determination to be conscious is hard work and life is no less a mystery.

I agree with you that self-improvement can become narcissistic. It's time for me to help others – one other would do. I'm working in the prison again next week, which will be rewarding but can hardly satisfy my need for relationship. I'm ready for something a little more intimate than a group of twenty inmates.

I'm not ready for a life of seclusion just yet. It takes such effort to feel complete on my own - my agent says that's because only old dogs are meant to be alone, but walking in the park yesterday, seemed to me that even old dogs prefer company.

Will book my ticket to California soon. Can't wait to see you all again.

Love.

❖

I withheld from my sister one secret sorrow which surfaced briefly at the same time each year. My nieces were born three years and one week apart, and it was one of my pleasures to visit the local toyshop and send a fat birthday package off to the United States. And every time I picked out their presents, I found myself regretting that I didn't have a child of my own to celebrate. This year the feeling hit me as I bent down to a bottom shelf to pick up a box of paints decorated with dolphins leaping from a crystal sea. A constriction in my throat heralded its almost predictable arrival, and there I was longing for the honesty of a child's voice and a trusting hand in mine.

I knew the paint box would appeal to my first niece. The secret drawer at the bottom of the box fascinated me and looking to see if there was anything inside, I backed straight into a carousel of paperbacks which tottered unsteadily as books flew to the floor.

'Dad, watch out!' a lean boy shouts, leaping away. The boy's father isn't so fast. He's still on his knees with his back to the falling bookstand when it hits him over the head.

'What the fuck was that?' he says, as he gets up – then goes on up and up. He's incredibly tall.

'I'm so sorry. I can't believe I was that clumsy.' I blush.

'We're fine, aren't we, Dad?' says the kid. The boy has clear blue eyes and pale skin. He watches his father intently to see that he isn't hurt.

'Sure. I'm okay,' his father says. He seems dazed and cradles his head with both hands clasped behind his neck as he wrinkles his nose. We stare at the books scattered on the floor. I drop to my knees to gather them up, and the boy is beside me pushing them into a pile. 'I'm sorry,' I whisper.

'Stop saying sorry. My dad's strong, he can take it. I read these books in school. This one's crap,' he says, holding up a collection of poems about frogs. He picked up another book. 'But you should read this one. It's wicked.'

The father towers above us, rubbing the back of his head, more from confusion at the scene than from pain. He is too tall and too remote to get back on his knees to help.

'That was some crash.' The woman who manages the shop runs towards us. 'Is your son all right? He isn't hurt?' she says to me.

'I'm the one. He's fine,' the boy's father grins and I'm grateful that he doesn't feel the need to correct her. 'Nothing like an early morning crack on the head to let me know I'm alive. But you should nail this thing to the floor before it kills somebody.' He lifts the bookstand up with one hand.

'I'll go find a hammer and nail right away,' says the manager.

'Wait a second. We came in for the latest Playstation.'

'Up there,' she points.

'Right beneath my nose,' the father laughs – it's more a humph – and pulls the game off the shelf.

'Dad, don't forget you said you'd get me some War Hammer,' says the boy, on the way to the till.

'Not now, Frank. I'll get you War Hammer next week.'

'I can buy it. I've got the money. How much have I got? Or did you spend it?'

'Hey.' I call to father and son, but they are locked in a discussion about finance. I hesitate, then call, 'Hey, Frank.' The boy turns, his brow crumpling as he's tries to figure out how I know his name. 'You forgot this.' I hold up his sports bag.

Frank's dad puts the money on the counter, leaving his son to pay, and walks towards me. 'Thanks,' he says.

We face each other. He is a man of such stature, I forget that I'm holding Frank's bag. He looks at me and in that second I sense the possibility of something more than goodbye. He waits, then takes hold of the dark green handle. 'I hope I didn't —

'Dad! I'm starving,' calls Frank and I let go of the bag. There's nothing between us now. Just formalities.

'We didn't get breakfast yet,' Frank's dad explains to me.

'Glad I didn't hurt you.'

'You didn't, not really.' His face creases into a kind of smile and I think that he winks at me. Then he follows his son out of the shop.

After I had chosen my younger niece a diamond hair band, I posted my package. There was still time to get to my favourite café for breakfast. Tom's was packed, the way it always is on a Saturday, and I stood in the queue waiting for a table.

'Breakfast menu finishes in ten minutes. Last orders for breakfast. Anybody on their own?' asked Lindsay, the headwaiter, moving down the line.

'I am.' Sometimes there are advantages to being single.

'You don't mind sharing?'

'No,' I lie because usually I love the luxury of a quiet table on my own in a busy café. But my urge for a latte and muffin overcame my preference.

'You can sit with us,' interrupted a small voice.

'Is that okay?' Lindsay asked. I checked the table, and there was Frank looking up at me with serious clear blue eyes.

'Hi, Frank. Are you sure you don't mind?' I asked, looking to his father.

'We're sure, aren't we, Dad?'

The boy's father was on the telephone, but he smiled and nodded in the direction of the empty seat. It was as though I had been commanded to sit, which I did.

'Snap?' offered Frank. A pack of cards was spread across his side of the table, set for a game of his own invention. 'Cards aren't much fun on your own,' he said.

Halfway through our first game, which he won, Frank said, 'You're Baby Bot's mum, aren't you? I've seen you on the telly in the commercials for those bum wipes.'

'That's me. But the baby isn't mine,' I said.

'So you're not married or a mum or anything?'

'No. That's all make believe.'

We played another game of snap. I got beaten again and ordered a latte and a blueberry and white chocolate muffin. Then Frank's dad came off the phone.

'You're following us around. What a treat,' he said, and this time he really did smile.

He was a man who didn't bother with hellos and his eyes shone – particularly when the food arrived. Frank had a marshmallow milkshake and waffles with maple syrup, and his father had a plate of fried everything and a short black coffee.

'Diet starts tomorrow,' the father sighed, tucking in. He was about to ask a question, or so it seemed, when his telephone rang. He talked as he ate.

Frank raised his brows and looked at me. 'Most days after school we come here for a snack because it's right by our bus stop.' He made loud gurgles through his straw as he sucked the last of his milkshake. 'You can have tea with us if you want,' said Frank, which was a suitable name for such a straight talker.

'Would you like another milkshake?' I offered.

'k,' he grinned. 'That's a meal in itself, that is. Number fifty-two is our bus,' he said, giving me the information as if wanting me to bump into them again. And I wouldn't have minded that at all. I liked the look of Frank's father and almost ordered another muffin to have a reason to stay until he came off the mobile. I stopped myself just in time. If the man wasn't interested enough to get off his mobile while I was there, I wasn't meant to get involved.

'See you,' I said to Frank, getting up and glancing at his father.

'Hope to see you again,' said Frank. His expression was so endearing I sat back down, wondering at what stage boyish enthusiasm is replaced by indifference.

'How old are you?' I asked.

'Eleven – in three months,' said Frank.

'Do you like school?'

'Most of the time. I like sports the best. Yesterday my teacher said I was athletic.'

'That's good.'

'I always want to be athletic. My dad needs to get athletic. He's a bit fat. Don't you think he's a bit fat?'

Frank's dad caught my eye over the top of his conversation and grinned at my predicament. We could all see that he needed to lose a few pounds. The question was whether I'd be honest or diplomatic.

'I think your dad looks cuddly.'

The dad winked at me and Frank laughed. 'He's good at cuddling, and cricket. Do you like cricket?'

'I've never played.'

'Dad! She's never played cricket. Dad, did you hear that? Let's go to the park.'

The boy's face exploded with excitement. He was tired of sitting around in the café. He wanted to be out in the bright day.

'Frank, I'd love to come to the park, but I've got to work this afternoon,' I said, checking my watch.

Frank's dad closed his mobile and sighed. 'Forget about the park mate.' Frank's face went blank, as though he'd been hit with terrible news.

My instinct was to step in, do anything to take away his disappointment, even though it wasn't my place.

'I'll meet you in the park later —' I started to say, but stopped. Frank's dad's mobile was ringing again. He winced, mouthed 'sorry,' answered the call. It was time for me to go.

'Listen, Frank I hope I do see you again.' I smoothed down his spiked blond hair. Frank's lips rolled together and he turned down the corners of his mouth. His eyes were round and heavy. 'We will play cricket one day I promise.' Frank didn't respond as I'd hoped. Perhaps he'd heard too many promises that didn't amount to much. 'I'll look out for you,' I said pointedly as I left the table.

At the café door I couldn't resist turning around. Frank's dad was off the mobile and receiving a well-placed kick in the shins. 'Dad – you didn't even say goodbye,' scolded the boy.

My breakfast encounter had made me late for my appointment in north London and I ran to the bus stop. Sitting on the top deck of the bus I thought how much I liked Frank. Then I thought about his dad and wondered how much I liked him. He'd certainly appealed in the toyshop but the telephone was a problem. And what about all that food? His breakfast plate had been stacked high. I didn't know anybody ate black pudding any more. All that dry blood and pork fat. But there was nothing a little exercise and a healthy diet couldn't fix. My mind whirred on, until I caught myself plotting to change a man I didn't even know. I stopped, took a deep breath and concentrated on accepting all things as they are.

The bus stopped to let city people on round ponies cross into Hyde Park. In the distance, the Park Lane traffic stood still. As long as it wasn't backed up on the Edgware Road, I wouldn't be that late for my 'go see' with a photographer for a mobile phone commercial – which brought me back to Frank's dad. When he was on the telephone I'd noticed the perfect shape of his forearms and the way the hair at the back of his wrist edged on to his hands. I wondered whether Frank's dad was married, single or had a woman languishing in the background. Nothing kills a new relationship quite like unfinished business from the previous one. Frank's dad didn't seem that interested in me over breakfast. Perhaps he did have a woman on his mind. He looked eccentric enough to nurture any number of female fantasies, and yet there was something very straight about him. Probably he was a single dad with a steady girlfriend he saw twice a week.

Frank's dad was on my mind for five stops before I began to think of Frank again. I wondered where his mother was. Something about the boy gave the impression she wasn't around. I sensed there was a vacancy for a woman in his life, which is why he'd liked me because he'd thought I was Baby Bot's mother. My obsessive thoughts were cut short when my telephone rang. Withheld number calling.

'Hello,' I said.

'It's me,' he said. The sound of his voice sent blood rushing into my head and heart.

'Hello,' I said, astounded at the power I still accorded the Billionaire.

'I'm in London this evening and was wondering whether you'd like to have dinner?'

The answer was no, I knew that, but it didn't come easily. I hesitated, part of me willing to be drawn into the Billionaire's world for one more glamorous night. Part of me dreaming that it could last longer this time because I had moved on. I wanted him to see the change in me.

'So where shall I pick you up?'

I imagined what it would be like to see him, as if for the first time. I wondered where we'd kiss, or whether we would. Then I heard myself say, 'I'm sorry, I'm busy. I can't see you tonight.'

'That's a pity. Perhaps some other time,' and just like that, after a polite goodbye, the Billionaire was gone.

For a second the desire to escape my reality had been as strong as it had ever been. But I had resisted. I was still on the bus. I was still in my life.

By the time I reached my destination I was almost fifteen minutes late. In a panic, I rang the bell. Red graffiti paint circled the metal door and 'all work and no play makes jack a dull boy' was scratched on a wood panel above it. I rang the bell again. The door opened.

'So you really are following me around,' said Frank's dad, squinting down at me.

'How could I possibly —' I sounded defensive and was happy to be interrupted.

'Of course. How could you? I'm joking.'

'I'm here to meet Gavin,' I said, trying to soften my voice, but couldn't help shrieking, 'You're not Gavin are you? That really would be too much.'

'Gav's got some business to sort out. He asked me to take the picture, if that's okay with you? It's only a test.'

'Sure. Whatever.' I was too self-conscious to face him.

'Whatever? What does that mean?' he said, quite gruff all of a sudden.

I dropped my bag to the floor. I had to look him in the eye. 'It's a bit strange to meet you again, that's all. But I'm glad it's you – as long as you really are a photographer.'

It was a pathetic attempt to flirt but we smiled. And then I saw that this wasn't a normal studio space. I was standing in a kitchen that had been constructed from stones and concrete and things from the street and on a shelf was a photograph of Frank.

'Do you live here?'

'We do. We all live here.'

'What with Gavin?'

'No, with my sons.'

I took a deep breath, the kind that happens when the body knows it's safe to relax before the mind does. 'I loved meeting Frank,' I said, feeling a lot happier as we walked through to the studio.

'Yeah, he's great. Do you have kids?'

'No. I live alone.'

'In perfect solitude?'

'Not always,' I said.

'Sooner better. Greater later. Now's the best. That's what I believe,' he said.

Such a constructive philosophy impressed me, and I warmed to Frank's dad as he prepared for the photograph, adjusting the light, getting down on his knees to look through the lens. Finally he turned to me. 'Okay. I'm ready. Are you?'

'What do you think?' I asked, walking onto the set.

'You look ready to me.'

He counted me into the shot and pressed the shutter, setting off the motor drive and that sexy sound. He loaded more film. This was going to be over in no time.

'It has to be better to live with people you love…' I stopped. He was adjusting my shirt collar and his touch at the back of my neck made my toes tingle.

'Love. It's the religion of the twenty-first century. Who doesn't believe in it?' he asked, now adjusting the reflector, turning back to see where the light fell.

'Amazing that we don't lose faith when you think how disappointing relationships can be,' I said.

'Love is all we've got left. But don't expect it to be perfect, because nothing is,' he said, as a particularly perfect young man in nothing but boxer shorts appeared from behind a curtain at the end of the studio.

'Morning,' he said, his hand ruffling the sleep out of his dark hair. He was wandering through the studio at two in the afternoon wearing little more than sleepy dust and he wasn't remotely embarrassed.

'Who's that?' I whispered to Frank's dad.

'Frank's brother. Well, half-brother.'

'So you've got two sons?'

'Two sons a life time apart, but it's working out.'

The young man was lean, with an almost concave belly and broad shoulders. He stood in the studio door watching, unaware that Frank was creeping up behind him about to tackle him at the waist. I smiled.

'That's nice. Hold that,' said Frank's dad, moving closer, the motor drive whirring one last time.

Frank gave up trying to bring his six foot five brother to the floor and came into the studio. 'Hey Dad…' Then he saw me and froze. 'Have you two met before today?'

'Never,' his father and I said together.

Frank's face screwed up in violent wonder. Then he laughed, 'That's weird.'

'I'm starving. Let's go get breakfast when you're done with the pictures,' said the older son, winking at me before disappearing to take a shower.

'We just had breakfast,' said Frank. 'We're going to play

cricket.' Frank spun round to face me. 'Why don't you come?'

'That's a great idea. You can be on my team,' said Frank's dad.

Walking with Frank's dad and his sons to the park, none of them believed that I was about to play my first game of cricket. They did their best to reassure me. Frank reached for my hand.

'You're lucky to be on my dad's side because he's the best and you're probably going to need help.'

'You're right,' I said, still glowing inside that he had placed his hand in mine.

'Sometimes things just work out, don't they,' said Frank, staring straight ahead, not needing an answer. His day couldn't have turned out any better.

Mine turned out pretty well too. After cricket, (we beat them by six runs), and a long lunch, I took the bus home. It had been a day of such sweet synchronicity I decided to send Frank's dad a text message. '**Goodness gracious**' was all I needed to say. I knew he'd understand.

A second later his reply came back. '**Goddess gracious. Toms café, Monday @ 5?**'

And I'd be there because he was right. Now's the best.

Acknowledgements

I would like to thank Toby Mundy for daring me to write this book. His faith fuelled mine. Also to Louisa and Karen in the London office, and Elisabeth and Judy in New York, thank you. Charles, Tai, Viv, Richard, Lucy, Nicole, T.S., Dijon, Nick, Jean, Loulou, 309, Alexandra, Arabella, Dorothy, Mark, Frank, Cyrano and my family – you don't know the difference you made. Thank you Precious for believing, and Terry for offering to break my leg to keep me in one place long enough to write – thankfully you didn't have to. And finally, I would like to thank Morgan for being a true friend and making this possible.